Verbivoracious Pr

Festschrift Volume Two

GILBERT

ADAIR

Reprint titles:

The Languages of Love
The Sycamore Tree
The Dear Deceit
The Middlemen
Next
Xorandor/Verbivore
Go When You See the Green Man Walking
by Christine Brooke-Rose

Three Novels
by Rosalyn Drexler

Knut
Erowina
by Tom Mallin

other Verbivoracious titles @

www.verbivoraciouspress.org

Verbivoracious Press

Festschrift Volume Two

edited by G. N. Forester and M. J. Nicholls

GILBERT

ADAIR

"I've always made it a point of honour never to repeat myself."

Verbivoracious Press

Glentrees, 13 Mt Sinai Lane, Singapore

First published in Great Britain and Singapore

by Verbivoracious Press

www.verbivoraciouspress.org

Copyright (c) 2014 Verbivoracious Press

Text Copyright (c) 2014 The Estate of Gilbert Adair

Text Copyright (c) 2014 Authors Listed Herein

All rights reserved. No part of this publication may be reproduced, stored in an electronic or otherwise retrieval system, or transmitted in any form or by any means, electronic, mechanical, digital imaging, recording, otherwise, without the prior consent of the publisher.

The Authors herein assert the moral right to be identified as author of their respective contributions to this work.

ISBN: **978-981-09-2169-9**

Printed and bound in Great Britain and Singapore

Contents

Introduction **Editors**	1
A Dare **Nicolas Tredell**	2
The Rape of the Cock **Gilbert Adair**	8
Interview & Profile **Kevin Jackson**	29
The Author, if Dead, is Not De Man But De Femme **G. N. Forester**	43
The Scottish Postmodernist Never Rings Once, Let Alone Twice, and Can't Even Be Bothered to Leave a Note **M. J. Nicholls**	48
Gilbert's Games and the Golden Age of Murder **Martin Edwards**	61
A De'Athly Confession **Kenneth Retrop**	69
A Letter to My Dead Friend Gilbert Adair About Having It Out **Alexander García Düttman**	75
The Death of the Reader **Lidia Ratberg**	81
Rereading Adair **Jonathan Rosenbaum**	87
The Hand and the Crocodile **Laura Guthrie**	90

Contents

Mysterious Transpositions: Adair's The Dreamers *and Cocteau's* Les Enfants Terribles
Warwick Wise — 95

An Open Book — 103
Alberta Rigid

Death and the Auteur: The Gilbert Adair Meta-Murders — 112
Sergio Angelini

Creative Licentious: The Real Cast of Buenas Noches, Buenas Aires — 130
Edited by Donna Kraschlong and Milo Wi

Disturbance at the Pastiche Playground — 137
Gianni D'Ane, G. N. Forester, Laura Guthrie, Mark Monday, Ian Monk, M. J. Nicholls, Geoff Wilt

A Reasonable Scheme — 162
Igo Wodan

The Glibread Affair — 169
Forest Gren

ACKNOWLEDGEMENTS

Thank you to Adair's literary executors, Miranda and Charlie Porter, and his agent, Carole Blake, for sourcing and allowing us to publish *The Rape of the Cock* in this volume.

Introduction

EDITORS

Our second festschrift celebrates the work of pasticheur, novelist, screenwriter, culture/film critic, and translator Gilbert Adair. This issue concentrates on Adair's literary output and contains a savoury range of pastiches, story homages, and essays on his formidable body of work. Opening the collection is Nicolas Tredell's excellent analysis of Gilbert's literary novels, followed by the first-time publication of a previously unavailable item haunting many of Adair's jacket bios, a parody of Alexander Pope's heroi-comic verse poem *The Rape of the Lock*. Kevin Jackson's profile and interview from 2003 is reprinted here, one of the most revealing portraits of the otherwise reticent and self-effacing writer, originally written during the arrival of Bertolucci's adaptation of *The Dreamers*. Lidia Ratberg and G. N. Forester riff on Adair's craftiest novel, *The Death of the Author*, a sly mystery speculatively influenced by Paul De Man with a tilt to one of Adair's heroes, Roland Barthes. Martin Edwards and Sergio Angelini have contributed two meticulous essays on Adair's popular take on Agatha Christie, the Evadne Mount Mystery novels, while Kenneth Retrop and Laura Guthrie explore alternate directions for *Love and Death on Long Island* and *Peter Pan the Only Children*. The volume culminates in an ecstatic outpouring of pastiches, including a nod to Adair's translation of Perec from Oulipian Ian Monk, followed by Forest Gren's spectacular post-meta-pastiche of *And Then There Was No One*.

A Dare

NICOLAS TREDELL

If the surname, rhyming with Astaire and debonair, seems to suggest an assured performer, it is also a homophone of 'dare', to take a risk, and both these elements are active in Gilbert Adair's novels. From one aspect, he is the postmodernist *par excellence*, the maestro of style, of surface, of pastiche, of multiple personae, parading a succession of masks with nothing behind them; from the other, he is the adventurer who dares to walk a tightrope, high above the city in buffeting winds, an Adair aware of the abyss below, the potential impact with the ground of transgression and mortality. This postmodernist always rings twice and if his first peal resounds with promise, the second tolls the bell that (as in the John Garfield film) reverberates with death and judgement—and, for Adair, there is no plea for an intercession that might end isolation ('make it like we're together'), only, at most, a defiant affirmation of a fragile community in adversity (as at the end of *Buenas Noches Buenas Aires* (2004)). It is this interfusion of these two modes of becoming, postmodernist and existentialist, that gives his fiction its peculiar quality, makes it both an instantiation and interrogation of postmodernism.

Postmodernism is characterized by pastiche rather than parody, not a mocking of previous styles but an imitation of them that, as it were, offers no judgement: a statue with blank eyeballs, in Fredric Jameson's phrase. The style which Adair was most often seen to pastiche was that of Nabokov, a likeness Adair himself repudiated strongly in a 1998 letter to the *London Review of Books* provoked by Lorna Sage's review of *The Key of the Tower* (1997); though fully aware that, as he put it, 'when a writer denies an alleged influence [...] the denial seems only to confirm the truth of the allegation'. He provided, instead, a checklist of influences he was happy to acknowledge: for *The Holy Innocents* (1988), revised and republished as *The Dreamers* (2004), Cocteau's *Le grand écart*, *Les enfants terribles* and *Thomas l'imposteur*; for *Love and Death on Long Island* (1990), Mann's *Death in Venice*; for *The Death of the Author* (1992), 'Henry James's stories of the literary life, as in *The Death of (the Lion) the Author (of Beltraffio)*'; for *The Key of the Tower* (1997), Alfred Hitchcock. The shift from high-cultural to cinematic influences in this list is significant. Postmodernism offered those relaxes that William Blake blessed, releasing culture from its constraining divisions of high and low. It permitted a mixing of levels, styles, and genres, and a raiding of past and present cultural constructions, not only of what the narrator and protagonist of *The Death of the Author* (1992), Léopold Sfax, calls 'the compacted immensities of literature' (20) but also, crucially in Adair's case, of the compacted immensities of film, the most powerful popular medium of the mid-twentieth century, about which he wrote widely. In *The Dreamers* it is the closing of the Cinémathèque Française in Paris and the sacking of its director Henri Langlois that sparks both the retreat of its youthful protagonists to a world of their own and *les_événements* of May 1968; it is through his inadvertent viewing of the wrong film (he had been expecting Forster's *Room with a View*) that the narrator of *Love and Death in Long Island* (1990) becomes obsessed with a young male movie star. The postmodernist release from realist constraints means that the improbable can overtly become (as it perhaps always covertly was) the very stuff of fiction, its incredibility highlighted rather than hidden, a situation epitomized, in Adair's novels, in this passage from *The Key of the Tower*:

> I couldn't believe it. Here I was, in Saint-Malo, held prisoner—inside a Rolls-Royce that was not my own—by a grotesque gangster and his punkish gunsel, hair radiating from his skull like a golden sunburst mirror above a mantelpiece. And now here he was, the gangster him-

self, spouting Proust at me. It was a joke, it was a horrible joke. (99)

Hitchcock famously used to say 'It's only a movie' and Adair's fiction may sometimes seem to solicit the same response. But, as with Hitchcock, the fiction can also summon intensities, draw monsters from the deep. In *The Death of the Author*, Léopold Sfax is a figure much like Paul de Man, autocrat of aporia, whose posthumous reputation was severely damaged by the revelation, unearthed by an assiduous biographer, that he had contributed to a collaborationist, anti-Semitic magazine and had written that it would be no great cultural loss if the Jews were expelled from Europe. This revelation, along with the Sokal hoax, was one of the unpredictable events that helped to bring the postmodernist era to an end. Adair's take on his fictional protagonist is an unsparing one: that his theory was designed as a sophisticated form of self-exculpation: if the author is, theoretically speaking, dead, an absent presence, how can he be held responsible for published utterances that might have fed into the cultural discourses which encouraged the concentration camps? Here the perspective is more Sartrean than postmodernist (and perhaps given an extra edge by the questions raised about Sartre's own role during the German occupation of France in WW2): the protagonist's fall to writing for a collaborationist journal is presented not as a conscious assumption of an anti-Semitic identity to avoid an existential void (as it is for Lucien Fleurier in Sartre's *L'Enfance d'un Chef*), but as an example of Sartrean *mauvaise-foi*: the protagonist knows what he is doing but does it anyway. And his awareness that his collaboration will—and eventually does—come back to haunt him, particularly since his growing fame as a literary theorist promotes increased interest in his life story and its potential for biography, creating a situation close to that of Sartre's *Huis Clos*, where Garcin poses the question: '*Peut-on juger une vie sur un seul acte?*' and hell is '*les autres*', those who fix you with a formulating gaze, sleepless with cold commemorative eyes.

In *A Closed Book* (1999), the past again returns to haunt the present, in the form of historic child abuse, a theme that resonates even more strongly in the post-Savile era. But in a novel told largely in dialogue, one of whose protagonists is a blind man, it is the voice rather than the eyes of the other that give judgement. The abuse has been perpetrated, in his early, obscure days as a master in a school for difficult children, by a now famous, knighted, Booker and Whitbread prize-winning author. He has already suffered the classical punishment for sexual transgression: on a sex tourist visit to Sri Lanka, he was blinded in a car crash, losing not only his sight, but also, literally, his eyes, making him hideous to look upon. The Miltonic term 'eyeless' and its variant forms occur recurrently. Wanting to dictate a memoir, he hires an amanuensis who turns out to be his nemesis, a former victim who finally confronts him with his crime, abrasively obtruding another story in the narrative that shares its title with the novel in which it features:

> It's all wrong, I know. For *A Closed Book*, I mean. Subject-matter's all wrong. After all those high-falutin ramblings of yours about eyes and blindness and eyelessness, it would come as too big a shock to the reader's system. Yeah, but that's life, you see, Paul. You said it yourself, remember? Life doesn't stick to the rules. It springs the sort of climax on you that you don't expect. (224-5)

John plans to execute a kind of wild revenge on Paul by killing him without being caught. But he has reckoned without the fact that the novelist, despite his blindness, is covertly keeping a diary which, as the novel ends, the police are about to open and read. The implication is that a closed book can always be opened again; that the attempt to achieve closure is always thwarted by other possible narratives; that the cycle of abuse and violence, once set in motion, may be impossible to escape.

Death enters Adair's fiction as both represented and unrepresentable, figured in but forever outside the text. For Guy in *The Key of the Tower*, it is represented above all by the haunting image of his wife just before her death in a car he was driving: 'Ursula's face at the point of impact, Ursula's face on which I had turned to gaze, helplessly, as it started to fissure into an unendurable network of crazy-paving cracks' (52). The crazy-paving image recurs near the end of the novel when he inadvertently kills Béa, who is desperately trying to protect a fake painting from destruction:

> I had hit bull's-eye. I had hit the female figure who was furtively handing the key to her male companion. I knew I'd hit her because she screamed—because, too, before my eyes, her face began to crumble into a crazy-paving network of cracks until all at once it was obliterated by her blood. (173)

The crazy-paving network of cracks—an image for postmodernist fragmentation itself—is drenched in blood, an image of primal vibrancy and violence.

In his final novel, *Buenos Noches, Buenos Aires* (2004), the visitations of death take the form of Aids—as the protagonist-narrator, Gideon, initially prefers to write it before, in the last word of the book, accepting the full capitalization: AIDS. Its inhibited gay narrator, teaching at the Berlitz school in Paris and spinning spurious yarns of his non-existent sexual exploits, starts to become aware of what is at first called a 'gay cancer' (73), though it seems, in the beginning, 'solely an American problem' (82). But then the signs show among his friends: an apparently healthy tooth falls out during a vigorous act of lovemaking; 'a row of prominent bluish bumps' appear 'on what were already abnormally reddened hands and wrists' (114). Confirmatory diagnoses follow. Gideon begins to wonder when his friends will start asking him (given the sexual exploits of which he has boasted) why *he* has not contracted Aids and, given the apparent withdrawal from same-sex activity by gay men in light of the disease, he is 'seized with terror at the prospect that if I didn't have my share of sex at once *I might never have it at all*' (126, italics in original). He thus embarks on an energetic pursuit of gay sex—

and, as he realizes, quite possibly also of death, culminating in the book's concluding declaration as he enumerates his lovers and addresses them in Baudelarian-T.S. Eliot mode as his fellows and brothers:

> So—Kim, Edouard, Didier, Enrique, Gaetan, Barbet, *mes semblables, mes frères*, all those members of the only set, the only family, the only brotherhood, to which I've ever felt I truly belonged or wished to belong, all of those of you with whom I've been privileged to share the splendours and miseries, grandeur and servitude, of the homosexual condition, let me salute you fraternally, wherever you are.
>
> I don't want to die—naturally, I don't—but, if I must, then I've now come to realise how proud I'd be, how utterly unashamed, to die of Aids.
>
> No, I take that back. To die of AIDS. (151)

It is fitting that Adair's last novel should end on this note of daring.

Works cited:
Adair, Gilbert, *The Holy Innocents: A Romance* (London: Heinemann, 1988); revised version published as *The Dreamers* (London: Faber and Faber, 2004).
- - -, *Love and Death on Long Island* (London: Heinemann, 1990).
- - -, *The Death of the Author* (London: Heinemann, 1992).
- - -, *The Key of the Tower: A Novel* (London: Secker and Warburg, 1997).
- - -, Letter to *London Review of Books*, 20:2 (Jan 1998), available at: http://www.lrb.co.uk/v20/n01/lorna-sage/the-view-from-the-passenger-seat
- - -, *A Closed Book* (London: Faber and Faber, 1999).
- - -, *Buenos Noches, Buenas Aires* (London: Faber and Faber, 2004).

Nicolas Tredell: 1 July 2014

The Rape of the Cock

GILBERT ADAIR

CANTO I

WHAT dire offence from am'rous causes springs,
What mighty contests rise from trivial things,
I also sing—This verse to POPE is due,
In like proportion as the theme is new:
Slight is the subject, but not so the praise,   5
If 's[1] genius consecrate my lays.
    Since coffee-tables altars have replac'd,
And are by coffee-table Bibles grac'd,
On these inferior shrines let me repose,
Sandwich'd 'twixt Avedon and Punch's nose,   10
There to support the silver-laden tray,
While tomes less functional in dust decay.
    Sol from th'ethereal dome eclipst the night,
And o'er the earth sent beams of radiant light;
Th'awak'ning day saw Gilbert still abed,   15
As stirring sights disturb'd his lovely head
(That puppet-playhouse of our brightest dreams,
Where all of life so elemental seems).
In vain loud musick, just at nine, arose,
And eccho'd down the neatly terrac'd rows: 20
Thrice rung the bell, the jingle chim'd in vain,
For Gilbert slept, and all was still again.

---

1 Blank space in the original manuscript.

When lo! a spirit thro' the curtain flew,
O'er bedsheets discompos'd, and limbs askew,
And tracing thro' the air a golden ray,   25
Shot it twixt legs in unpropel'd array,
Thence to behold Creation's noblest work,
Propt up on pillows, languid as a Turk.
All spying done, he near'd the rumpled bed,
Cough'd lightly once, and in a whisper said: 30
   "Fairest of mortals, thou the cherish'd prize
Of ev'ry heart, and twice as many eyes,
Learn that thou art, beyond this narrow care,
The cynosure of more unearthly air!
What tho' great wits in ev'ry age have striv'n   35
To make a soulless desart out of heav'n,
What tho' half-truths and theories just reveal'd
Cause angels from the world to be conceal'd,
Yet know that sylphs, and gnomes, and airy things
'Gainst Arctic zephyrs bravely bend their wings,   40
Or shivring tread the skies above the Pole,
Or tremble o'er the Carib's smoking hole,
(Where kindred souls lie deep in wat'ry graves,
And just their fus'lage dances on the waves)
Or rove the fields in tiny insects' guise,   45
In search of nymphs commens'rate with their size,
From flow'r to flow'r rare specimens pursue,
Till the long grass glitters with more than dew.
   "Some sprights, reposing from celestial courts,
Like hanging judges in Bermuda shorts,   50
No more thro' musty annals pleas'd to roam,
Or stablish precedents in some dank tome,
To earth descend on chariots of bronze,
There to disport like Bacchanalian fauns.
'Tis these that steal into a virgin's bed,   55
Prompt her foul words, and quick rotate her head;

Or spew huge monsters from the plangent deep,
With jaws that tear the flesh, or make it creep;
Or raise up 'gainst mankind with equal glee
A tempest in a tea-pot, or at sea! 60
　"Oft, when the world imagine young men stray,
The sylphs thro' mystic mazes guide their way,
Till ev'ry innocent become a whore,
And to the streets be damn'd for ever more.
What gentle youth thereafter cou'd resist 65
Satan himself, if limping at the wrist?
What lusty hero cou'd for long withstand
His hissing sibilants, but be unman'd?
Nay, soon the nat'ral laws wou'd he confound,
His neck within a silken knot be bound, 70
His cheeks to paint be due, to coal his eyes,
And ev'n his hair to varying wigs and dyes.
This erring minds effeminate may call:
Oh blind to truth! the sylphs contrive it all.
　"Of these am I, who thy protection claim, 75
A watchful spright, and Ariel is my name.
The secrets I divulge thy unlock'd eyes
Shall soon dispel, as keener instincts rise,
But airy ecchoes of my speech shall stay
To guide thy wandrings thro' this fateful day. 80
For late I saw, without a gypsy ball,
A dread humiliation thee befall,
But heav'n reveals not what, or how, or where:
Warn'd by the sylph, impious youth, beware!
This to disclose is all that Ariel can: 85
Beware of all, but most beware of man!"
　He said; when Gilbert from his slumber woke,
And twitch'd the ear in which his guardian spoke.
Up flew the sylph, and vanish'd full away,
As minst'ring spirits hover'd o'er the tea: 90

Some in the rich bohea their wings immerst,
And to the liquid's edge its gold disperst;
Some tasted it with confidential sips,
Then help'd to raise it steaming to his lips.
    The solemn bev'rage at its journey's end,   95
Now o'er the mystic mirror does he bend.
'Tis there he spies, the image to his cheek,
A pimple rise abrupt upon its peak.
Strait to the flaw converge two fingernails,
But first, ill-judg'd, the operation fails.   100
Twice, thrice, the cruel, unbending nails return:
Three times his eyes o'erflow, his temples burn.
Not with more valour 'gainst th'offending Greek
Did Troy withstand, than this unyielding cheek!
Belinda now, a nymph of pity known,   105
Approaches to the naked youth alone,
And pulling from her curls a shining pin,
Impales the boil, and gently sucks therein.
    Now Gilbert swiftly o'er his face applies
The bracing soap, and just as swiftly dries.   110
The genie of perfume he now unlocks,
And all cologne breathes forth from yonder box.
Then 'neath each arm extends the cooling spray,
And, tho' not clean, smells lov'lier ev'ry day.

CANTO II

THIS youth, whom all consented to adore,
Nourish'd a cock, that graceful hung before.
On this inspiring vision suitors gaz'd,
And all dimensions in a glance apprais'd.
Men with this bodkin ease their own desires,   5
And others cause to burn with fiercer fires,

Op'ning their legs its volume to divulge;
Closing, to trace the contours of the bulge:
If to their share some nat'ral errors fall,
Look on that bulge, and you'll forgive 'em all. 10
    A Baron long th'elusive cock admir'd,
Long had he wish'd, and to the prize aspir'd,
Contain'd his rage as he himself was spurn'd,
And billets-doux unopen'd were return'd,
But fail'd to gain by pedigree alone 15
What all the coronets in Burke won't own.
    Oft wou'd he sit, and musing o'er his fate,
That sweetmeat, vengeance, wou'd he meditate.
Unhealthy visions swam before his eyes
Of doubtful youths with sexes in disguise. 20
Soon these to nobler chimeras wou'd fade,
In crumbling wigs, and shreds of silk array'd,
And all his ancestors, an ancient strain,
Now dusty phantoms, swell'd his fever'd brain;
But chiefly one—a sacrilegious Peer, 25
Long dead, but living in a poet's air:
Lord Petre! who just once the sylphs defy'd,
Who but for that, an honest man had died :
From him the Baron, if report say true,
Receiv'd the notion—and the scissors, too. 30
    With careful thoughts the spirit is opprest;
Th'impending woe sits heavy on his breast.
That not his favrite charge be led astray,
He calls all heaven's angels to the fray.
The fragile legions to th'alarm reply, 35
Their brittle pinions fluttring in the sky.
Sylphs first in slender filaments unwind
Bright banners all inflated by the wind
Which wafts them o'er th'aerial terrain,
Cool zephyrs mingling with the soft-hued rain. 40

Then to and fro amid the boistrous swell
They dart; and prince among them, Ariel,
Who silence with three cryptic words enforc'd,
And to th'assembled spirits thus discours'd.
    "Ye sylphs and sylphids, to your chief give ear!   45
Fays, fairies, genii, elves, and daemons, hear!
No more sweet stupors shall our senses daze,
Nor silken wings in balmy tropicks glaze;
Too long did we in easeful comfort bask:
Be present now, and equal to the task!   50
But let no trust to which a sylph might own
Take precedence o'er this: the British throne.
Make mischief, sprights! on that usurping reign,
Ere the sun sets, and ye the skies regain.
Compose rude lim'ricks on the Queen's discourse,   55
Or spread unseason'd rumours of divorce,
Untimely show'rs on garden-parties spill,
Or 'By Appointment' grave upon the Pill,
Or Corgis mate with an inferior line,
And by such acts o'erturn the right divine.   60
    "Our humbler province is to tend the fair,
Not a less pleasing, tho' less glorious care;
To shelter hapless mortals from the danger,
Here of rain, and there of heav'nly anger;
Gyrate in clockwise wheels the idle thumbs,   65
Or to chaf'd lips apply soft pomatums.
    "Oh sylphs! black omens threat the brightest fair,
That e'er deserved a watchful spirit's care.
This is the purpose of our just crusade:
To stay the arm that lifts a fateful blade,   70
And has, moreo'er, a martyr ready claim'd:
A saint whose hair (he sigh'd) was cruelly maim'd.
But fair Belinda was not long disgrac'd,
For sever'd locks are in due course replac'd,

As nimble digits o'er the ringlet dart,   75
And vagrant wisps along the middle part.
But now behold a more enduring theft,
With Gilbert soon of all his pow'r bereft!
So lend an ear, your own assignment learn,
And be forewarn'd that few shall e'er return.   80
   "To a commando, famous for its grip,
We trust that perilous slope, the trouser-zip :
Step lightly, sylphs, upon that silver stair,
That not the ogre waken from his lair,
And, lac'd together, let it not uncoil   85
From rung to rung; and so the en'my foil.
   "The rest a no less dreadful task awaits:
On Gilbert's body join to thwart the fates.
Haste, then, ye spirits! to your ward repair:
The handkerchief be Nylonetta's care;   90
The shirt in Terylena's charge we place;
Do thou, Brillante, shield the colour'd glass;
Crispissa, let the pubick locks be thine;
Ariel himself shall guard the Vaseline.
   "Whatever spirit, careless of his charge,   95
His post neglects, or leaves the fair at large,
A ladder'd stocking shall his tread-mill be,
Or round a soup-tureen pursue a pea;
Wedg'd tight between the motors of a watch,
Hear frail wings crack at ev'ry wheel's approach;   100
Or dangling craven from the morning-clock,
Fall, just at half-past six, when both hands lock.
Let Gilbert's hand-bag be his narrow tomb,
His crucifix the cruelly scallop'd comb,
In the soft butter be condemn'd to sink,   105
Parch'd, a nose-drop, or his own urine, drink;
And if such punishments be not enough,
We'll brew thick fogs inside the powder-puff!"

He spoke; and sent the spirits on their way,
As anxious, but as resolute, as they.   110

CANTO III

CLOSE by the town, where yet meads moist with dew,
And forests, and fair vistas fill the view,
There stands a structure of imposing frame,
Which takes from neighb'bring Kensington its name.
Here Lords, with these who love a Lord, consort,   5
Tasting awhile the pleasures of a court;
Here thou, dear MARG'RET! dost with envy'd ease
Emit an endless stream of royal we's.
   Hither on Dag'nam's fiery chariots flock
Lovers of am'rous, or instructive, talk,   10
To praise the Bottoms of theatrick Dreams,
Or these Aldwych ushers, and such themes;
One waxes lyrical o'er Lucan's death,
With just the wat'ry vortex for a wreath;
And one describes in unabash'd detail   15
His wife's anatomy, from head to tail;
A third to calumny serene replies,
And, drest in white, tells nicely matching lies.
   Mean while, declining from the noon of day,
The sun obliquely shoots his burning ray;   20
Dieting secret'ries long labours stop,
And gorge on babas in Ye Olde Tea Shoppe;
While Hampstead mammas count each sweet in fright,
Lest little Tristram dull his appetite;
Till homewards all the world in peace repairs,   25
To softer duties, and to slighter cares.
Gilbert alone, whom thirst of fame invites,
Burns to encounter two adventurous knights,

And play strip-poker to decide their doom,
With gains more tantalizing still to come.   30
But om'nous shadows o'er the Palace build,
And with misgivings are the spirits fill'd;
The Baron's eyes are red inflam'd with hate,
His lust half-hidden 'neath a crested plate:
"Insulting youth! (disdainfully he vows)   35
Soon shalt thou suffer fair Belinda's loss,
But lower down, in that secluded place
Where latent hairs imbrown thy second face!"
    Ariel, in fear of his obscure designs,
Swift to each royal suit a sylph assigns.   40
Not swift enough! The Baron first reveals
A pack from which, without a cut, he deals:
Tho' hid from view their parti-colour'd pride,
The shining icons o'er the table glide.
    Gilbert with awful care his portion fann'd.   45
An op'd the cards that lay within his hand.
There sate three kings upon themselves enthron'd.
(Or twice three monarchs at the middle join'd)
The king of diamonds, shewing half his face,
And these of spades and clubs, a darker race.   50
Alas! no sooner had he joyful play'd
The club, the diamond, and th'imperial spade,
As many aces then the Peer put forth,
Th'aeternal emblems of all pow'r on earth:
These Hoyle declar'd the mightiest of 'em all;   55
To these ev'n kings an easy conquest fall.
    While heapt with scorn disperst th'inferior band,
The king of heart still lurk'd in Gilbert's hand:
At once his consort and her knave appear,
And two plebeian hearts bring up the rear;   60
But in the Baron's palm a troop of spades,
In dusky legions of superior grades,

Spite of the army of the sanguine race,
With broken hearts bestrow the verdant baize.
The red artill'ry to its en'my lost, 65
Then on th'ascending pyre the fair youth tost
A broider'd handkerchief, a shirt from Blades,
Chas'd out (oh irony!) in hearts and spades.
    The battel rages, and the war prolongs,
As troops debate the field in hybrid throngs: 70
Here kings from common cards exact their toll,
And ties from necks, like heads from bodies, roll;
There pious youths prefer to shew white pricks
Than e'er remove a sparkling crucifix;
While these less young who, drest, their years belie 75
See in an hour their reputations die.
    A pair of knaves spring forth, of count'nance bold,
And two fair queens, each doubly crown'd with gold,
Whose pow'rs combin'd of diamonds and of hearts
In Gilbert's cause engage their wily arts. 80
The Baron, mean while flying to th'attack,
Falls his own victim: from the perjur'd pack
A mob of indiscrim'nate rank and dye
Greets his just wrath, and unforgiving eye.
With artful ease his smouldring brow he fans, 85
Nor heeds the nigh destruction of his plans.
Sudden he starts, and seems to doubt his eyes:
"Oh Lucan! is it thou (the villain cries)
Who, spite of having murder'd once in vain,
Resolv'd to kill thyself—and mist again?" 90
As ev'ry head towards the vision rears,
And ev'n the sylphs o'erlook their former fears,
The Peer, of more than once device possest,
A matching pack swift summons from his breast,
Plucks out five cards, which ancient laws endow'd 95
With sov'reign pow'rs, and wins the game by fraud.

    No more did disaccord the play'rs divide,
At once all rally'd to the victor's side
"Off with his pants!" in gen'ral voice they said,
"Off with his pants!" as tho' it were his head;   100
" . . . His pants . . . his pants . . ." came th'incomplete reply,
As the dom'd roof re-eccho'd to their cry.
    Impatient now, the Baron stretch'd his hand:
"The prize is mine!" he cry'd, and seiz'd the band,
Th'elastick band that still the cock conceal'd,   105
Then, pulling fast, its hard, bright knob reveal'd.
White thighs, and undrest limbs around it shone,
But ev'ry eye was fix'd on it alone,
And ev'ry eye its swelling forms pursu'd,
(Swelling that from their lustful gaze ensu'd).   110
Only the Peer this tender vision spurn'd:
To have for ever that for which he burn'd,
A glittring engine on his fingers spread,
The same that once profan'd Belinda's head:
A tiny pair of shears, of purpose dire,   115
'Fore which in disarray the sylphs retire.
    Arm'd this, the Baron to his victim nears;
The crowd is mute: opprest with nameless fears,
A thousand sprights draw in their breath as one,
To see their charge stand shivring and alone.   120
At forty-five degrees around the cock
The scissors now diverge, now neatly lock:
Snick! and the Baron disunities his prey,
While Gilbert (like the reader) faints away:
For when great Sheffield forges steel to steel,   125
Its edge no mortal shou'd so closely feel!
    "Let wreaths of triumph now temples twine,
(The victor cry'd) what I long sought is mine!
While fish in streams, or birds delight in air,
Or men deposit all their refuse there,   130

As long as th'Irish question is discust,
And ash to ash return'd, and dust to dust,
As long as royal lovers make good press,
And Julius Caesar plays in modern dress,
And lying witnesses their right hands raise,   135
So long shall live my honour, name, and praise!"
    But soon th'affrighted youth shall ope his eyes,
Soon shall the comp'ny shudder to his cries—
Enough! O Muse, permit me to retire,
Sicken'd by scenes that no lampoon inspire.   140
What boots the careful crib of ancient times,
The'Augustan rhythms, and th'Augustan rhymes?
Not ev'n Alexis in his noblest strain
Cou'd in ten syllables such grief contain.

CANTO IV

Now anxious cares the pensive youth opprest,
And secret passions labour'd in his breast.
Not rash Antonio as his debt came near,
Not kidnap'd heirs who forfeited an ear,
Not poodle-dogs whose testicles are tap'd,   5
Not ev'n Belinda when her lock was rap'd,
Not surgeons who a living limb extract,
And not Conundrum's author when intact,
E'er felt such rage, resentment, and dismay,
As thou, pale monster, on that fateful day.   10
    Put in a rage to see the sylphs all fail,
And Gilbert broken like a fingernail,
A spright Italianate, whose mincing grace
Did little honour to that manly race,
One Zephyrelli, to his haunt repairs,   15
A gloomy vale of onion-scented tears.

No cooler zephyrs do these halls aerate,
For spirits, if they rise at all, rise late,
From reveries of some attractive gnome,
Or of the cupid on the painted dome.   20
Erotica in leather volumes bound,
Tight trusses, and reviving whips are found;
The nat'ral pow'rs this dismal pit avoids,
'Cept Spanish Fly, and cures for haemorrhoids.
   Two servants wait the throne: alike in place,   25
But diffring far in figure and in face.
Ill-nature here, in heavy chains array'd,
Whose eyes dark glasses from the daylight shade:
A mighty iron crucifix he wore,
That sylphs, in various ways, learn'd to adore.   30
   There Affection thro' the grotto flitts,
With simpers, moues, and awful screaming fits.
A num'rous court about his presence moves
Of acolytes, all slaves to shameful loves.
Now to the Phallus does the genuflect,   35
And pray, with head bent low, and cock erect;
Now seraphim in turn him entertain,
Who penetrate, or hold aloft his train.
   A constant vapour o'er the palace flies;
Strange phantoms rising as the mists arise;   40
Unquiet, as madman's ravings in their ills,
Or missionaries' dreams on pagan isles.
Now headless visions, and marauding apes,
Pale virgins, vampire-bats, and wolves in capes:
Now gilded totem-poles, Tahitian songs,   45
Green sheltering palms, and dancers in sarongs.
   High o'er the living lab'rinth flew the spright,
Swift thro' unnumber'd caves aswarm with night.
Here by a jealous sylph turn'd Pekinese,
A desp'rate lady calls in vain for trees;   50

There babes, germs, carbs, and allergies fly past,
Old men are born, and embryos breathe their last.
    Close by the Goddess, solemn-fac'd and proud,
The gnome approach'd, and rev'rently he bow'd.
Then thus addrest the pow'r—"Hail, wayward Queen!"   55
Who male and female rule, and all between.
A Lord there is, that all thy pow'r disdains,
And thousands more in equal mirth maintains.
If e'er a sylph might mischief better place
Than make a statesman runny babes embrace,   60
Or, elf-green, dangle from a royal nose,
While all her retinue in concert blows,
Or dunces of their coronets deprive,
Or iron crosses as a mode revive,
Or at the play a maiden discontain: 65
Thrice from her chair to rise, and thrice regain:
Oh hear me, and thy mystic musk inhal'd,
Let me succeed where all the sylphs have fail'd."
    The Goddess with a discontented air
Seems to reject him, tho' she grants his pray'r.   70
First from the throne she wearily descends,
And with a mighty creak her whole frame bends;
Attendant sylphs her ample robe then raise;
And two huge buttocks meet the goblin's gaze.
She waits, that neither haste nor caution vain   75
Essential gases from the air retain,
Till mounting vapours nicely are amast,
And all their force is concentrated fast,
Then all at once th'imprison'd winds discharge
With such report that sylphs are knock'd at large,   80
Jars crack, and ev'n the automatic clock
Unwinds, its spirals straiten'd by the shock.
Only the gnome rejoicing braves the fart,
Whose essences, inhal'd, rare pow'rs impart.

Then rising up, he circles once the scene, 85
And bids adieu to the recumbent Queen.
   Sunk in Sir Cecil's arms the youth he found,
His eyes dejected and his hair unbound,
O'ercome with shame and robb'd of earthly joy,
A Bowdleriz'd edition of a boy! 90
"O wretched lad!" his confidant exclaim'd,
(As in a Pieta unwitting fram'd)
"Was it for this I took such constant care
To hide 'neath wide-brimm'd hats my shrinking hair?
For this a course in calisthenics pay'd, 95
For this long ages at the hammam stay'd?
Renounc'd for this charms of wedded life?
A gelded boy no better than a wife!
Methinks already I the mock'ry hear
Of those who claim to hold my int'rest dear; 100
Or see the cock in a satiric skit,
Like that which for Belinda's lock was writ;
Or, like a trophy, if it were display'd,
Its beauties on a mantel-piece array'd,
Pickled in brine, with burning acids serv'd, 105
And by the taxidermist's art preserv'd,
There in the clarifying glass encas'd,
To lure uncensur'd eyes, and lips unchaste:
How shou'd I, then, my hapless fame defend?
'Twou'd then be infamy to seem your friend!" 110
   He said; and to the Baron swift dispatch'd
The stunted youth, impermeably patch'd,
Who with protruding eyes, and tear-streak'd face,
His en'my met, and skilful lay'd the case.
He thus broke out—"Hey, man, but there's a limit! 115
I mean . . . Y'know . . . Y'gotta gimme it!
Fuck! Where's the cock? Now give it back, you poof!
Or . . . Or . . ."—he said, and thought he spoke enough.

"It grieves me much" (reply'd the Peer again)
"Who speaks so well shou'd ever speak in vain.   120
But by this cock, this sacred cock I swear,
(Oh let it long enjoy my single care,
Wrapt in old lace, in Asprey's finest box,
And cur'd for ever of the rav'nous pox)
That while I live, while wits remain intact,   125
My judgment to correct, or on it act,
'Twill be my purpose to defend from harm
What 'gainst ill-fortune has become my charm."
    But lo! the gnome upon a cloud appears,
And with one puff dispels all Gilbert's fears.   130
Now see the youth from out his torpor rise,
Hot tears no longer rolling o'er his eyes,
With bright auroras burning in his cheeks,
And arms imploring heaven, thus he speaks.
    "For ever curst be this detested day,   135
Which snatch'd my best, my favrite toy away,
Which pluck'd me of my proud, my forky horn,
And made a eunuch of a unicorn!
No more to oily hands my limbs t'entrust,
To soothe my aches, and satisfy my lust;   140
No more mid'st drowzy vapours to recline,
With gay companions on the knotted pine,
Or, acorn-like, my sprouting member shew,
Which to a mighty oak ere long wou'd grow!
What mov'd my mind with ancient Lords to roam?   145
Oh had I stay'd, and improvis'd at home!
'Twas this, no doubt, that haunted me all night,
Thrice from my bed I started up in fright;
A sylph, too, whisper'd warnings in my ear,
Subtle, and pitch'd too fine for me to hear;   150
Ev'n the live grains lay silent in the bowl:
Nay, Snap was pale, and Crackle seem'd to scowl!

"Now see the stump where late my bodkin grew,
(He said; and op'd his legs that all might view)
And think again what you have robb'd me of: 155
A horn of plenty fill'd with liquid love,
Whose double stream ooz'd warmly o'er my thighs,
Now graz'd by other, ev'n less wholsom files!"

CANTO V

THUS he: the pitying audience melt in tears,
But fate and Jove had stopp'd the Baron's ears.
Not all the shrieks of rage or passion born
Cou'd help him now so abject and forlorn!
Sir Cecil to the cause return'd again, 5
And Gilbert sobb'd and sobb'd, but all in vain.
Then grave Conundra three times tapp'd her chair,
And call'd for silence from th'assembly there.
"Say, what gives men prerogative of place,
And makes them honour'd most of all the race? 10
Why to their member do they proudly cling,
As tho' it were a rare and precious thing?
Why bow and scrape in awe of Phallus' pow'r?
Why phallus seek in ev'ry dome or tow'r?
Oh! if to wave that wand cou'd halt decay, 15
Charm the cancer, or chase old-age away,
Who wou'd not male extremities prefer,
Or who wou'd still think ours superior?
But since, alas! the passing years divest
A prick of all the pow'r it once possest, 20
Since that which once so vig'rously uncurl'd
To rival all the wonders of the world
Shall like a tyrant, old and pow'rless grown,
Curl up in fear, and shrink into its throne,

Be grateful, dear, that like Belinda's lock,   25
A foster-parent shall conserve thy cock
In its first purity, and pristine state,
And thank, not curse, the heavens for thy fate."
   So spoke the dame, but no applause ensu'd;
Sir Cecil frowns, and Gilbert calls her rude.   30
The short-liv'd pax in mounting bedlam dies,
And tearful passions streak mascara'd eyes.
Battel is join'd, the marble halls resound
To "Come on, girls!", and ev'rywhere is found
A throng of greazy Figaros with Pekes,   35
And spavin-legged dealers in antiques.
"To arms, to arms!" in unison they cry,
And tweezers, rings, and safety-pins let fly.
Thus (if small things we may with great compare)
Did Albion send her eager sons to war;   40
When grim Leviathans tall sails unroll'd,
And hearts were hot, tho' steel was cutting cold;
When galleons galleons crush'd; o'er nodding tow'rs
The hovring arrows sudden dropt in show'rs.
   Gay Zephyrelli in amber haze,   45
Drugg'd by his mistress' fumes, the fight surveys:
Here pictures, hangings, tapestries are sack'd,
No chair is left upright, no vase intact;
There Donatello's David topples o'er,
His vitals lie in fragments on the floor.   50
   'Gainst Ronald, Clive; 'gainst Percy, Julian arms,
And all Belgravia rings with loud alarms.
Now Rudolf leaps into clam'rous fray,
Wounding Sir Cecil with a fouette:
"Encore! Encore!" the smitten aesthete cries,   55
And from a second blow contented dies.
Conundra casts a glance o'er all the scene,
Regretful now of what she once had been,

And ponders pleasures only men can know,
Until a flying dildo brings her low!   60
   See Gilbert keenly thro' the comp'ny fly,
With more than usual lightning in his eye;
Tho' sylphs and gnomes and men together pray,
No thoughts of heav'nly retribution sway
His awful purpose: to regain the limb   65
The fates for ever judg'd to keep from him.
   But first the Baron seiz'd the dainty case,
Wherein the cock repos'd on ancient lace,
Then fled towards the door, but tackled low,
Unwitting past the trophy to a foe: 70
A crowd of fierce contenders on him fell,
All slid across the Aubusson, pell-mell.
"A foul! Afoul!" shrill righteous voices cry'd,
And with his bodkin Ariel blew off-side.
A scrum was form'd, 'gainst shoulder shoulder prest,   75
The prize no sooner dropt, was re-possest;
Till Gilbert, stirring from the tumbled heap
'Neath which he lay, made an heroic leap
Obtain'd the case, unlock'd it with a snap,
And pos'd the cock erect upon his lap.   80
   "Indecent Lord! (he cry'd) Boast not thy gain!
What thou did'st rob me of, was robb'd in vain!
Thou might'st have any limb but this possest,
Or left but this, and taken all the rest!
But thy defeat from thy own greed is born;   85
What! shall the cock thy vulgar case adorn?
Nay, let my curse re-eccho thro' this hall:
What I may ne'er embrace, no other shall!"
   He said; then launch'd the casket on the air,
But when it fell, 'twas empty of its care,   90
Which like an arrow labour'd up the skies:
O'er Selfridges late shoppers watch'd it rise.

Some thought it mounted to the lunar sphere,
Since all things lost on earth, are treasur'd there.
There humble Pam may hear her dogg'rel scan,   95
And Col'ridge ev'ry verse of Kubla Khan;
There statesmen's wits are grav'd on heads of pains,
And expletives strung out on lengthy skins;
There, too, the lover's sighs, the husband's snores,
The death-bed rattle, and the birth-bed roars,   100
Cudgels to brain a flea, and chains for mites,
Elephants' pills, and tomes of Leavisites.
    But trust the Muse—she sees it from afar
Stream thro' the heavens like an infant star,
(So man just crawling from the apes' embrace   105
Cast bones that chang'd to satellites in space)
Show'ring with sparks the orb-encrusted sky,
Sparks that seem dew-drops to the naked eye;
It rises up e'er farther, e'er more true,
And glows like gossamer in mortal view,   110
Till sylphs, assisting its divine re-birth,
Direct its even beams o'er all the earth.
    This the gai monde shall as a cult adopt,
And as a relique keep the box that dropt.
To this ev'n Paisley shall enlighten'd pray,   115
And hail in Latin its propitious ray.
This Thatcher from the rostrum shall proclaim
As Britain's saviour; and th'egregious dame
Shall fix on ev'ry wall uplifted thumbs,
And ev'ry Sabbath ring with Te Deums.   120
    Then cease, fond youth! to mourn thy ravish'd limb,
Which hence shall reign o'er all its kind supreme:
Belinda's lock shall be its Dantean guide
Thro' silent wastes where sick'ning stars subside,
Whence to the purest spheres it shall ascend,   125
Where sylphs ablaze in gold and white attend,

Wing'd amoretti shall o'erflow the air
With high, exalted strains; and then, and there,
This cock, the Muse shall consecrate to fame,
And mid'st the heav'ns inscribe our common name.   130

Interview & Profile

KEVIN JACKSON

Two or three things I know about Gilbert Adair: He is a cinephile of the most ardent order, who cares so much about what films have been and might still become that he can hardly stand what they (mostly) are these days, and seldom sets foot inside a cinema. He is a fastidious and exacting aesthete, with a Flaubertian disdain for vulgarity, yet has been one of this country's most influential pioneers in writing about popular culture: Dennis Norden, Tintin, 'Don't forget the fruit gums, Mum . . .' He tends, in person, to be a rather quiet, self-effacing sort of chap, but his prose can be supremely dandyish and ostentatiously brilliant: Clark Kent transformed into Super-critic. There are passages in his work, both fiction and non-fiction, that hint at a temperament shot through with veins of deep sorrow and even despair, but he is a richly gifted entertainer and a genuinely funny wit: hence his love for Charlie Chaplin, whom he once celebrated in an essay with the delicious title 'On first looking into Chaplin's humour.'

If you try to pin down what is it that makes Gilbert Adair's writing so different, so appealing, you'll probably discover that the virtues which come to mind are rather old-fashioned ones. Craftsmanship: whether at the level of lapidary sentences or ingenious plots. (At least two of his novels, *The Death of the Author* and *A Closed Book*, owe something of their structure, if not their style, to the example of Agatha Christie.) Learning: he has an uncommonly broad cultural range, which suavely encompasses the most recondite literary theory and the most humble ephemera: Michel Serres to *The Sun*. Elegance: he once said that his ambition was to write as fluently and finely as Fred Astaire danced. And a few other, comparably unfashionable graces—panache, eloquence, a penchant for the aphoristic: 'Taste is, in short, the style of the public.' You can point to a lot of writers who have worked and played in similar veins—Wilde, Nabokov, Queneau and the late Anthony Burgess (a great Adair fan, by the by)—but to none who have quite his particular admixture of musicality and brio.

Next month sees the British première of *The Dreamers*, a feature film by Bernardo Bertolucci freely adapted from Adair's first, quasi-autobiographical novel *The Holy Innocents* and set in Paris during the "*evenements*" of 1968. Adair has not only written the screenplay but—dissatisfied with some elements of the novel as it stood—has substantially rewritten it in a form which, as he puts it, is 'a twin of Bernardo's film, but not an identical twin.' Shortly after the movie opens, Faber will be publishing Adair's latest novel, *Buenas Noches Buenos Aires*: a very different fiction, though also one which, despite its teasing title, has precious little to do with Argentina's capital city and plenty to do with France's. It is, characteristically, the only novel of which I can think where the emotional power of the last line—which is considerable—turns on a question of typography.

This double-barrelled blast of accomplishment is gratifying both for Adair and for his long-term admirers, but it scarcely amounts to a case of overnight success. Adair, who will be sixty at the end of this year, has been working steadily at the construction of his highly idiosyncratic "oeuvre" for over two decades. I first encountered his unmistakable prose style in the early 1980s, when he was mainly employed as a film critic, contributing reviews and articles and squibs to *Sight and Sound*—pieces which stood out from most of the surrounding texts (often worthy and learned, often plodding) like bright sparklers in the autumnal gloom.

If memory serves, the first Adair piece I ever read was a rhapsodic account of a young actor's incisive fossa—the small groove that lies between the nose and the upper lip. (As he has put it elsewhere: 'The incisive fossa is that short vertical furrow, the face's navel, as it were, that divides the nose from the monogrammatic M of the upper lip.') I was an instant convert. 'He writes', a friend said to me at the time, 'as if he were making a thousand angels dance on the head of a pin.' Just so.

Since that time, Adair has been about as prolific as is compatible with an innate fastidiousness: five novels, half a dozen critical works, two books for intelligent children (sequels to the *Alice* books and to *Peter Pan*), a mock-epic, semi-pornographic poem, translations from the French of Truffaut's collected letters and—Adair's single most astounding technical feat—of Georges Perec's lipogrammatic novel *La Disparition*, which runs for hundreds of pages without ever using the letter 'e'. Adair's version is called *A Void*; some readers think it improves on the awe-inspiring original. All that, plus hectares of film reviews, including plenty for the *Independent on Sunday*, and assorted cultural journalism for the *Sunday Times* and other papers.

Outsiders to the literary racket might well think that a track record of such ample proportions brings a substantial fortune and a pile in the Home Counties as well as critical acclaim: cue bitter laughter from the direction of the Society of Authors. No, Adair continues to live in a modest, slightly austere one-bedroom flat, albeit in a modish district of West London, and the only signs of material indulgence I noticed when I went to interview him for this profile were a few rare-ish books. Aspirant Lloyd Grossmans, if such sorry creatures exist, might care to make something out of the fact that he has two shelves of books by and about Jean Cocteau (a major influence on *The Holy Innocents*) set immediately above two equally sized shelves of books on mathematics—some for the general reader, others for the hyper-numerate only. For Adair, maths is the Road Not Taken: he had the chance to read the subject at university, but opted for modern languages instead. In glum moments, he has been known to lament the choice: 'I missed my vocation, I wasted my life . . . '

*

We begin by talking about *The Dreamers*, not only from Adair's perfectly respectable desire to promote the film, but because so much of his life is implicit in its story and its images. The basic narrative is fairly simple. A handsome, slightly naive and virginal American youth, Matthew (played by Michael Pitt), new and lonely in Paris, falls in with a similarly good-looking brace of siblings, Isabelle and Theo (Eva Green, Louis Garrel) who share his extreme cinephilia; they meet, as cinephiles of that time and place did, at Henri Langlois's justly mythologised Cinémathèque Française. (Bertolucci's film is crammed with clips from the films they adore, from *Shock Corridor* to *Bande a Part*.) When the Cinémathèque is closed down by the French Government, thus provoking film buff riots, the three young people retreat to a world of their own fashioning. They live together in a rambling flat, conveniently vacated by the twins' parents, and spend their days playing increasingly strange games: movie games, erotic games, power games, identity games. But the new French Revolution, taking place quite literally in the streets below, finally breaks in on their hermetic rites . . .

Though not strictly autobiographical, *The Dreamers* does draw on Adair's experiences of that time and that place. He had arrived in Paris about three months before the *"evenements"*. (He is deeply reticent about his life before that time, doesn't even want me to mention the university he attended, but is just about willing to let it be known that he grew up North of the Border.) The exhilaration of mass revolt was all the greater by contrast with the sadness of his Parisian life before the May eruption. 'I had some money at first and I went to Paris with someone, and at first I had a good time. And then the money ran out, the "someone" ran out, and I was alone, I was incredibly lonely and disoriented . . . I actually went to the English Catholic church, to convert. And there was a wonderful old priest there, Father Murphy. I had to read the catechism and so on, and then I had to confess my sins before my first communion. Now, today it's different—they give you a standard statement to read—but in those days you had to confess "all" your sins. Now, I was, what, 22?, and I said "Father Murphy, let's be reasonable, I can't even remember all my sins." "Well," he said, "it's not so complicated. Let's just think of a sin . . . now, you touch yourself, don't you?" "Well, um . . . " "Yes, yes, you touch yourself." And then he pulled out a little pocket calculator. "Now, let's say you've touched yourself four times a week, since you were, say, 13, now that's 52 weeks a year . . . " And the notion that I had to say "Please father forgive me, I have touched myself 4 times 52 times . . ."; it was ridiculous. Now, fortunately I didn't have to tell poor Father Murphy about my response, because that was just when May '68 exploded . . .'

And was it a case of 'Bliss was it in that dawn to be alive?'

'Yes, it was . . . I was a Maoist, an absolute Maoist, for about three weeks, which was the going rate. I truly believed that the world was going to change, truly, truly believed that.'

Did you throw rocks? (A highly incongruous image, for those who think of Gilbert as one of the gentlest of souls.)

'I did, but . . . I had to be slightly careful, like Matthew in the film, because I was a foreigner, and I was a teacher, I taught at the University, so I was also employed by the French state, and would have instantly been deported if I had been caught.'

But you hadn't gone to Paris specifically in search of Revolution?

'No, not at all. It seems me that in the sixties, cinephiles went to Paris—Paris was the capital of cinephilia. [Indeed, though the two never ran into each other, Bertolucci was there at the same time, and for much the same reasons.] So I went there, started attending the Cinémathèque screenings, and the people I got to know there were fellow cinephiles. Then this thing happened with Henri Langlois, he was ousted, and there were these demonstrations, and the amazing thing was that they "worked". Sometimes it's been said that it was the Cinémathèque affair which triggered off May '68; other people have pooh-poohed this, but perhaps it was like the assassination of Franz Ferdinand on the eve of World War One. It seemed to have little to do with what followed, but the essential thing was that young people discovered that taking to the streets worked. Langlois was reinstated by Malraux [De Gaulle's Minister of Culture].'

So you hadn't been at all a political creature before Paris? You were politicised overnight?

'Politicised *and* eroticised . . . To me, that's what this film is all about. It's not just about the sex inside the apartment: *everything* was eroticised. Today the idea of being a cinephile seems a bit nerdy—it wasn't at all then. Sitting in the same row was Truffaut, sitting behind was maybe Chabrol or Resnais or Rivette . . . all great film-makers. It was a very sexy thing, and romantic, being with these young people watching old American movies, or being in the streets arm-in-arm . . . The whole thing was like a collective orgasm—a mini-orgasm in February with the Cinematheque, and then the real thing in May.'

And how long did the delirium last?

'Two or three weeks . . . the real delirium was when the workers and students joined together. That was incredible, that was unheard-of, and that's when we truly believed that this time it was going to happen. And then the Communist Party saw that its constituency was being seduced away from the party line, and its leaders began to clamp down on this extracurricular activity, and then De Gaulle, who had vanished from the scene, came back. I remember being at the Berlitz School and someone came running along the corridor shouting "De Gaulle has reappeared! De Gaulle has reappeared!" We all rushed into the staff room and listened to a little transistor radio, and heard De Gaulle talking about this *Chien Lit*—this "dog's dinner"—France has become a dog's dinner. And then within a few days there was a great demonstration down the Champs Elysee with Malraux and all the other members of De Gaulle's government, with thousands of his supporters . . . and that seemed to be it . . .

'But it didn't really end at that point. There was talk of staging another uprising in May 1969, May 1970. A lot of young people continued to be militant, continued to work in cells; they were no longer perhaps Maoists, but they were still Marxists, Trotsykists, followers of [the Italian Marxist philosopher] Gramsci and so on. A number of people of that generation ruined their lives, because they did not complete their studies, did not go through the conventional paths and then, when it was finally over in the mid-seventies, when we knew that it had died, they were completely unequipped for life. There were suicides, there were stories of left-wingers going completely in the opposite direction, towards the National Front, which is a classic trajectory . . . '

And your own trajectory? You stayed on the Marxist left?

'Yes. I despised the Communist Party: the French Communist Party is rather sleazy, actually . . . But I read all the holy texts, the sacred texts: Gramsci, who was incredibly important to us, Bakunin. And then, I suppose that before I finally left Paris in 1980, I began to be more of a pragmatist, and was sort of rooting for Mitterrand and the Socialists, because militancy outside the structures of government had so manifestly failed.

'Something that Bernardo has also been saying in interviews recently is that young kids today, for example the actors in the film, who were 19, 20, 21, know next to nothing about that time. Their parents' generation, the generation of '68, never wanted to talk about the sixties, because they felt that it had been a failure. They'd all become lawyers, estate agents. But in fact it was *not* a complete failure. It was like a time bomb . . . or, a bomb that explodes and sends out all these little seeds, seeds that took time to blossom. Gay Liberation really started in those years. Feminism . . . Well, there had been feminism since before the twentieth century, but the notion of a modern Feminist movement came out of '68. It was the crystallization of a lot of things in the sixties, and we wanted the film to resonate beyond the French events, which is why Bernardo wanted lots of music like Jimi Hendrix.'

Twelve years, from 1968 to 1980, is a fair slice of anyone's life. What kept you in France so long?

'Good question . . . Well, I went native, I began to think of myself as French. And in those days, Paris was just so much better than London. Paris now needs to reinvent itself, it's a little boring at the moment, but at the time it was wonderful. It was also the period of the New Theory—all these books were coming out, Deleuze, Guattari, Barthes, Foucault, which were all very exciting. Social life was also exciting. I got very friendly with David Hockney, and was part of his sort of entourage, and I kept waiting for David to say, "Gilbert, just sit over there and look sideways", and draw my portrait, but he never did . . . And I knew a lot of people in cinema, and was very caught up with that, and I had a very good time. But no film-maker ever invited me to write a script.

'I was a single man, and, to use an expression from *Beunos Noches*

Buenas Aires, I had neither roots nor branches: no roots because my parents had died, no branches because I had no family of my own. I was sort of floating. I lived for many years in the hotel room in which Gideon [the narrator of *BNBA*] lives, the room in which Baudelaire had lived and wrote some of *Les Fleurs du Mal*, I had a job to go to, I had friends, but . . . I felt more and more that I had to produce something. I'd been consuming for years, I now had to produce, and to produce I needed a whole back-up system. I was writing in Paris, I'd written some poems in French which were published in a collection, I'd written quite a lot of *Alice*, but I had no agent, no contacts, no publisher. I had to come back to Britain for all those. I always think that writing is to publication what love is to marriage. I needed to come back to England to "get married" to writing, to officialise it. So I've always thought that the real date of everything I've published is ten years earlier. My first book [*Hollywood's Vietnam*] was published in 1980, but in my mind it's 1970.'

*

Back in England, he began to work hard. Besides criticism, he also wrote a number of screenplays, only one of which made it to the screen—*The Territory*, a philosophical thriller directed by Raúl Ruiz and produced by Roger Corman. '*The Territory* is basically *The Blair Witch Project*. It's about a group of people who go into a forest where their friends have disappeared, and they get lost, and they heard voices . . . and it ends with cannibalism. We just didn't market it properly.' Movie buffs may care to know that Wim Wenders' *The State of Things* is a *film à clef* about the shooting of *The Territory*.

Adair's debut novel, *The Holy Innocents*, was followed by *Love and Death on Long Island*, a sort of replay of Thomas Mann's *Death in Venice* in more comic mode. In place of Von Aschenbach, Adair's narrator-hero is one Giles De'Ath, an elderly, querulous author of slender fictions so finely drawn as to make Henry James seem gross and fleshy; in place of Tadzio, the love object is a nice but dim young Hollywood actor called Ronnie Bostock. After accidentally catching a glimpse of Ronnie on screen in a Hampstead cinema (De'Ath thought he was going to be seeing an E. M. Forster adaptation—itself an experience perilously close to slumming), De'Ath develops an overwhelming obsession for the young man, which ultimately takes him to the young actor's American doorstep. *Love and Death on Long Island* was successfully brought to the screen with John Hurt in the role of Giles and—brave man!—Jason Priestley, the young star of *Beverley Hills 90210* as sweet, dopey Ronnie. Incidentally, Adair has since written a brief monograph on the boy who was, as its title says, *The Real Tadzio*.

Then came *The Death of the Author*: a murder mystery (one of the precursors in Adair's mind was the Henry James of 'The Figure in the Carpet' and such tales) which was partly inspired by the real-life career of Paul de Man—the revered Yale-based literary theorist who, late in his career, was discovered to have written some damaging, more than damaging, articles for the collaborationist press during the Second World War. Gripping as well as thought-provoking, the novella has been turned into a small-scale opera by a German composer: Adair was flown in to act the part of the narrator.

Next, two more thrillers: *The Key of the Tower*, something of an homage to Hitchcock in his *Strangers on a Train* mode, in which a freak accident (here: a tree falling across a road, so blocking traffic in either direction) causes an innocent English biographer to be plunged into a world of international art theft and conspiracy; and then *A Closed Book*, the tale of a blind author and his sinister amanuensis, in which the twists are so gleefully ingenious that you're just going to have to read it for yourself. It has been adapted twice for radio, once for the stage, and became a surprise bestseller in Germany. A German production company wanted to film it with Klaus Maria Brandauer in the lead, 'but I said no, because we thought there was the possibility it might be filmed here...'

Throughout these years, Adair was also being published on several fronts as a pundit: he was the first writer, or at any rate one of the very first, to bring the sort of analytical, free-ranging essay form developed by Roland Barthes for the French press in the 1950s to the mainstream of British journalism. In fact, one of his pieces—an amusing fantasia on the *Carry On* series, jokily published by *Sight and Sound* as a translation of a previously uncollected Barthes essay—was such a triumphantly convincing pastiche that it has been known to crop up in Barthes bibliographies; those compiled by the terminally humourless, presumably.

Unlike most journalism of the kind, Adair's is sufficiently thoughtful and well-honed to stand up to reproduction in book form. He has compared his first collection, *Myths and Memories*, to a centaur: it has a long first section that, precisely, does for Britain what Barthes's *Mythologies* did for France, and then a short second section made up of tiny shards of reminiscence and recall—a few strictly personal (such as the youthful Adair's mistaken belief that a 'blow job' had something to do with breathing on erogenous areas), but more to do with the trivia of mass culture that are briefly ubiquitous but then all but universally forgotten: comedians' catchphrases, novelty toys and novelty songs, advertising campaigns, slogans and crazes. This part was a tribute to Georges Perec's *Je me souviens* (which was itself derived from an earlier source.)

Two further collections, *The Postmodernist Always Rings Twice* (enviably sharp title) and *Surfing the Zeitgeist* (horrible, vulgar title; deliberately so; the preface explains why) corralled more of Adair's Barthesian aperçus; while for *Flickers*, his contribution to festivities for the 100th birthday of cinema, he chose one image, one movie still, from each year of the first century, and used it to say a hundred different things about what the cinema has been. Adair now says that he will never write film criticism again: partly from weariness, but partly because his experience working on *The Dreamers* has softened his heart. Having experienced at first hand the toils and trials of practical film-making, he can no longer take the side of the reader against the producer and director.

*

His commitment to fiction, by contrast, remains undiluted; has, if anything, deepened. The impetus for his latest novel, *Buenas Noches Buenos Aires* was unusual. At around the time of the publication of *A Closed Book*, which, like some of his other novels, has a subplot about male homosexuality, a friend hinted to Adair that at least one tranche of his readership would be pleased and grateful if he would write a book in which one of his recurrent subsidiary themes became the main theme. In short, if he would write novel directly about gay experience. Shortly afterwards, another friend made exactly the same request. *Buenas* answers those pleas. It tells the story of a young gay Englishman who arrives in Paris in 1980, lonely and horny and hoping for love, or at least some hot sex; he finds plenty of gay friends among his fellow language teachers, but little in the way of erotic adventure. Shamed by his lack of success, he starts to tell his eager colleagues elaborate tales about his wild nights with wild boys, and they happily believe these lurid fantasies. Then comes the first news of a fatal illness which appears to target homosexual men...

Like *The Dreamers*, *Buenas* isn't simply worked-up autobiography; like *The Dreamers*, it does draw on many of Adair's own experiences. By publishing it, Adair has, in effect, come out as a gay man (though not, he insists, as a Gay Writer). It probably says a lot about his discretion, or maybe just about my gaucheness, that we have known each other as colleagues and friends for twenty-odd years now, and that this is the first time we have ever discussed or so much as alluded to his sexuality.

Well, Gilbert, I cough, I've always sort-of assumed that you were gay (this provokes an immediate qualification: Adair has had his share of heterosexual encounters, has indeed come close to marrying on at least two occasions), but somehow the subject never seemed to come up. On the other hand, it's not as if your novels don't drop the odd hint or two.

And with that much, Adair does agree. 'I've always thought that there is no more powerful truth serum than fiction—you simply cannot keep out the truth. Obviously there are gay themes in a lot of my novels, though not all, but I really wouldn't be happy to be thought of as a Gay Writer... It should be clear to anyone who knows me at all that *Buenas Noches Buenos Aires* is not purely autobiographical, in the sense that I was never that nerdy, and I was never that much of a stud either.'

It's also shifted significantly forward in time...

'Yes, I'd left Paris by that time—the narrator, Gideon, and I cross in mid-Channel, so to speak, because I have Gideon going to France in 1980, the year I left, as though he were taking one steamer, I was taking the other, and we might have waved to each other. But I decided that if I were going to write a book about homosexuality, there was no point in pretending that this had no personal interest for me—although a lot of the practices I write about, and a lot of the boys, would not have interested me at all . . .'

The novel has something of an mini-encyclopedic quality—almost every mode of male homosexuality, every form of male homosexual practice, is at least mentioned if not lavishly described.

'Yes; there was a technical challenge there as well: writing about certain physical acts in a language which was never designed to describe those acts. There's a lot of pretty disgusting sex acts, but the language is such that even if you'd normally be disgusted by the idea, the spectacle, or even by another description in a raunchy gay novel, in this book you won't. To use a French term, it's very imàge, full of metaphor, even puns sometimes—I like the idea of words "meeting cute" . . . Despite the fact that it talks at some length about AIDS, I didn't want it to be glum at all. There's a certain kind of mawkishness in some gay writing that I find impossible—all that stuff about gays wasting away and making brave wisecracks with their last breath, I just can't bear that.'

One way of describing the plot is to say that it's about Gideon's transition from being awkward and furtive about his sexuality to being open and defiant and pleased. Does that echo your own experience?

'Yes. One scene in the book which is absolutely autobiographical is the one that takes place outside the gay club. The name of the club—the Four Hundred Blow Jobs—is my own gag, but there really was a club like that where I was taken by a friend, it was very fashionable, it had just opened, and we had to queue up to get in, and we saw these straight couples walking past and sneering, and I said to him, "I just can't do this". And my friend looked at me and said, "Are you ashamed? I thought you were Out . . ." Now I'd never been a militant, and in fact because I saw myself as bisexual, there was a sense in which I "wasn't" really Out. I suppose that, for someone like Peter Tatchell, I've never been Out. My favourite move in chess is the Knight's Move—two steps forward, one to the side—and I just don't have the temperament for the kind of directness that activists want. I've also experienced all sorts of things vis-à-vis the gay world, and sometimes it has just disgusted me, the thought of being associated with some of those people. Being gay hasn't defined my life, I'm not one of the people I describe in the book for whom a man is something attached to a cock. I've always had more straight friends than gay friends, and I just never see the need to declare myself, I always assume that people assume . . .

'It's funny, when I wrote the book I thought, OK, I'm old enough now, I don't give a shit any more. And when I was writing, the subject matter somehow didn't matter, I was engaging with all the usual problems of sentence structure and style. Then I sent it off, then I got a set of proofs, and then suddenly it hit me that—my God, a lot of people around me are going to read this! And I began to have a certain queasy feeling . . . not so much about friends, but about, well, my dentist's receptionist, or the newsagent, or the nice Indian man who launders my shirts—what are *they* going to think of this? And then I tell myself that, of course, this is the standard delusion of professional writers, who think that when they've published a book, the whole world is talking about them or gazing at them. If I'm realistic, I know that my dentist's receptionist is not going to be reading the novel. Even so, I *am* a little nervous . . .'

*

Needlessly so, I'd hazard. Anyway, even if his worst fears about the local newsagent prove justified, he won't have to face the fellow for a while, because he's off to Rome tomorrow to work with Bertolucci—now a good friend—on a new project. Another happy spin-off from *The Dreamers* is that Adair is also working on a novel which will take a real-life person—Louis Garrel, who plays Theo in *The Dreamers*—and use his appearance and personality as the basis of a major character. 'I took Louis out for lunch and asked his permission to "cast" him, so to speak.' There are several other film projects in the offing, too, including an adaptation of Wilde's *Picture of Dorian Gray*, 'completely faithful to the original, and stuffed with epigrams. The only difference is that not one of them is by Wilde. They're all by me. And—this is an obvious anecdote, but it's authentic—the first producer to whom the script was sent, *did not notice* . . .'

Before I leave, there's just enough time to tackle him on the sizeable collection of books about maths. He looks a little wistful: 'I really left it too late. Today, at my age, it's hard for me even to read properly the more advanced sort of mathematics books I've got. It's just such a beautiful, beautiful world, it's so perfect, but . . . Mathematics is a bit like one of those beaches where you wade in and suddenly you're in up to your neck. In fact, I do have the idea to use certain mathematical ideas —specifically, Cantor's Diagonal Method—to see if they can work in a fictional context . . .' And his Parthian shot is typically Adairian: 'But one of the real reasons I love reading mathematics is that I know it will never be contaminated by the sound-bite, the Starbucks culture. I know I'll never have to read what Julie Burchill thinks about the Riemann hypothesis, or Michael Winner's opinion of the Hodge Conjecture . . .'

First published in *Talk of the Town*, 2003

The Author, if Dead, is Not De Man But De Femme

G. N. FORESTER

Gilbert Adair's *Death of the Author* has long been regarded as one of his masterpieces. What readers and critics have either disdained or ignored, through a seeming lack of perspicacity or a wilful avoidance and misconstrual of textual hints and contrivances, in a manner reflecting the very subject matter and the protagonist around whom the story develops, such that the void of comment represents the absence suggesting presence, is the actuality of this novella being a mistresspeace, a homage to the one woman he truly admired, and dare it be said, loved.

It all begins with a novel published in 1957 in which two characters, one a homosexual of refined and cultivated tastes, yet given to an appreciation for popular culture, the other a bisexual, older and sophisticated, at times quick to apprehend injury but generous in sharing intelligence as much as sharing invitations to bed, receive light but generally flattering treatment, in what is effectively a satire of the day, and which will propel the writer of the fiction on a path of immediate if moderate success.

Not content with introducing sexuality differing from the conventional and expected norm in one work, three subsequent satires, all published by the beginning of the sixties and either notionally or specifically focused on the subjects of literary criticism, psychology, academia, writing, popular culture, Art and art, history, politics, and philosophy, woven together in such a variety of ingenious means and methods that only readers of a certain level of erudition will perceive the scale of intellect and learning masked by the seeming frivolity of the texts, will contain sympathetic character studies of supporting homosexual roles, and never the key protagonists, who bear the brunt of the comic lash and ape the social follies of the day. The reading of these works will have a profound influence on the young Gilbert, for the narrator of each text mimics his own, as yet unheard, voice; its playfulness, mocking tones, self-deprecatory notes, willingness to up-end conservative idiom and lampoon mindlessly repeated banal ideals, skewering wit, and self-aware realism. It will also plunge him in a thirty year unrequited love affair, much like Michelangelo and his adoration, unfulfilled, of Vittoria Colonna. How do these events come to pass?

Despite the impact of these four novels, read avidly before 1966, as a young man of twenty-two fresh from having studied modern languages at university and already seduced by the medium of film, it is the publication of the author's astonishing new work, taking a completely unexpected and challenging new direction, in the style of the *nouveau roman* and capturing the camera's fixation with detail, in an alternative world where the status quo of pale skin hegemony is dismantled and reversed, and dark-skinned humans are privileged and powerful. It is a metaphor not only for oppression built upon and sustained by the level of pigment in one's skin, but for vilification predicated upon the extent of attraction to members of the same and/or opposite sex. The young Adair, already primed for the visual appeal of cinema, is fascinated by this written evocation of discrimination in a text defiantly exploratory, labelled, even, postmodernist, a term with which he finds an immediate affinity. When he discovers the author of these treasured anti-novels has left London, amid rumours of a marriage riff and gossip about affairs, always such stuff as to keep literary parties well-attended, to take a lecturing position at the new experimental university of Paris, Vincennes, he accedes to his own plans to travel there, taking lodging in the Hôtel de Lauzun, as Baudelaire before him, teaching English at the Berlitz school and lecturing at the university, and, shy and retiring as he is, determining how best to approach his idol. It will be, however, a painful pursuit, eventually, after evenings and early mornings spent in protracted and heated discussions with fellow cinephiles at the

Cinémathèque Française about the finer points and limitations and all-too-quickly entrenched standards of the medium miring it in the mundane, resulting in Gilbert's desultory and disappointed return to England, after a decade-long, desperately difficult and frustratingly futile endeavour to prevail upon the heart and mind of his muse, aloof as ever, a Persephone to his Hermes, a Cassandra to his Agamemnon.

But it is not without profit, because it is in Paris, apart from perfecting his French (letters, kisses, toasts, and leavings) that Adair encounters the theorists and philosophers that will shape his own literary leanings: Derrida, Barthes, Deleuze, Foucault, lectures jammed to the rafters with students, academics (including the rose among thorns), the enlightened and enamoured public. Paris is ablaze with the glory of the new and the re-imagining of the old, the reconstruction of the deconstruction of the Formalists and the Structuralists and the Posts of what follows, in Art, in Literature, in Film, in creative and critical expression, seen as two sides of the same coin and not conspiring in opposition. It is the first time students will prevail upon the state, the removal of fiercely independent Henri Langlois from his position as Cinémathèque Française Director inspiring the riot that inspires the uprisings, from a simple street march of students carrying placards inscribed "Films pas flics" (Films not fuzz) metamorphosing to the surreal landscape of baton-wielding riot uniforms beating François Truffaut, Jean-Luc Goddard, and Yves Boisset's wife.

It is here Gilbert will conduct and publish a first interview, propelling him towards his later career of film critic and literary reviewer, on the set of Rivette's *Les Filles de Feu*, meeting and forming decades-long friendships with Eduardo de Gregorio, Alain Resnais, and Raúl Ruiz, as well as learning the intricacies of rendering imagination celluloid, although he will never hanker to wield the camera, rather create the dialogue that shapes the characters as a flask contours the fluid poured within it. The many hours spent watching films, thinking films, talking films, and observing the making of films (itself worthy of being filmed) will combine to produce his signature storytelling style, that of meta-narrative infusing infra-narrative, the ostensible plot suborned to the puzzle of guessing the paraphernal *hors de texte*, intertext, and intratext, pitting the wily Reader against that unruly creature, the Author. Although he will pen innumerable non-fiction collections (notably no essays concerning the works of his *amour secret*) and pastiche Lewis Carroll in *Alice Through the Needle's Eye*, J. M. Barrie in *Peter Pan and the Only Children*, and homage Jean Cocteau in *The Holy Innocents*, it is not until 1992, twelve years after his despondent departure from Paris, his experiences there cached as memories he will plunder most evidently and bitterly in *Buenos Noches Buenos Aires*, that his true literary voice is fully heard with the simultaneous publication of *The Postmodernist Always Rings Twice* and *The Death of the Author*, the latter being his first attempt to grapple with the fact of his unreciprocated love.

The central conceit cunningly disguised with his trademark obfuscation, Adair's principal character Leopold Sfax appears to mimic the life of Paul de Man (architect on one side of the Atlantic of the theory which banishes authorial intent from the text, post-dating the theory already espoused by Roland Barthes and highly influential upon Jacques Derrida, who in turn influenced Paul de Man), the latter denounced after the fact by several years for having propagated anti-Semitic texts in service to the Nazis. Sfax, however, has yet to be exposed, and like Paul de Man, develops a "grand theory" imported from his Continental origins which achieves iconic status, impelling Sfax into academic limelight, and which argues for the divorce of a writer and her/his story and past with the texts and theories s/he produces. But unlike Paul de Man, whose wartime articles were revealed after his death by a researcher, it is the biographer's discovery that precipitates both her own and Sfax' death (to elaborate further would deprive future readers of the pleasures found within *Death of the Author*) and confirms Sfax' reason for having invented the theory. Moreover, as Sfax is the narrator, and continues to recount events after his own demise, the reader is provided further "evidence" for discounting the entire novella.

This is, in point of fact, all so much metaphorical sand in the eye of the beholder.

Adair was intimately acquainted with the theories of Barthes, Derrida, and de Man, and cognisant particularly of the differences distinguishing each. Sfax' life might be said to resemble, or even be based upon, that of Paul de Man, but Sfax' supra-theory is wholly Barthesian. So if Adair didn't intend a tongue-in-cheek jab at the folly of US literary academia i.e. Sfax is only superficially meant to appear as proxy for de Man, who and what is actually being protected by this castle of artifice?

Adair himself. By having ultimately convinced the reader of the lack of credibility of the author in this novel, he achieves that status for himself in every subsequent one, and hidden in each are the tragic references to a love spurned (let the discerning reader discover these for her or himself) which he cannot acknowledge, but fails to deny, just as Sfax can neither acknowledge his egregious past nor deny it (thus confirming its existence), and can only aspire to a prestidigitation capable of cuckolding the reader. As to the identity of the woman he adored and by whom he was scorned, who, like Adair, finally succumbed to a condition described presciently in a story written years earlier, as if both condemned themselves by the articulation of the sufferings of their respective affliction to experience its ravages, consider a minor alteration to the title of his *A Closed Book*.

The Scottish Postmodernist Never Rings Once, Let Alone Twice, and Can't Even Be Bothered to Leave a Note

M. J. NICHOLLS

1

I first encountered Gilbert Adair's work in the former Writers' Room at Edinburgh Napier University, where I elected to abandon a paid career in pursuit of an MA in Unshite Writing. The Evadne Mount books, proud property of the course organiser and her Thomas Young power-reader of a husband, sat on the shelves in an enticing hardback trio. At this stage of my reading life, I went into orgasmic spasms over any book tagged postmodern—i.e. writers writing about writing in tones of narcissistic self-reference—i.e. the sort of fiction I was peddling in those days (and still struggle to avoid despite habitual dousings in Victorian opulence or the sentimental hygiene of Waterstones 2-for-1s[1]). I softly fingered *And Then There Was No One* (not then released in paperback) and set about fellating the book on a four-hour bus trip from Edinburgh to Inverness. Alongside that towering masterpiece of metafiction *Mulligan Stew*,[2] Adair's novel was my introduction to the kind of witty and candid authorial self-insertion and self-flagellation

---

1 In Jan 2012, Waterstones dropped their apostrophe (formerly Waterstone's), altering the name of the firm's original owner to incorporate the spelling mistake. Fictional Adair defines the difference between bookstores in Switzerland and the UK in *ATTWNO*: "Your bookshops sell fifty types of books and one type of coffee, while ours sell fifty types of copy and one type of book." My local branch of Waterstone[']s has no titles by Adair, except the Perec translation.

2 Gilbert Sorrentino, Grove Press, 1979. That my first two postmodern crushes were named Gilbert is a happy coincidence.

that enhances the reader's interest and affection for the author's works.[3] This chimed with my fondness for attention-seeking and making a fool of myself in a comedic way to drum up readerly affection for myself through prose.[4]

Adair's final novel is a fictional literary memoir, written in the arch-affectionate style of his nonfiction, hilariously characterising a variety of literary types, from the wheedling Hugh Spaulding, author of "a cycle of thick-eared thrillers each of which was set in a different sporting milieu", who pesters Adair for ten thousand francs after the failure of *Doctor Zhivago on Ice*; the outrageous egotist and star guest Slavorigin (based on . . . ?), whose collection of ill-timed 9/11 essays *Out of a Clear Blue Sky* launched his reputation as an outspoken anti-American terror; and Meredith van Damarest, "a hellish Hellenist from an obscure Californian college."[5] The depiction of writers as a gaggle of grotesques holds appeal. I have always viewed writers as the damaged patients in a worldwide therapy group, sharing their manias in the form of stories and novels, hoping and praying for someone to comprehend their pain in between the hourly ingestion of other nutters' fictions. The creative process is nothing more than feverish scribbling in one's padded cell. This notion of writers as far-gone crazies squabbling for love, understanding, and teaching posts in a stifling matrix of insane saboteurs and bile-stirrers was the truth hammered home to me by my MA tutors.[6]

Adair's blend of fiction and self-reference (several characters are named after real people, events and names from his past are scrambled as fiction), alongside his striking finale—the last gasp of a late-period postmodernist—seemed like a devilish and self-replenishing method of telling fiction. The only problem, as the resurrected cut-out Evadne flings at Adair: "Nobody gives two hoots about self-referentiality any longer, just as nobody gives two hoots, or even a single hoot, about

---

3 Note from my co-editor: "This presupposes an equally self-absorbed reader."
4 Second note from my co-editor: "Otherwise missing in all aspects of Nicholls's life (and for good reason, which requires no adumbration here)."
5 My co-editor and I have debated (heatedly) regarding the existence or otherwise of misogynistic undertones in Adair's writing (present book especially). This being a festschrift, all negative comments have been struck in favour of propagandist praise.
6 And, indeed, Martin Amis' funniest novel *The Information*.

you." I had arrived at my literary fascination in its dying or long-dead days, twenty-one years since David Foster Wallace (also recently dead) had attempted to retire the literature of exhaustion with his rambling Barth homage 'Westward the Course of Empire Takes its Way.'[7] Could a literary movement be considered passé if it never even reached the country in which I was born and raised?

My immersion in the postmodern took me to France and the Americas, where novels are still (according to various undercover sources) being written outside the realist mode with a view to smashing the capitalist superstructure and bringing forth an era of humanist utopia with extra sprinkles and chocolate sauce. I looked in vain for the Scottish metafictionists. I was, of course, already conversant in the oeuvre of Alasdair Gray—*Poor Things*, a *Frankenstein* pastiche and beautiful marriage of art and text, was required reading at my progressive Catholic school, and the opus *Lanark* with its index of plagiarisms and Author-God appearance in the fourth book was an imaginative blast-off into the outer limits of what Scottish people might do with techniques already explored by Queneau, Vonnegut, O'Brien, Sorrentino (two of whom are cited by Gray as plagiarisms). These books aside, Gray's stories and novels are in the fantastical or realist mode—he's a postmodernist whenever it fits the form. This leaves the 1990s novels of Janice Galloway, notably *The Trick is to Keep Breathing*—a dark feminist novel à la A.L. Kennedy making use of typographical play à la Raymond Federman —and Ali Smith, whose novels are the least Scottish and therefore the most postmodern.

Self-conscious fiction is inherently unScottish. I was surprised to learn Gilbert Adair was a writer *comfortable* with the postmodernist label[8] (not a common position among the Americans, Sorrentino preferred the label "high modernist" as did others). I was not surprised to learn that Gilbert Adair was a writer uncomfortable with the Scottish label.[9] The Scots are a nation of cherub-cheeked teamworkers and

---

7 In *Girl With Curious Hair*, W.W. Norton, 1989.
8 See *The Postmodernist Always Rings Twice*, 4th Estate, 1991.
9 Adair was raised in Kilmarnock and (purportedly) studied in Edinburgh. He left for France and re-invented himself as an Englishman (with a tinge of Scots). Scots often appear in his books, such

campfire storytellers—the solipsistic and vainglorious are not indigenous traits to this fair land. The commingling of culture, science, and philosophies from other nations is unpatriotic. We have our own thinkers here. We don't need ideas from outside creeping in our cosy idyll when we have David Hume and the miserable internal monologues of J. Kelman for companionship.

This, despite Scotsfolk having a foot in founding the pomo. Walter Scott was among the first to publish under comedic synonyms (Jebediah Cleisbotham, Captain Clutterbuck[10]) and use the found manuscript frame for his otherwise abysmal historical novels.[11] James Hogg's *The Memoirs and Confessions of a Justified Sinner* also makes use of a spurious editor and found manuscript—a technique later used incessantly by Gray, and in historical novels such as James Robertson's *The Testament of Gideon Mack* (an homage to Hogg). These novels, however, still present provincial concerns. Scottish provincialism has been a problem for Scottish writers looking to explore new forms and challenges without having to bear the burden of Caledonia's past. Their response is usually to scarper.

Glaswegian novelist Alexander Trocchi, author of the outsider's classic *Cain's Book*, left for Paris in the 1950s to mingle with the French new novelists and help edit Beckett's *Watt* for Olympia Press, publishing a torrent of grotty and unsexy S&M novels, all written for cash, under that imprint. He moved to Beatland in Manhattan, wrote *Cain's Book*, and downed his pen for the next three decades due to heroin-inflicted impotence. The 1960s British avant-garde scene, populated by B.S. Johnson, Eva Figes, Christine Brooke-Rose (who fled to France in 1968) *et al*, never migrated north. Trocchi's famous spat with Hugh MacDiarmid at the 1961 Edinburgh International Writers' Conference (resuscitated in 2012), where the venerable poet dismissed Trocchi and Burroughs as drugged-up whippersnakes (not that he was *wrong*), high-

---

as the housekeeper in *A Closed Book*. It is hard not to speculate on his closed-book childhood. See also his take on Perec's 'I Remember' in *Myths & Memories*.

10 Along with Malchi Malagrowther, Crystal Croftangry, Jonas Dryasdust, and, more boringly, Lawrence Templeton.

11 See *Scott-Land: The Man Who Invented a Nation*, Birlinn Ltd, 2012, for an alternative opinion.

lighted the close-mindedness to new forms developed by the postmodernists (an aversion to the young?). It would take Gray's *Lanark* (1981), for some of this creative energy to trickle through the Scots literary landscape (Gray was 47 upon publication).[12] Even then, the multimedia one-man renaissance Gray was quick to pooh-pooh the label. Rodge Glass, Gray's secretary, recalls in his biography asking if *Lanark* was "a postmodern work, or merely one that has been called postmodern by critics,"[13] to which Gray replied with a temperamental glower and refusal of a free gin and tonic. Polygon, a defunct Edinburgh publisher,[14] released works from poets-turned-novelists such as Frank Kuppner and Robert Alan Jamieson in the early 1990s, that while "poet's novels", with their focus on lyrical and opaque language, were Calvino-tinged enough for an intrepid or desperate PhD student to rush them inside the Scottish pomo camp.

At any rate, this preamble proves the field was not crowded when I began this fruitless pursuit. I found myself pleased to be a postmodernist (if not pleased to be Scottish). While other deprived terrors from working-class backgrounds sought to become the new Irvine Welsh, clacking out rambling monologues in dialect about snorting speedballs and shagging Sharons and other unhinged yawns of passage, I was working on fictions about M. J. Nicholls persecuting his characters and characters persecuting M. J. Nicholls in a glorious masochistic loop. My characters mocked my Scottishness, teasing me for refusing to take part in the crime fiction *kulturkampf* (Ian Rankin's novels litter used bookshops)[15], and snubbing the Scots self-love-a-thon by failing to tip the hat to the Bard (Burns) and the Laird (Scott), and the Other One (Louis Stevenson). It seemed my acceptance as a postmodernist rested on tossing away the baggage of my Scottishness.

---

12 By Canongate. *Lanark* remains the most ambitious and risky book published by this Edinburgh-based press. Their new fiction output today consists of short works written for younger readers with short attention spans, or books with film tie-in potential. Not an unshrewd business move, only disappointing for pomoheads seeking chocolate novels knitted on ox skins.
13 In fairness to Gray, Glass asked this ingratiating question when serving him in a pub.
14 Now Birlinn Ltd.
15 Crime novelists comb the *Edinburgh Evening News* hoping for something scandalous with sufficient plot hooks to turn into gold. Discuss the ethics of this practice.

And so Adair, the most prominent Scottish postmodernist whom no one identifies as Scottish, writes his European and deeply English novels, each drip-feeding moments from Adair's past through intertextual winks and private pranks. The results being an exquisite sequence of slyly personal thrillers and pastiches, with Adair doppelgänging Lewis Carroll, J. M. Barrie[16], Jean Cocteau, Thomas Mann, and Georges Perec, like a less cracked Peter Sellers slipping on another skin and making magic. I worked my way through the Adair oeuvre, eating up the novellas in a few days, missing the subtleties in the first-person monologues, and decided the best course of action as a postmodernist-in-waiting was to turf the hearth and proceed as an acultural nomad who can write in whatever tradition he damn well pleases (or can convincingly imitate), aware that, at some point, I would have to plunder my Scottish childhood for material. But as a postmodernist, I had no obligation to the truth.

2

Fast-forward several months and I encounter Adair himself at a conference in Edinburgh. The title? 'The Resurrection of the Author'. Guest speakers: Gilbert Adair, Tom McCarthy, Katie McCrum, and David Polmont. I had read Tom McCarthy's *C* with a degree of boredom— Ballardian "death of affect" transposed to a WWI setting was not exhilarating (no doubt I missed the point—Tom writes highbrow lit-fic in a post-Derridean mode, whatever that might mean—shall we ask the panel?), and hadn't heard of the other two participants. Katie McCrum was a *Guardian* book critic who had slammed Adair's *And Then There Was No One*, Tom McCarthy's *C*, and David Polmont's *From Juvenal to Jonathan Franzen—A Concise History of Postmodern Satire*. Polmont was the foremost writer on postmodernism in the UK, having published *Stop Me if You've Heard This One Before: A Concise History of British Postmodernism* (with a chapter on Trocchi), and *Like Modernism, Only More So: A Blockhead's Guide to the Postmodern World*. His books had been roundly criticised for their inclusiveness—sitcoms and dense novels were on a par artistically in his uni-

---

16 A Scot, it's true, but *Peter Pan* is about as Scottish as a pot of Earl Gray in a Kensington Palace hot tub.

verse. Soap operas and sonatas were the same. "Postmodernism freed culture from the chattering classes, creating a world where the lowliest blog could be as brilliant as a Shakespearean sonnet," is an example of his drivel.

Katie McCrum was on the panel as devil's advocate. She had completed a work called *Yeah But No But Yeah But Shut Up*—a scathing assault on the exalting of trash that David was proposing in his books. Both of their voices were irritating. David spoke in a sort of laid-back transatlantic drawl like Peter Sellers[17] on 1970s chat shows, a monied affectation that made him sound kitsch and false. Katie was a reformed ladette unable to shirk her undergraduate inflections—with each sentence, it seemed she was edging nearer an *awesome* or *totes amazing* outburst and squeeing up and down in her plastic chair. Tom and Gilbert were lacking in chemistry, made worse by them being positioned at opposite ends of the interviewer, Hugh Pegges—a smirking Irish imp with inexhaustible levels of enthusiasm for any words printed on any paper (and the only person man enough to act as arts ambassador for Clackmannashire council). The discussion began with the assumption that the author *was* dead in the age of mass communication etc., and how best to resurrect him [sic]?

The question was posed to Gilbert. David made a move to speak but stopped himself when he saw Hugh looking at Gilbert. "Well . . . " he replied, taking a moment to reflect. "If the author is really dead, we can reanimate him from the parts of other authors. A limb or two from James, Flaubert, Larkin. We can stitch them together to make a series of Frankenstein's authors." A slight ripple of laughter for this. Gilbert appeared content with his ripple and the buck passed to David. "If the novel is dead . . . let it die, I say. I mean, us writers, we're like crazed doctors hunched over our manuscripts with defibrillators [defibillayters] screaming 'Live! Liiiive!' What we need to do is euthanise our books." His unfunny outburst made the room uncomfortable, allowing them to forget the lapse in logic that if the author is dead there is no

---

17 At the time of writing, I am reading Roger Lewis's 1152-page bio *The Life and Death of Peter Sellers*. Hence the second ref.

one around to write the dying manuscripts in the first place.

Tom McCarthy went on to speak for a minute about something Derrida said that summed up the topic to a tee and made further discussion irrelevant, however the point sailed over everyone's heads, so Hugh carried on. "I reckon Gilbert is right," Katie said. "Only, writers like Gilbert have been graverobbing authors for most of their careers—pastiches of Mann and whatnot. I reckon it's time to enter the age of the lost masterpiece. I reckon [sic] authors working as a team could recreate the prose style of a James or a Flaubert, using computer technology. We have the means to recreate at the level of syntax the style of these immortal authors—The Greats. Why not work on a sequel to Madame Bovary? Complete Bouvard et Pécuchet? Why do we need new works when we can enhance the canon?" Hugh allowed Gilbert a chance for a riposte. "In the same way we can tell a genuine Picasso from an imitation," he said. "For one thing it would bugger the rare books market." More laughter.

This was an untypical remark from Adair, who seemed to be in a curmudgeonly mood. Perhaps sharing a panel with a reviewer who had shredded his latest novel, a writer who had dismissed Adair's books as "too throwback to be pomo" (David), and another who had never read a word of his (Tom), was a tad irksome. The conversation moved to Barthes's original posit in 'The Death of the Author', i.e. writer as scriptor, displaced from his text, and Tom spoke about the 1968 essay for five minutes with stops at Lyotard and Baudrillard, which went above everyone's heads (except Adair's). Adair politely kept silent about his 1992 novella named after Barthes's essay, which he expected someone to namedrop, and the conversation took surreal turns with David suggesting authors should be hung up on hooks like meat in slaughterhouses and tortured to encourage them to express their fullest creative potential (no one knew if he were kidding), and Katie suggested all writers become transvestites, with both penises and vaginas, to create a sort of "gender neutral all-inclusive unisex fiction."

The conversation meandered until the Q&A, where things picked up. The first question: "What if I were to tell you right now, you really were all dead?" a rakish man asked, to some nervous laughs. David took a sip from his water as Kate answered. "Do I look like a zombie to you?" she asked, expecting laughs. As she said this, David slid from his chair and collapsed on the floor. We all chortled. "This is the liveliest he's been all night," Hugh said. The panel waited for him to end the ruse, but David was playing dead. Because he was dead. The water had been spiked. Adair crouched down to take David's pulse and a look of horror appeared on his otherwise unflustered features. Pandemonium ensued. The man who had posed the question was seized by the audience and was heard shouting: "I only meant it as a gag! I didn't know, I didn't think . . . " We were instructed to stay put while the medics carted the unfortunate critic to the morgue. The police arrived for the interrogations.

3

— What are you doing at this event?
— I came to see Gilbert Adair, mainly. And Tom McCarthy.
— Why?
— I'm a big fan of Adair's works. I like what McCarthy has to say about fiction even if I didn't like his latest novel.
— You came to see a novelist you don't like?
— I disliked *C*, but I like McCarthy's essays.
— What about the victim, David Polmont?
— I hate to speak ill of the deceased, but I think he's—was—an idiot. His books are apologias for cartoons over novels, music videos over operas. He's popular among the liberal intelligentsia because he absolves them of their guilt for slumming in front of TV sitcoms instead of reading War and Peace.
— What's wrong with watching TV?
— Nothing. Only you can't claim Loose Women[18] has the same artistic merit as Shakespeare.
— Sounds like snobbery to me. Sounds like you have a chip on your

---

18 Interminable daytime gossip show presided over by four loudmouths who exchange mildly salacious banter, sweeping moral judgements on subjects about which they know nowt, and pull mock-earnest expressions whenever required.

shoulder over this David's opinions. Do you write, Mr. Nicholls?
— Yes.
— What sort of books?
— I know what you're angling at.
— Just answer the question, please.
— Experimental.
— So unpopular, then? The sorts of books no one reads?
— I haven't published most of them, so clearly . . .
— Yes, and don't you think you'd get more readers if you wrote something less snooty, less highfalutin'?
— You sound like my last girlfriend. And my mother.
— Just answer the question.
— Sorry, I don't see what this has to do with the murder of David Polmont.
— Jealousy, Mr. Nicholls. You were so wound up that David had written a popular book promoting the popular literature that you despise, you poisoned his water to exact a public revenge.
— First off, David Polmont is, was, not popular. As I said, he's a hero among a certain group of intellectual slobs who get their rocks off thinking Sonic the Hedgehog is the same as John Milton. Gibberish. No one in the academic world took him seriously. Even lowbrow readers took the piss. It was a pose. Secondly, I haven't the faintest inkling how to make a colourless poison, never mind the skill to sneak it undetected in a glass when conference workers are everywhere setting up the room.
— Come off it, Nicholls. It's simple to plot a poisoning. You're the strongest suspect. We've been reading your blog. How do you think this entry, from last year, sounds to us? *Tossers like David Polmont are propagating the belief that picking up the nearest available book with a pastel cover will increase one's intellectual understanding of the world, sensitivity towards others, and ability to empathise, and that the sentimental lyricism of middlebrow drum-bangers like Jhumpa Lahiri or Khaled Hosseini constitutes High Art. Polmont is the sort of pandering populist who was the first to tout reality TV over novels. In his pseudo-scholarly ramble, he defends the copout*

that in a postmodern world there are no cultural barriers—novels can be about slackers in their pants or viscounts in their pools—unspellchecked drivel from a subliterate teen has as much merit as a polished masterpiece from a genius. Polmont is a first-class buffoon who should be killed with a brick.
— Clearly kidding from the tone.
— Oh? Then what about this later entry? *I hate David Polmont. His stupid book is going to keep experimental writers out of publishing forever . . . I will never be published because of dickheads like him. I want to stab him in the nose with an ice-pick and hack him to bits with one of those big Japanese swords.*
— I was venting. Clearly kidding again.
— You think a murderous threat is kidding? There are twelve more posts where you state your intention to murder David Polmont. We don't consider this 'kidding' in light of what has happened here. Do you?
— It was unfortunate. But you're wrong.
— Oh?
— Yes. Because it was Adair I intended to kill.
— Was it now?
— You missed the most pertinent detail. Polmont had taken Adair's water by mistake. Adair was too polite to correct him and that's what saved his life. I tried to kill Adair because I wanted to sever the line between fiction and reality in his works entirely. It would be the perfect postmodern murder—slain by a fan at a conference, only a year following the publication of his book where a writer is a slain at a conference. Can you think of a more perfect postmodern send-off? I wanted to make him a pomo martyr! That twerp Polmont had to ruin things with his uncoordinated lunge for the wrong water. Got what he deserved.
— Jones, better call the nut doctor.

4

I was released to private care a few months later, having successfully pleaded insanity. Now a hero in the postmodern community, I received cards of congratulations and hundreds of animated gifs on my Facebook wall. It seemed that my (accidental) murder had precipitated a "renaissance" of the postmodern novel. John Barth sent me a bouquet of hyacinths with a nice card as his backlog was now being purchased in the millions by the residents of Scotland. I published several of my novels with the emerging firm Metabooks who were receiving submissions of novels from fresh-faced writers the nation over. The Scots had "caught" postmodernism at last! Irvine Welsh wrote a novel in which he, Irvine Welsh, remixed *Treasure Island*, only to be haunted by the ghost of R.L. Stevenson who exacted his revenge by remixing *Trainspotting*. A.L. Kennedy wrote a novel about the hellishness of being A.L. Kennedy (unrecognisable from her previous novels, except the protagonist was named A.L. Kennedy). Alasdair Gray sulked, claiming he'd had these ideas first.

Books about books were hip. Kids wore 'I am a character in your novel' T-shirts (with 'And you in mine' on the back). People protested at being considered "people", preferring the term unreliable narrator. Flann O'Brien's *At Swim-Two-Birds* became the ur-text of a generation. School kids took things a step further, living lives as though hopping from one "novel" to another, acknowledging no subjective reality, drifting from scenario to scenario and acting as mere vessels (scriptors) for the texts they produced. A novel comprised of the 444th word of each postmodernist novel published in America between 1960-1980 was a bestseller for two months. Mugs with the slogans 'Eat my performative utterance', 'Sign my signifier', and 'Deconstruct my deconstructors' were sold in the millions. My own self-published novel *A Postmodern Belch* became a standard on college campuses.

I now had a clear picture of what Scottish postmodernism looked like. Ian Rankin wrote himself into his novel as a rookie detective who outsmarts the ailing Rebus, John Burnside completed an experimental novel on 4,000 beer mats in 4,000 pubs, wherein he imbibed ten pints to create a "fragmented horrologue." James Kelman characters interrupted their usual streams of consciousness to question their purpose in his miserable novels, hopping inside cheerier works like the New Feminist satires of Louise Bagshawe. Alexander McCall Smith began writing literature. When word spread that Gilbert Adair was Scottish his sales also skyrocketed (which pleased me as in his last novel he complained about being out of sight and out of mind). I was now in a pomo-saturated Scotland. This, of course, all took place in a novel I was constructing in my head, entitled *My Sad and Implausible Wet Dream*, to be published in my head in a few weeks. I wasn't allowed to leave my straight jacket, so I dribbled the novel across sheets of paper, having bitten my tongue to create red ink.

Gilbert's Games and the Golden Age of Murder

MARTIN EDWARDS

Gilbert Adair's last three novels reflect a fascination with the crime fiction genre also evidenced in his earlier work, notably in his take on the novel of psychological suspense, *A Closed Book* (1999). *The Act of Roger Murgatroyd* (2006) introduced Evadne Mount, and is a pastiche of Agatha Christie's work in particular and Golden Age detective fiction in general. Adair said that he liked to think of *The Act of Roger Murgatroyd* as the 67th full-length Agatha Christie murder mystery, and wrote it after spending two years reading the 66 written by Christie herself as preparation for his work on "a celebration-cum-critique-cum-parody of what remains perhaps her most ingenious and celebrated thriller, *The Murder of Roger Ackroyd*."[1]

The novel's premise was summarised by Andrew Taylor, himself a crime writer of distinction: "The scene is a house party at ffolkes Manor on snowbound Dartmoor in the 1930s. On Boxing Day, the corpse of the gossip columnist Raymond Gentry is found with a bullet through his heart in the attic. There is no trace of the gun and the door is locked inside. The weather insulates the house from the world: the murderer must be one of house party (servants don't count, of course). The phone isn't working, the nearest police station is 30 miles away, and the roads are impassable. Fortunately, help is at hand in the form of a pipe-smoking neighbour, ex-Chief Inspector Trubshawe, and his faithful labrador Tobermory."[2]

The cast includes detective novelist Evadne Mount, author of mysteries such as *Faber or Faber* (concerning "identical twin fratricide"), *The*

---
[1] Gilbert Adair, "Unusual suspect: Gilbert Adair discovers the real secret of Agatha Christie's success", *Guardian*, 11 November 2006
[2] Andrew Taylor, review of *The Act of Roger Murgatroyd*, *Independent*, 17 November 2006

Mystery of the Green Penguin (green being the colour Allen Lane chose for Penguin paperback editions of crime novels) and *Oedipus v. Rex*. Her unpublished work includes a lesbian novel in the Radclyffe Hall tradition, *The Urinal of Futility*. The recurrent exclamation "Great Scott Moncrieff!" references Proust's translator, who gave his name to the Scott Moncrieff Prize. Awarded annually for French into English translation, the Prize was won by Adair in 1995 for *A Void*, his translation of Georges Perec's lipogrammatic novel, *La Disparition*.

Adair was by no means the first writer to recognise the potential of the detective story form for parody and other forms of literary experiments and games. The "Golden Age of detective fiction", a term commonly associated with the cerebral whodunits written in Britain (but also in the United States and elsewhere) during the period between the two world wars. This was an era when intellectual game-playing became exceptionally popular. The craze for crossword puzzles was matched by enthusiasm for "fair play" mysteries in which readers pitted their wits against writers, in the hope of solving murder puzzles before the Great Detective—Hercule Poirot, say, or Dorothy L. Sayers' Lord Peter Wimsey—revealed all. "Rules" for writing detective stories were proposed by such unexpected authorities on the genre as T.S. Eliot and A.A Milne, as well as by the American aesthete Willard Huntingdon Wright (who wrote mysteries as S.S. Van Dine) and, most famously, by Ronald Knox, who laid down ten "commandments" for authors.[3] Knox's "rules" have often been misread by critics, who occasionally suffer a sense of humour failure when assessing Golden Age fiction, but he meant them as a joke. The reality is that he and his fellow detective novelists did not take themselves too seriously. They enjoyed playing games with the whodunit form, and would surely have enjoyed the games that Adair played with their genre.

Agatha Christie herself wrote a series of short stories early in her career which poked fun at "Great Detectives". Her sleuthing duo Tommy and Tuppence Beresford ran a detective agency and, in solving cases,

---

3 In addition to half a dozen whodunits, Knox was also the author of a Sherlockian pastiche which earned praise from Arthur Conan Doyle himself.

invoked the methods of fictional sleuths ranging from Sherlock Holmes to ... Hercule Poirot. The parodies were eventually collected in *Partners in Crime* (1928), and at around the time the book appeared, Christie and a group of fellow detective novelists were invited by Anthony Berkeley Cox (better known by his pseudonyms, Anthony Berkeley and Francis Iles) to a series of dinners, which led to the formation of the Detection Club in 1930. Christie, Sayers, Knox and Milne were among the founder members of the Club, which retained exclusivity as a result of electing new members by secret ballot and seeking to restrict the intake to writers of "admitted merit". The Club raised funds by publishing collaborative mysteries, including *The Floating Admiral*, a renowned "round robin" novel in which each chapter was written by a different member. In *Ask a Policeman*, half a dozen members contributed chapters parodying the methods of each other's detectives. Berkeley's chapter featuring Lord Peter Wimsey supposedly displeased Sayers, but she did not mind when her friend, the Club's second President, E.C. Bentley, was prompted by her magnum opus *Gaudy Night* to produce a parody called "Greedy Night."

For good measure, two middlebrow novelists, Margaret Rivers Larminie and Jane Langslow (a pseudonym for Maud Diver) collaborated on a full-length parody, *Gory Knight* (1937) in which Wimsey as well as Poirot and other major sleuths of the period were guyed. Dylan Thomas, who enjoyed and reviewed detective fiction, co-wrote a parody, *The Death of the King's Canary*[4], that remained unpublished until long after his death, while the most memorable of countless post-war parodies of the classic whodunit include Tom Stoppard's *The Real Inspector Hound*, and Anthony Shaffer's *Sleuth*, which is dedicated to a list of "omniscient, eccentric, amateur" detectives, starting with Bentley's Philip Trent.[5]

Adair was, therefore, working in a long-established tradition, but the postmodernist touch that he brought to *The Act of Roger Murgatroyd* sup-

---

4 Co-written with John Davenport, *The Death of the King's Canary* was eventually published in 1976.
5 Shaffer shared Adair's fascination with classic detective fiction, and with his brother Peter co-wrote three now forgotten detective novels. He also wrote screenplays for three films based on Christie's novels.

plied an extra dimension for those familiar with "Golden Age" whodunits. He concluded that:

"If an Agatha Christie novel appears to become increasingly suspenseful as it approaches its denouement, it's because the reader himself, already keyed-up, begins to grow as nervous as one of the suspects in the novel. This curious transference of narrative tension from the text itself to the reader made me realise, too, that Christie is arguably a more modern writer—even a postmodern writer, as we used to say—than she's ever given credit for. Consider a few of the more abstruse critical methodologies of the last four decades—psychoanalytical, semiological, ideological, etc. If there's a single characteristic shared by all of them, it's what might be called an allure of improbability . . . [but] Implausibilities, psychological or other, cease to matter. What does matter is that, like two players hunched over a chessboard, reader and author lock themselves in combat, each openly acknowledging the adversary's existence and skill. And, at their best, Christie's denouements are comparable to elegant chess endgames, if of a type whose aphoristic concision has next to nothing to do with the authentic parameters of the game."[6]

Adair described *The Act of Roger Murgatroyd* as an "entertainment", and the book is, like the Golden Age mysteries to which he doffed his cap, best read as entertainment. The novel was generally approved by readers and reviewers alike, although Andrew Taylor argued that "this type of parody works best as a sprint and is difficult to sustain over the marathon of full-length novel." There is a good deal of evidence to support this view. *Gory Knight*, for instance, has too many *longueurs*, whereas the short story "The Murder at the Towers", by E. V. Knox, brother of Ronald and editor of *Punch*, is witty and effective from start to finish. Taylor concluded that: "Adair gives us some excellent jokes but, in the end, his paradoxical achievement is to make us appreciate the solid literary virtues of Agatha Christie."

Scathing dissent from the appreciative consensus came from Michael Dibdin, whose review dismissed the book as "Half-smart and immensely

---

6   *op. cit.*

self-referential", and for good measure added: "Tom Stoppard is . . . cleverer and funnier than Gilbert Adair when it comes to this sort of thing."[7] This was harsh, especially given that Dibdin, an accomplished and intelligent crime writer and well-read[8] but occasionally mean-spirited critic, had begun his own career as a novelist with *The Last Sherlock Holmes Story*, a pastiche not universally admired by fans of Arthur Conan Doyle. Indeed, in 1993, Dibdin had published a pastiche of the Golden Age murder mystery, *The Dying of the Light* (also published by Faber), which makes all the more surprising both his attack on Adair's book, and his Channel Four TV programme, *J'Accuse*, which amounted to a feebly reasoned rant about the alleged shortcomings of Agatha Christie.

At first Adair rejected the suggestion that he should write a sequel to *The Act of Roger Murgatroyd*, "on the grounds that I've always made it a point of honour not to repeat myself", but—characteristically—he was struck by the notion that, in the circumstances, for him to write a sequel would in itself be a new departure. Accordingly, he produced a second book in the same vein. *A Mysterious Affair of Style* (the title refers to Christie's debut novel, *The Mysterious Affair at Styles*) reunites Evadne and Trubshawe, more than a decade after their first case. Their investigation of the poisoning of an actress allows Adair to deploy his knowledge and love of films, and to invent Alastair Farjeon, a movie director based on Alfred Hitchcock. He makes enjoyable use of Christie's favourite device of "the least likely culprit", a plotting technique discussed at length by Evadne during the course of the novel.

When she and Trubshawe meet again, in the tea-room of the Ritz, Evadne argues that: "the real tension, the real suspense, of a whodunit —more specifically, the last few pages of a whodunit—has much less to do with, let's say, the revelation of the murderer's identity, or with the untangling of his motive, or anything the novelist himself has contrived, than with the growing apprehension in the reader's own mind that . . . the ending might turn out to be, yet again, a let-down . . . what generates the tension . . . is the reader's fear not that the *detective* will

---

7 Michael Dibdin, review of *The Act of Roger Murgatroyd*, Guardian, 4 November 2006.
8 Dibdin also compiled a wide-ranging anthology, *The Picador Book of Crime Writing* (1993).

fail—he knows that's never going to happen—but that the *author* will fail."⁹

Bearing in mind Andrew Taylor's argument about the challenges posed by a full-length Golden Age parody, one might add that readers of Adair's first two Evadne Mount books may worry that the quality of the entertainment cannot be sustained for the whole span of the novel. Adair seeks to maintain interest, and to compensate for any shortcomings in plot when his book is compared with the work of Christie and company, in two distinct ways. First, he has a good deal of fun with the tropes of the Golden Age whodunit, rather than merely parodying the literary style (or, some would argue, the lack of literary style) of Agatha Christie. Second, he piles on the jokes, often in the form of sly cultural references. One of Evadne's novels, for instance, is *Murder without Ease*—which neatly combines a nod to Christie's *Murder is Easy* with a pun about *A Void*, a book without the letter "e". These techniques prove largely successful, but although Adair succumbed to temptation and wrote a third Evadne Mount book, he recognised that it was time for him to take a more radical approach. He found the answer—naturally, as the author of a book of essays entitled *The Postmodernist Always Rings Twice*—in a storyline more daring, and more overtly postmodern, than any other novel drawing on the traditions of the Golden Age detective story.¹⁰

The title of *And Then There Was No One* represents another hat-tip to Christie (author of *And Then There Were None*), to whom the book is dedicated. It was published in 2009, and the events of the story are set in 2011. This time, the story is told in the first person. The narrator is Adair himself, and he proves to be no more reliable than the narrator of *The Murder of Roger Ackroyd*. Adair attends a Sherlock Holmes festival in Meiringen, Switzerland, close to the Reichenbach Falls, where Holmes grappled with Moriarty before (apparently) plunging to his doom. A pastiche Sherlock Holmes story, more effectively done than the over-

---

9   Gilbert Adair, *A Mysterious Affair of Style* (Faber, 2006), p.11.
10 Another contender for Best Postmodernist Take on Agatha Christie is Pierre Bayard's *Who Killed Roger Ackroyd?* (1998), which offers a solution to the mystery different from Poirot's.

whelming majority of Sherlockian pastiches, is included, and there are plentiful references to G. K. Chesterton, creator of the priest-sleuth Father Brown, and first President of the Detection Club, as well as to Ronald Knox and his "rules". But the main literary inspiration remains Christie. When Evadne Mount appears in the narrative, having hardly aged since the events of *The Act of Roger Murgatroyd*, Adair reminds us that Hercule Poirot too managed not to age in the course of his long career as a detective.

The murder victim is a Gustav Slavorigin, a controversial novelist whose unpleasantness enables Adair to indulge in a little catharsis when they discuss the first two Evadne Mount novels:

"Clever contraptions, both of them. You really caught the cardboard quality of her characters. Anyway, they helped pass the time."

"Thank you."

"Got good reviews, too, I noticed. Deserved to."

"Thanks again."

"Also a couple of stinkers."

"Just one, I think. In the *Guardian*. Michael Dibdin."

"Who died not long afterwards. *Spooooky* . . ."[11]

Adair probably did not realise it, but even here he was following in the footsteps of a master of Golden Age detective fiction. Anthony Berkeley, regarded by Agatha Christie as the most ingenious of her colleagues in the Detection Club, also took revenge in his detective fiction[12] against the American man of letters, Alexander Woollcott, who once gave him a disobliging review.

At the heart of the story, however, is Adair's extraordinarily skilful fusion of elements of reality, the fictional mystery of Slavorigin's death, and the literary tricks of Christie and Conan Doyle. In the bizarre yet strangely poignant final scene, Evadne taunts Adair: "Postmodernism is dead . . . Nobody gives two hoots about self-referentiality any longer, just as nobody gives two hoots, or even a single hoot, about you. Your books are out of sight, out of sound, out of fashion and out of print."

---

11 Gilbert Adair, *And Then There Was No One* (Faber, 2009).
12 In *Panic Party* (1934).

And the story ends with Adair diving into the Reichenbach Falls.

The most insightful review of the novel came from Jake Kerridge in the *Daily Telegraph*[13]. He thought it superior to the first two books about Evadne, "which, for all their allusive larkiness, replicated the main fault of most classical whodunnits: after the discovery of the corpse, the writer is simply killing time for the bulk of the book until the revelation of the murderer . . . This novel is an immensely entertaining *jeu d'esprit*, a ragbag of puns and allusions that literary trainspotters will delight in rummaging in, but is there anything to distinguish it from a dozen other such books? I would say, yes: its quiet poignancy. Adair's criticism of his previous Evadne novels is just one example of the honesty with which he writes about the shortcomings of his life and work here, and this lends the novel, for all its meta-fictional tricks . . . an emotional charge rarely found in whodunnits, parodies, postmodern fictions or any combination of the three."

Kerridge's acute remarks about poignancy proved sadly prescient. Adair never published another book. A stroke cost him his sight, a strange and shocking echo of *A Closed Book*, whose protagonist is a blind writer, and he died, far too young, in 2011, the year he had chosen for his fictional demise. For anyone else to say that these tragedies were themselves somehow ironic and postmodern—let alone "spooooky"—would be unforgivably tasteless, yet one suspects that Adair might have been unable to resist saying it himself. He was a witty and brave writer, and although the fact that he cast new light on the old ways of classic detective novelists represents only a fraction of his literary achievements, this is a feat that has eluded the vast majority of orthodox commentators on the genre. Like the misunderstood and underestimated whodunits they teased and celebrated, his last three books and above all that extraordinary final novel deserve respect, admiration, and to be remembered.

---

13 Jake Kerridge, review of *And Then There Was No One*, Daily Telegraph, 7 January 2009.

A De'Athly Confession

KENNETH RETROP

When approached to contribute to this festschrift, I considered writing a piece on the gentleness and good grace of the writer in question. On his kindness and generosity towards his colleagues and friends. But, of course, this is wishful thinking. He was notorious for being a selfish prig and stubborn old mule, a militant prescriptivist and baroque stylist, and a connoisseur of prewar cognacs and sherries. An oft-quoted (apocryphal) story about him is how he took a publisher to court for an incorrect footnote. (The truth is he attempted to start proceedings, but no lawyer would take on his case). When my father died, I took over as his literary executor. I knew about his prickly nature, wild tempers, and snap decisions to bequeath his savings to deeply inappropriate organisations (he once rang me in the middle of the night telling me he wanted to leave everything to the Shoreditch Morris Dancing Society). To counter this perception, I want to write about an unusual occurrence in the last year of his life—not to cause shock or controversy—but to reveal an unexpected all-too-human side of his character.[1]

I took over as executor in 2009. At this stage, he was writing solely academic works, and had finished a book on how to read Pope in relation to the French Renaissance, along with a poststructuralist (he never acknowledged the existence of the deconstructionists) analysis of Eliot's *Four Quartets*. His long-term housekeeper had died a few months before —she was loyal, long-suffering, and something of a second wife to him, despite being kept at remove (due, no doubt, to her "paucity of passable

---

[1] I do so knowing his aversion to sentiment and literary "softness", and consider this my one and only act of (affectionate) revenge for the rudeness to me in that final year.

breeding.") When I arrived he was arguing with the "replacement", a Portuguese student who had little time for his fusspottery, and made the rookie mistake of moving papers in his study to dust. "You don't understand!" I heard him shout as I arrived. "These papers must not be moved! I have spent a long and exhausting number of years arranging these papers in the wrong order so I can spend a long and exhausting number of years trying to arrange them in the right one!"

I tapped on the door to his study, having let myself in (the doorbell had been deactivated). He continued scolding Jess, who put up more resistance than his last housekeeper (whose name was never disclosed—there is some debate as to whether Giles ever asked for her forename in over ten years), and took five minutes to acknowledge my presence. He was clearly taking pleasure in having someone to spar with again and Jess met his crankiness blow for blow, dodging his sallies on her bad English by sniping his fondness for dust. I had last seen him in my late teens when I turned up stoned to one of my father's formal author lunches, and poked some salad around my plate, planning the moment I might ask my father for an extra few hundred (to buy an ounce of hashish, or "the complete set of Proust", as I called it then). Giles was unimpressed and spent the entire lunch hinting (outright stating) that I should leave and "attend to homework" (I was nineteen at the time—although I *did* have homework), and as I arrived he fixed me with the same disapproving glance. "Well, at least you've tucked your shirt in this time," he said. I laughed, although he intended it as a reproach. He allowed himself the faintest of grins and I was at ease as much as I ever would be.[2]

Giles De'Ath had become a parody of the ivory-tower academic, socially bereft in his tweed blazers with elbow patches, although as a younger man he had partaken of his share of zestful and exuberant living. His antiquarian prose style and decades spent inhabiting the 19th century had left him ill-equipped for the technological revolution when it arrived with unrelenting pace in the '80s and '90s. So the last person I expected to turn up on his doorstep was the former "teen heartthrob"

---

2 Later he asked me if I was "finished smoking Proust", and I had to marvel at his memory.

Ronnie Bostock. The actor, now prodigiously middle-aged, appeared the afternoon I sat down to discuss Giles's latest intention to leave his savings to the Kakapo and Other Endangered Parrots Collective, and had made himself incongruous on Giles's banquette, looking in wonder at the 10,000+ books. Bostock had starred in '90s "comedies" *Hotpants College II*, *Tex Mex*, and *Ketchup With Me*, each execrable in a different way, and in the '00s sank to erotic films and hardcore pornography. The former doe-eyed dreamboat had put on a kennel or two of puppy fat and wore an offensively colourful shirt with several buttons undone, bronzed chest and hairs on display, unaware of his general slovenliness and unmistakable appearance as a purveyor of pay-per-screw sleaze. Giles, of course, did not introduce us, and I spent the first hour bashfully avoiding the question as to how Giles ever came to promise to write a script for such a hasn't-ever-been. After some false starts, Giles stuttered out a request that I return later. I asked if he was sure; he snapped an affirmative.

I returned a fortnight later. Ronnie had holed himself up in Giles's largest spare room and created an extra workload for Jess, leaving his laundry strewn around the house, including his soiled floral underpants, behaviour to which Giles was turning a blind eye. If I had so much as left a coffee ring on his trestle table, he would have seen me beheaded. Giles was hard at work on a script for Ronnie, with the intention of "relaunching" his career in Hollywood. Giles was defensive and would not discuss the matter, or the script, with me, clearly in a muddle about how to behave (as was I). He hadn't written a movie script in his sixty years in the business, but here he was, hammering nervous sentences onto his Corona for the bloated mess lying in one of his beds upstairs. The most he would tell me was that he was "returning a favour", and that he would have the script done in a few weeks (and Ronnie's removal). As he waited for his masterpiece, freeloading and being excessive with his insincere thank yous, Bostock prowled around the house in a maudlin state, confiding to me that he had fallen into "bad movies" since his *Hotpants* heyday and was ecstatic for the "second chance". Since he appeared to be operating under the delusion a hashed-out script by an octogenarian Leavisite would bestow him with the acting talents of Olivier, I began to soften to his plight.

I looked up Bostock's filmography, and that pity evaporated by the time I arrived at *Rimming When You're Winning* (2007), his directorial debut (on 8mm cameras), and tried to fathom in what parallel universe Giles might have ended up owing a favour to this self-pitying schlong-slinger. I tried to squeeze the truth from Bostock. I approached his "room", and found him sitting on the edge of the bed staring at a grunting video on his phone. (Watching his own movies?) "I made a mistake twenty years ago in letting him go," he told me. "But he told me not to tell anyone about how we met each other. I can't break that promise, man. All I can tell you is what I said before, that he's doing me a huge favour. I need to get out of this . . . porno slump. Just consider what he's doing an act of charity." He pronounced "porno slump" in a cringing whisper. He wasn't half as embarrassed as I was.

How do you act when you are responsible for ensuring one man's reputation is kept intact (and in tact) without turbulent last-minute embarrassments that could linger far longer than a literary legacy? I chose to do nothing. In two weeks, Giles had finished the script (the quickest he had completed any work) and delivered the product to Bostock's hands. I was present for the farewell. Giles urged Bostock to leave at once, to take the script straight to Hollywood to pitch, trying to convince him not to use his name to help sell the script, to use a pseudonym. Bostock was adamant, of course, that a script by famous author Giles De'Ath (had he ever read one of his books?) would take him far. I managed to catch a glimpse of the title, *Budding Brooks*. Consulting some scribbled notes upon Giles's death, it seemed the plot concerned a washed-up actor mentoring an up-and-coming young star, who goes on to achieve more success than the hasbeen had as a young man, and the hasbeen actor's attempts to sabotage his protégé's career. The film (as yet) remains unmade.

Giles would only live another eleven months after Bostock's departure. His final book—a Marxist reading of Longinus—remained unfinished. The script was his last completed project and my attempts to contact Bostock about returning the material have proven futile (it was likely Giles waived the copyright). In those peculiar post-Bostock months (my time with Giles has been mentally filed pre- and post-Bostock), I sought to unravel the mystery of this episode. There were moments of light humour in our interactions when I might have let fall the question, but I always feared a reproach and destroying the confidence I had built, so I let the matter drop, expecting there would later be a confession or another "right moment" to bring it up. The moment never appeared and Giles died of complications in surgery a few months after we had finalised his will (he left, at my insistence, his money to distant relatives and several ailing publishers). I inherited his formidable library and have yet to decide whether to auction the books to charity, or keep them safely guarded in their two hundred boxes, in the event any hidden notes or revealing slips of paper might present themselves.

An explanation finally arrived itself in the form of an unpublished manuscript, *Love and De'Ath on Long Island*, an astonishing piece of confessional writing about an aging novelist's infatuation with teen heartthrob Ronnie Bostock, completed in 1991. On a rainy afternoon, Giles took refuge in the cinema with the intention of seeing an adaptation of Forster's *Where Angels Fear to Tread*, only to find himself before *Hotpants College II* due to a particularly indolent projectionist who had fallen asleep after popping one too many Snooze-Eaze pills. About to walk out, he found himself entranced by the childish eyes and chiselled jawline of Bostock and began a long infatuation with the actor, collecting cut-out pictures and his movies on VHS. It was the awakening of some dormant or new sexuality in him and some palpable excitement in his life. He travelled to Long Island and contrived a way to introduce himself to the actor and his wife (crashing against her in the supermarket and blundering some cringing cant about mutual friends), and took Bostock under his wing and helped the actor move from the comedies to serious acting roles. Finally, unable to suppress his affection for the actor, he blurted out his true feelings and Bostock left in a macho huff. He wrote Bostock a long and impassioned farewell letter, cursing

Bostock with the realisation that he would never get the chance to star in a script of any substance without Giles's guidance, and he would regret ejecting him from his life. (The latter proved to be true, the former, not unhumorously, proved false).

How do we explain such unGileslike behaviour? Is it fair to speculate or even discuss an embarrassing secret that Giles wanted hidden until his death? By keeping the manuscript in his papers, he must have wanted people to know the story of his folly, of this beyond-mid-life mania—as an artist, the story was too irresistible, too classic a tragedy to be passed over, and his manuscript is indeed subtitled "a novel", leaving a tantalising question mark over the accuracy of the events inside (despite real names being used). Why didn't Giles, after being spurned, send Bostock packing? He must have softened at the memory of his former infatuation's return and taken an uncharacteristic pity on him. The pain of having this wound opened again must have driven him to sentiment. Perhaps he also took a certain pleasure in seeing his infatuation in such a dire state (his wife had left him when the porn career started) and no longer beautiful. Does this cast our author in a new light, dispelling the myth of the fustian pedant and professional curmudgeon? Not particularly. He too was prey to illogical crushes, like the rest us, and as much a victim of desire and the madness of lust as you or me. Anyone who has read his most beautiful works already knew this.[3] Let us celebrate the art, not the infelicities, or as Giles put it, "the tedious business of suffering for one's material."

---

3 See the wrenching scene between Abetta and Laurence in *Unlucky James* (1959).

A Letter To My Dead Friend Gilbert Adair About Having it Out[1]

ALEXANDER GARCÍA DÜTTMANN

If I had to state, in a nutshell, where we differed, and where we did so in a manner that mattered, or that was relevant to our friendship and to our understanding of what a friendship should entail, and that was not just a question of temperament, my first impulse would be to say: we had opposing views when relating to what we perceived as a wrong. I mean, of course, a wrong done to the friend. But I am not alluding to an unintended wrong, committed out of a lack of knowledge in a particular situation, or out of the kind of thoughtlessness that comes with our human condition of separateness and that so often seems unavoidable. Nor am I alluding to a minor wrong that seeks the generosity of forgetting, or that demands not to be turned into an object of obsession, as if it could become the pretext for some deeper resentment to go about its business without showing its ugly face. The wrong I have in mind is the wrong that puts the friendship itself at risk and that may lead to an irreversible loss, to a rupture from which the friendship may not recover in the future.

When I say that we had opposing views, I am not being accurate enough. For in truth, it was less a question of views, a word that suggests the possibility of change, as if a convincing explanation could always make one come around to the other's way of seeing the world and comporting himself within it, than a question of something much more entrenched, of something that had almost a bodily dimension. We seemed to have been shaped by diverging dispositions towards the

---

[1] This is my second letter to Gilbert after his death. The first letter was published by the online journal *Lola* in May 2012: www.lolajournal.com/2/letter_dead_friend.html

world and others, so I wouldn't hesitate to claim that the difference I am trying to describe is one that concerned our respective feelings of life, which in other respects seemed so similar. And I conclude, provisionally, that the feeling of life may not have the kind of unity or simplicity we would expect it to have, and that feelings of life may communicate and at the same time remain impermeable to each other. Perhaps the importance of tact in a friendship, unneeded when one coincides with the other in all significant aspects, should be understood as the consequence of such elusiveness or intractability.

How did we differ, then? If your opinions and your behaviour were not consistent in every single instance, and if you could surprise me at times by saying or doing something that, in my eyes, implied a disagreement and even a contradiction when referred to something I remembered you saying or doing in the past, regardless of a firmness of tone that intimated an equality of attitude throughout adulthood, or a steadfastness of principles held since coming of age emotionally and intellectually, there was at least one conviction that you never renounced during the time of our friendship and that you defended with a fervor that did not admit of any debate. You believed that, should a friend have a grudge against the other friend, whether rightly or wrongly, the only thing to do was to have it out. Nothing was more reprehensible to you, more threatening to the spirit of friendship, more unfriendly and more selfish, more unforgiving, than keeping the pain of an inflicted wound to oneself. Silence, the hope that the friend might notice what he had done before being alerted to it, perpetrated the violation and was not a remedy. It was an obtuseness. The friend owed it to the other friend not to leave him in the dark about what he had experienced as the rawness and even cruelty that disregard may involve. "You must tell me when you feel that something is wrong." Telling, for you, and talking about it was the only way to restore the friendship to its own ambition, to a common outwitting of an acknowledged solitude—and in your case to outwit must be understood literally, as a cunning use of wit.

I recall that the first time I felt alienated from you we had known each other for two or three years at the most, though I believe that we were already carried by the confidence that I take to be a distinctive feature of friendship. We had been willing to behave from the start as if we had always known each other as friends, not because we shared so many friends and acquaintances in Paris, not because I had experienced an affinity with you when reading your weekly film criticism for *The Independent on Sunday*, and not because, in the late nineteen-eighties, we had been briefly introduced outside a French cinema as you were coming out of a screening of Edgar Ulmer's *Detour* on your own and I was about to see the film with Hugo Santiago. All these reasons may have played a historical role in our friendship, yet ultimately the principle of reason does not apply to what makes friends into friends.

What had happened? After working, as so often rather secretively, on a script that the Famous Director was to turn into a movie, you had left for Paris, where the shooting was to begin soon. I did not hear from you for much of your absence. Perhaps you got in touch once or twice when you were in London for a short period to deal with bills and correspondence. I cannot remember whether it was on one of these occasions that you told me not only about the occurrences on the set but also about all the visits you were receiving from curious friends. It is possible that you only told me after returning to England in the autumn, when once again we had regular dinners in your neighbourhood. What is it that put me off? The fact that I had been waiting for an invitation that you never extended, as if in my case the secret of the writer's work had encompassed the continuation of this work by a third party, the filmmaker? Or the fact that I could not help but find myself excluded when you kept mentioning the friends who, almost casually, had been granted the privilege of witnessing you on the shoot? I assumed that you were playing games with me, turning on a curiosity that had been disappointed in advance, as it were, though I could not fathom what the reason for such cock-tease might be. Ten years later, you made a point of asking me to the wintry shoot of *A Closed Book* in Oxford and we even convinced Raúl Ruiz to include us in a street scene on New College Lane. The sequence was cut short by the producers, who massacred the film, and all the spectator sees now, for the briefest lapse of time, is a fleeting appearance of our backs.

We had it out eventually because you had noticed my reluctance to remain as close to you as you had thought we were. And you explained to me that the cause for your withdrawal while in Paris had been connected to my loose entanglement in a web of fidelities and betrayals, hopes and disappointments, declarations of love and jealousies amongst friends. For it was out of this affective web that the work adapted to the screen had originally come into existence. It had done so in the guise of a first novel. An urgent request for protection against public exposure had then prompted you to extract the novel from wider circulation. Hence you were worried that, if permitted onto the set, I might report back from the front and, without fully realising what I was doing, unsettle the precarious balance that you had managed to establish between you and your friends after the debacle. Did you not fear that you were jeopardising the balance yourself by allowing, and perhaps encouraging, the Famous Director to base his film on your novel?

After giving me an account of your behaviour, you asked me to reassure you and to confirm that having it out was always the best option when a friendship needed to be preserved. To be honest, my endorsement of your view was less motivated by your art of persuasion than by a strange form of superstition on my side. I had the impression that the mere fact of addressing the issue had made it almost irrelevant and that therefore there was no reason to dwell upon it, as if the absolving power had emanated from hitting a key on the piano, not from listening to the reverberating sound it had produced and asking oneself whether the chord was out of tune or not. I did not really believe that clarifying contents could ever do the trick, and I did not think your explanation compelling, given how little I considered myself a potential go-between in the whole affair. However, I must admit that my skepticism was unfair, a sign of sulkiness unprepared to open up to your own concerns and ambivalence, to assumptions, suspicions, and anxieties that might not have been as unwarranted as I imagined. The film, I told myself, would soon be screened all over the world, and your friends, the ones who had felt exposed by the novel's first version, would not be able to ignore its existence. Still, you desired a reprieve. Or was it that you did not want anyone to meddle with the film before it was finished? Let me return to my scepticism, no matter how unfair it proved to be. Where does my disbelief in the sufficiency of a clarification of contents originate? Why am I not a supporter of having it out? To some extent my disbelief stems from a dubious attachment to innocence: innocence lost cannot be recovered. Once the web of appearances has been torn to pieces, once a slit has ripped it open, it will never be mended again. From now on a smaller or bigger gap will separate the appearance from the truth. The truth will no longer lie in the appearance itself. Truth and appearance will have come into conflict. To some other extent, my disbelief stems from a distrust in language as a means of information and communication. Words, employed pragmatically, or in view of bringing something home, rarely amount to more than an assurance. They weaken the truth even though they may be stating it. Lovers can have sex after a fight, friends cannot. Yet to some further extent my disbelief also stems from shame, shame at having forced the other to justify himself. This, then, is my bad faith when it comes to friendship. On the one hand, I wish the other to recognise that I feel puzzled and disenchanted; I wish to do something, I wish something to be done about what I take to be a wrong; while, on the other hand, the justification, when it is offered and when it triggers additional queries, seems a futile and demeaning endeavour in which I do not want to have any part.

Does the breakage, the tear in the web of appearances, require some kind of reparative action that, paradoxically, it must disavow at the same time, though perhaps not entirely, not if the justification can be regarded as a gesture? Is the tear the result of the "dire deformity" of one's own attitude towards the web of appearances, to quote from Henry James's *The Golden Bowl*, so that such an action can only be meaningful if it is directed at oneself? There was something I admired about you, something hands-on. The undisturbed belief in having it out with your friends when necessary was like a frankness, or a straightforwardness, that bestowed the freshness of youth upon you, the impetus of Enlightenment. You were not an obscurantist. You were not tortured, did not lack for the right thing to say because of too many considerations and hesitations. You were there, willing to engage in difficult conversations, possibly at your own expense. You were ready to try and remove the poison from the injury so that, in the open, it would cease to produce its evil effect. In short, you were a man of surfaces, a wit in the ethics of friendship. For what is a wit if not someone who moves swiftly on the surface of language and life?

The Death of the Reader

LIDIA RATBERG

As we advance towards bolder frontiers of technological innovation, evolving hundreds of new ways to communicate vital (or trivial) messages to each other, so we evolve a hundred new ways to wipe nuisances from our lives through the convenient (and essential) block, blacklist, and banish buttons. I had set up firewalls, brickwalls, redirectors, and pop-up blocks to prevent Hertie Scooner from contacting me—short of hiring an armed sentinel outside my office, I couldn't have been farther from her presence. I had, however, no means to stop her letters arriving through my mailbox, each attempt disguised using altered handwriting or resized envelopes, forcing me to open and take a glance at the pleading contents before placing them in the shredder. Hertie Scooner was the first student to undertake a serious critical dismantling of the Dead Reader Theory I had developed and she was desperate to present her findings to me in order to make her own impact in academia. She had unearthed, or so she claimed, some striking revelation in my theory requiring my urgent attention. After placing her latest envelope in the shredder, I sat down at my Toshiba to type the very paragraph I have been reading.

I had arrived at Craigmount College after a long period struggling to publish several supposedly 'experimental' novels with tatterdemalion small presses—one-man operations run by well-meaning simpletons with photocopiers and a head full of quixotic notions—where several fatal accidents brought me to the brink of obscure success, only to deny me that petite pleasure. I had written a novel, *Loop de Loupe*, a bilingual whodunit where each sentence alternated French and English languages (swapping viewpoints and tone), to create entirely different versions of events for mono- and polyglots (from both sides of the Channel). The editor at Bottom Feeder Press, Chris Alpine, was opposed to publishing the book, terse in his dismissal ("mono punters won't shell for half a text"), while the sub-editor Jerzy Glacial raved and praised its qualities in private mails to me. A few weeks later, when I had abandoned any hope for publication at this press, Chris Alpine was found dead in his Quebec apartment. I waited a respectful month-long period before I entered into negotiations with Jerzy about the prospect of publishing my novel, after he had taken over as head of Bottom Feeder. Jerzy took the view that since Chris's decision was to oppose the publication he couldn't disrespect his dead friend's wish—and so the novel remained drawer-bound until my later success.

I accepted the need to compose a more 'accessible' novel and failed to do so by writing *Gravid Syntax*, a typographically complex text where paragraphs became 'pregnant' with litters of sentences of less linguistic complexity, splintering into stories upon stories in various styles—this also was too radical for Lexicon Artists Press. A month after the refusal, their Head Reader emailed me to say that he had adored the novel, but their editor had conservative tastes and disliked the 'brain strain' the reader would be required to endure while reading. A month later, their editor was found dead in his Seattle apartment, and once again, I waited the respectful month before contacting their new editor about possible publication. He parroted the last—it was bad taste to publish a work his editor had opposed and so on. These frustrating knock-backs made me reconsider my outlook on the production of the one sort of fiction I believed still had worth—the *sui generis*, cliché-crushing kind.

Rather than attempt to contrive a way forward for the reader and writer, I decided to sever the relationship with a metaphorical guillotine. In my critical work, *The Death of the Reader*, I argued for the extinction of the reader from critical discourse, how the text-combers had been achieving interpretive murder for the last fifty years, dismissing the author's intentions and contorting texts in laughable shapes until their creator's original intentions no longer mattered. I decided it was time to return the reins to the writer, to write the sort of texts that coded their meanings in the work itself and left as little room for interpretation as possible. (Of course, mass market fiction offers this option—I was proposing more of an artistic totalitarianism in works of intellectual value). I proposed in my groundbreaking thesis that writers ought to make their intentions blatant, either by including explanatory passages within their texts, or afterwords, setting out the *one and only* '*meaning*' (or series of '*meanings*') of the text, shunning the reader's free interpretive reign and driving them to that ur-text of over-interpretation, *Finnegans Wake*. This was a response, also, to the indifference of publishing houses and readers to 'experimental' works—if readers had no time for these sorts of books, why should writers invite their participation? Writers should write self-enclosed texts with no attempt to involve or include the reader—to write and publish for themselves, and deny the reader the opportunity to theorise on the work. (My theory allowed for the *possibility* of readers, so these new texts could be sold to others—however, the theory aimed towards a complete abandonment, towards not publishing at all).

Due to some twist of cosmic irony, my book was a critical success, read by millions. I accepted a position at Craigmont College teaching literature, where the Dead Reader Theory made my role untaxing. I encouraged students to dismiss the entire history of literature up until now, apart from the books whose meanings could be understood without further interpretation (from author interviews or explanatory essays), and to concentrate on reading the newest of the reader-shunning texts, and to praise them on their qualities *as reviewers*. The reader became the reviewer—permitted to comment on how well or poorly the author had performed his or her experiment, never permitted to stray into the realm of textual analysis. The only person to whom the author had to answer was him or herself.

Hertie Scooner had been a student of Carlton Curp's (actual name), for whom the New Criticism was still considered an anarchistic form of approaching texts, and who was overseeing her thesis on Barthes until her line of thought led him to the brink of incomprehension, and I took over as 'auxiliary' tutor. She had made several interesting comparisons between 'The Death of the Author' and *The Death of the Reader*, positioning herself in limbo between the two poles, taking potshots at both. At some point she would have to come down on the side of the reader or the author—in fact, as she approached her decision, I hadn't heard from her for weeks. Then I received the bombardment of messages. I can't say why, exactly, I chose to remain in hiding from her (to the extent I avoided the campus that summer)—well, I can say, only not in this paragraph. After placing her latest envelope in the shredder, I sat down at my Toshiba to type the very six paragraphs I have been reading.

Before I began the business of writing novels, I lived in Yardley, Birmingham where I fell in with a group of radical writers and pamphleteers. Inspired by their fiery views on literature, I became a part of this thriving scene, taking weeks to realise their sole output consisted of propaganda for the British National Party. I too began writing pamphlets for the BNP, condemning immigrants and dredging up colonialist clichés for the not ungenerous remuneration offered. I later learned that the pamphlets were being used to stir hatred among a group of renegade nationalists who bullied immigrants in attempts to force them to return to their homelands. I wrote increasingly fulminant pamphlets, espousing outright hatred through doggerel, and spent the money on a new Volkswagen. I was invited to make a speech during one of their demonstrations at Dover, where they had barricaded the harbour to prevent immigrants arriving by ship. The bile flowed quite freely from my lips.

I became a spokesperson for a splinter group, Britain4Brits (later dubbed the UKKK), pocketing the lucre for fuelling these people with the hatred that seemed to give their otherwise useless lives meaning. The strong sense of community forged through hatred led me to a relationship with a woman in the organisation, where the raucous exchange of ethnic insults became a binding agent for our love (or hate-love). I came to believe what I preached—rhetoric as art form, preaching as a means of being respected and adored, the thrill in stirring others to believe with conviction in my words. Falling asleep to the sweet racism murmured in my ear every night also didn't help me wise up. This madness reached breaking point when I took part in several acts of violence against immigrants at the docks, flinging bricks and bottles alongside subliterate skinheads, whose respect I had won as a 'warrior' among them. When the group asked me to go on television to defend the organisation, I panicked and knew this would seal my fate. I left the woman and fled Yardley.

I moved to Aberdeen, where I co-managed a bookshop, landing the position by sinking most of my ill-gotten profits in the business. It was there I knuckled down to write proper literary works, free from rhetorical flourishes, experimental in form, and began my frustrations with publishers, as adumbrated earlier. I can't possibly hope to defend my time as spokesperson for B4B—the only logical explanation I can offer is that my selfish, nihilistic approach to life (one I had always regarded as a form of wry detachment), made it simple to disengage from the inhumanity of persecuting other humans. In Aberdeen, I saw the composition of meaningful and original fiction as a chance to atone for past actions by devoting myself to making the beautiful, to emotionally replenishing works of art. Having completed these works to my satisfaction and meeting with persistent crushing failure, I felt a little redress to be harmless.

When I read the first chapter of Hertie Scooner's thesis, I became suspicious of her criticisms on *The Death of the Reader*. She noted a certain "blustering" tone in my style, and remarked on my "fascistic urge to immigrate the reader from a text"—not a phrase I re-read without highly raised eyebrows. I had been aware of her hints for some time, those little nods to her awareness of my past indiscretions. Now, with me deliberately absenting myself from the university, I was beginning to appear paranoid. After placing her latest envelope in the shredder, I sat down at my Toshiba to type the very ten paragraphs I have been reading. And a moment later, Hertie stepped inside my study.

"How did you get in here?" I said, startled.

"Picked the lock. My people are very crafty with locks. I need to talk to you about my thesis," she said, sitting on a stack of papers. "See, the reader is very much alive."

"Get out."

"Or, at least, the readers of the email I have just sent denouncing you as a hate criminal and responsible for driving me to my death."

"What are you talking about?"

"In a few minutes I'm going to shoot myself and ruin your life. Because you ruined mine."

"I don't . . . "

"The UKKK. You were there that night my parents were trying to cross the border, egging on your friends to smash my family's brains in with rocks. And that's exactly what you and your fascist friends did. My parents were pummelled with bottles and rocks and had to be taken to the hospital and treated for severe brain damage. And they died two hours later in surgery. I was brought up in care."

"My God, I . . . "

"And I devoted my life to finding the person behind this hatred and violence, and bringing him to justice. Unlike you, I don't believe in violence. But the violence you etched in me can't be erased, the memory of what you did to my parents will never leave me. Which is why you must live with the memory of what you did and your life in ruins, and the memory of me in this office as I take my life at the end of this sentence."

Hertie shot herself with the gun she had been holding in her pocket. I looked away as she fell to the floor. As if on cue, I heard sirens in the distance, and logged onto my campus email. The entire history of my time with the UKKK, with incriminating photographs, and a longer version of Hertie's story, had been emailed to every department on campus. I had mere minutes to make a decision before I was tried for manslaughter. I reached inside Hertie's coat for the bloody revolver. I placed the weapon inside my mouth and pulled the trigger. If you are wondering how I could have written this story if at the end I blew my brains out with a revolver, consider this, Reader, my way of returning the narrative to your hands. The author is dead: it is now your turn to make sense of this mendacious and meaningless story.

Rereading Adair

JONATHAN ROSENBAUM

Ever since Gilbert Adair died three weeks short of his 67th birthday, in London, I've been rereading him compulsively. And I've had a lot to choose from—not only many online articles (including pieces written for this magazine and for *Sight & Sound*), but all but one of the 18 books listed on the flyleaf of his nineteenth and last, *And Then There Was No One: The Last of Evadne Mount* (Faber and Faber, 2009)— the final volume in his inspired trilogy of Agatha Christie pastiches, which somehow manage to combine his taste for pop entertainment with his more avant-garde impulses, to riotous effect. Even though I eventually lost touch with Gilbert as a friend—whom I'd met in the early 1970s as a fellow habitué of the Paris Cinémathèque, and who years later was kind enough to broker my friendship with Raúl Ruiz (with whom he worked on several projects, including three that were filmed, and who tragically and prematurely died just a few months earlier)—I remained a steadfast fan who collected all his books.

For *Film Comment*, Gilbert made his first appearance in an interview with Jacques Rivette, conducted jointly with myself and Lauren Sedofsky for the September-October 1974 issue.[1] After that, from 1977 through 1982, he contributed six London Journals, nine Paris Journals, a final journal "from a country manor", a "cliché expert's guide to the cinema", and an especially memorable Mae West obituary—which includes a definitive tribute to *Sextette*, her 1978 swansong, which he called "the most extraordinary *compliment* ever paid by the medium to one of its stars" and "the most chivalrous film ever made", adding that its "extreme fascination . . . derives not merely from its star's age—she

---

1 Available online at both jonathanrosenbaum.com/?p=28298 and jacques-rivette.com

was 86 when she made it—but from the fact that the film pretends not to notice it." ("To paraphrase Cocteau's oft-quoted aphorism about Victor Hugo, Mae West is a madwoman who thinks she is Mae West.")

A singular and highly gifted literary dandy, Gilbert was also a seasoned and voracious film buff—uncharacteristic for a writer in the U.K. (born in Scotland, but in fact a fully self-created English dandy and francophile), yet part of his essential baggage as a frequent Channel-crosser. Characteristically, in Paris he used to discard all the books he read except for those by Cocteau, whose volumes filled the shelves in his hotel room on Quai Voltaire, and one of his sadly unfulfilled dreams was to write a biography of his role model. (Check out his superb audio commentary to *Les Enfants Terribles* on Criterion.) Equally ambitious and self-critical, he often rewrote his own books when they went into second editions.

Almost half his books qualify as impressive pastiches: sequels to Lewis Carroll's *Alice* books and *Peter Pan*, spins on *Death in Venice* and *Les Enfants Terribles* that later formed the basis for the film versions of *Love and Death on Long Island* and *The Dreamers*, a thriller conceived as a tribute to Hitchcock (*The Key of the Tower*), a joint takeoff on Barthes' *Mythologies* and Perec's *Je me souviens* "translated" into an English context (*Myths and Memories*), and the only book listed on his flyleaf that I don't own—a brilliant Alexander Pope pastiche called *The Rape of the Cock* which I read in manuscript circa 1974. (In fact, I once strongly suspected that this remains unpublished; the only other bibliographic reference I've come across, "Caen: Editions Dom, 1991," suspiciously sounds like a half-buried Adairian pun, caen+dom equaling "condom", although I've subsequently been informed that this book actually exists.)[2]

Most of his other books are film-related: obviously *Hollywood's Vietnam* and *Flickers*, but also many entries in his two wonderful collections of "cultural" columns, *The Postmodernist Always Rings Twice* and *Surfing the Zeitgeist*. His adapted his own novel *A Closed Book* for a late Ruiz feature (subsequently retitled *Blind Revenge*) that was poorly received but deserved more attention than it attracted (and could still be purchased,

---

2 Editors' Note: This book never existed—it had not been previously published until now.

the last time I checked, at amazon.co.uk), and even *The Death of the Author* features a telling interlude related to Lubitsch's *To Be or Not to Be*.

He will be missed—but thankfully, he can still (and can always) be read.

The Hand and the Crocodile

LAURA GUTHRIE

The crocodile lay waiting beneath the waters of the Amazon river beside a bank. A tasty-looking piece of meat with a string attached to it, suspended from a crudely-bound log raft, drifted downstream with the current past the crocodile. Upon this raft sat three people: a man, a woman and a small boy. The crocodile could barely distinguish their features—the images undulated above the rippling surface—but the man seemed tall and muscular, with a long black beard and wild, curly hair. The woman was smaller, with pale skin and dreadlocked blonde hair. She was sitting cross-legged, the boy on her knee. The crocodile smacked his jaws shut, heaved his body off the silt, scattering tadpoles as he did so, and paddled out towards the tempting feast. His head barely rippled the surface of the water, and he made no sound, his approach remaining unnoticed.

The woman was named Mary. She was enjoying the wonderful coolless of the water lapping against her trailing hand. As for the man, his name was James R. I shall not divulge his family name, as he has committed such atrocities in the intervening time that it would be tarnished forever. This would do the family a gross disservice, as every other one of its members is both noble and notable. At this time, however, he was still innocent, and his attention was fixed on steering the raft. James and Mary had deserted London as young lovers, seeking to rid themselves of the endless social obligations and petty restrictions placed upon them by their elders. It was James's idea: he had proposed to Mary after courting her as she played the piano at balls, and, with her consent, subsequently spirited her away. This behaviour, which in retrospect was appalling in the unresolved worry and grief it must have caused her loving but overbearing parents, would later prove to be family traits: an adventuring spirit and resistance to the obligations of adulthood.

The couple had sailed to the Amazon on a vessel called the HMS *Steerforth Civilian*, the purchase and fitting-out of which had been funded entirely by a like-minded group of rich but disillusioned heirs to unwanted fortunes or family businesses. It had foundered in a sudden and violent tropical storm, but the young couple, having conceived the child illicitly whilst on board, and having thus been put off the ship in a lifeboat to meet their fate three days previously, had survived. The lifeboat had drifted to the mouth of the river and there they had built their home and raised their child—whom they named Peter—using whatever tools they could fashion from the materials at hand. Precisely how much time had passed since then neither could say, since there was no way of keeping track; but Peter was now swift on his feet, could carry on a conversation, wield a weapon, cook a fish on an open fire, make clothes out of leaves and feathers . . . yet was still in possession of all his baby teeth. At any rate, it must have been a few years.

Suddenly, the little vessel erupted out of the water as the crocodile reared underneath it and Peter was flung out of it. In contrast to all his land-based skills, he had not at this stage learned how to swim. Now he splashed wildly, gasping equal quantities of air and water. As the crocodile advanced upon Mary, James was placed in a terrible predicament as to who he should rescue first, but after a fraction of a second's deliberation he struck out for Mary and thrust his right arm between her and the crocodile. The water turned a fearful red and everything was arms and legs and leaves and feathers and logs, and finally only James, swimming to the bank holding Peter in his good left arm, his right hand flapping limply on the end of his wrist. Mary was nowhere to be seen.

When he reached the bank, James turned an unconscious Peter on his side and watched as he shivered and vomited vast quantities of water. James screamed Mary's name, but did not dare wade back in the river for fear of the crocodile. He sank to his knees beside his half-drowned son, as the upturned raft grounded itself. Tears dripped from his face to the mud.

Within minutes, Peter began to regain some of his strength. He pulled himself to the lush greenery of the riverside and continued to recuperate in the soft shade. Meanwhile, James tried to move his hand. Nothing happened. He tried again. Still, nothing happened. Now that the danger was past, he was aware of a dull, throbbing ache in his arm. He looked down. A chunk was gone from his forearm muscle and blood oozed down, dripping from his fingers to the grass. A length of white bone stuck out. With a howl, he tore off his upper garment and bound it in a tourniquet around the wound, before hauling Peter up and stumbling further inside the forest with him.

Despite staunching and careful care, James's right hand did not regain movement, and over the next few weeks it began to wither. One night, Peter noticed that the tips of the fingers were turning black. As James slept, he lifted the hand gently and put it to his nose. It smelled putrid, like a dead capybara he had once found in a shrub, flies burrowing within its flesh and its eyes pecked out. He imagined his father looking like that, felt the bile rise in his throat, and swallowed it back down. He remembered salvaging and eating a piece of meat left over from a fire two days ago. It had a similar odour to the fingers and the capybara, and had made him ill with fever and vomiting. If this decaying hand was still attached to his father, could it not poison him too? Peter had only just survived that. His mother had put his resilience down to his being 'young and fit'. His father was older—that must mean he was more likely to die—and then who would look after him and tell him stories? Peter crept to his bed and put his hand under the skin and grass mattress. He retrieved a heavy, wooden-handled, flint-headed axe his father had used to cut down trees. He stole back to where his father was sleeping . . .

James was dreaming that he was a potato plant in a vegetable patch and a farmer was standing over him, garden fork in hand, ready to plunge the prongs into the soil and dig up his roots. Therefore when he awoke, it did not at first seem strange to see a silhouetted figure kneeling down, hand raised with an implement. The figure came into sharper focus. At the same moment as James leapt up, Peter brought the axe down with all the force his childish arms could muster. The blade fell and the hand dropped cleanly onto the grass. James roared and clutched at his stump, as Peter caught up the hand and ran with it to the river bank.

The world spun and for a time, James knelt on the ground, unable to see, hear, or think through the raging pain. Slowly, through an intense effort of will, he pulled his mind back, and tried to make sense of what had happened. He had fed his son, sheltered him, and cared for him all his life—and how had he been repaid? By having his hand cut off while he slept. An unprovoked attack, carried out when he was at his most vulnerable, by someone he trusted. "Betrayed by my own flesh and blood!" he snarled, as he bound his stump. "You are no child of mine! You are an evil fairy—a goblin—a changeling, and changelings must be cut down!"

As he stood to leave, something flashed at the empty fireplace: a hook once attached to the tarpaulin of the lifeboat when it had lain on the deck of the *Steerforth*. Now the hook was used to string up clay pots of water for boiling. It glinted in the moonlight: a suggestion—no—an invitation. James snatched it and lashed it to his bandaged stump, grimacing and sweating as he did so. He looked down at the hook and swore an oath:

"Henceforth, I renounce James R. I, James *Hook*, will never rest until the changeling, Peter Pan, is hunted down and destroyed—even if I die in the attempt!"

When he reached the river bank, Peter threw the hand in the water with a splash. It landed in the reflection of the moon and splintered it. The raft, which still floated in the shallows, bobbed on the ripples.

"That's for you, Crocodile!" he cried out. "I hope you die from the poison. Serve you right for eating my mother!"

A shape in the water stirred. The hand floated briefly before being pulled under by a dark mass. The reflection of the moon re-formed over the place where it had been.

Something crashed through the bushes. Peter braced himself, ready for a wild animal, but instead saw his father charging at him through the undergrowth, right hand raised and the hook from the fire tied to it. Upon seeing Peter James roared. For a second, Peter stood completely still. As he did so, he banished forever all thoughts of this man as his father and any care he once had for him, and picked up a stone. He hurled it at James, who dodged, so he threw a second, smaller one, hitting James squarely between the eyes. James toppled over, not dead but stunned.

Taking his chance, Peter jumped on the raft and, breaking off a long branch from a fallen tree, pushed off from the bank. He headed towards a segment of the river as yet undiscovered by all who return from the Amazon—a segment where the fairies live, and where, when two stars align on a certain night each year, a gateway opens to Neverland...

Mysterious Transpositions: Adair's The Dreamers and Cocteau's Les Enfants Terribles

WARWICK WISE

> Only those who have to translate ideas from one language into another will be sensitive to such nuances. —The Dreamers

As Gilbert Adair pointed out, somewhat irritably, in a letter to the London Review of Books, he drew on several Cocteau novels for the writing of The Holy Innocents (1988; later The Dreamers, 2003), including Le Grand Écart and Thomas l'imposteur (both 1923)[1]. But the most conspicuous model remains, quite deliberately, Cocteau's 1929 masterpiece Les Enfants terribles. Not that Adair wrote a straightforward adaptation, much less a translation; rather, the relationship between the two books is not unlike the relationship Matthew in The Dreamers sees between the room he's given in Théo and Isabelle's house and the room that belonged to his beloved best friend in San Diego, the elements of one 'mysteriously transposed' to the other. Matthew's

> sensation of déjà vu, [...] the obscure conviction not only that he had been here before but that something had taken place here of import to him (p.64)[2]

... is likely to be shared by readers of Adair's book who are also familiar with Cocteau's. Both works concern adolescent Parisian siblings who live in a private world of sexualised ritual and oneupmanship; in both, one or more outsiders enter that private world and catalyse an emotional escalation that ends in tragedy. But important changes to the

---
1 LRB vol. 20 no. 2, 22 January 1998, Letters.
2 Gilbert Adair, The Dreamers, Faber & Faber 2004. All subsequent quotes from this edition.

pattern are also made, some of which expand on Cocteau's themes and some of which argue against them in revealing ways.

First of all, Adair simplifies the cast into something more archetypal. The central siblings become twins; and of the two outsiders invited into the dreamworld, one male and one female, Adair retains only the male, thereby reducing a fairly complex web of relationships to something more nearly resembling the classic love triangle. At the same time, the relationships involved are made more physical and more sexually explicit.

One thing that becomes immediately apparent in the wake of these alterations is that homoeroticism has been highlighted much more directly than in Cocteau. There are practical considerations behind this (Adair can be upfront about things that were more difficult for Cocteau writing in the 1920s), but there are also thematic consequences. In *Les Enfants terribles*, homosexuality is evoked through a series of ostensibly hetero dynamics whose boundaries are constantly shifting and whose participants teeter always on the edge of androgyny. On the face of things Gérard loves Élisabeth and Agathe loves Paul; but Paul also loves his male school-friend Dargelos, so long as we understand that this constitutes 'un désir chaste sans sexe et sans but'; meanwhile, Agathe, the recipient of Paul's surface affections, resembles Dargelos so closely that she mistakes his photograph for her own, and Paul simply uses her as a more acceptable stand-in:

> Paul se sentit remué en présence d'Agathe. [...] Or, il venait, sans le savoir, de transporter sur Agathe les masses confuses de rêve qu'il accumulait sur Dargelos. (p.69)[3]

> [Paul felt stirred in Agathe's company. And yet he had, without realising it, shifted on to Agathe the confused mass of dreams that he had built up around Dargelos.][4]

---

3 Jean Cocteau, *Les Enfants terribles*, [1929], Livre de Poche 2013. All subsequent quotes from this edition.
4 The translations of Cocteau here and elsewhere below are my own, including any mistakes.

The relationship of Paul and Élisabeth contributes to this sense of gender fluidity; they are in some sense aspects of the same person, 'comme deux membres d'un même corps', and it is from this basis that the theme of incest arises. In Cocteau's book incest is a mood, not a physical act: all we are told is that 'aucune gêne n'existait' between the two siblings, and that they sleep, dress, wash, together. But, more fundamentally, incest as a concept also allows Cocteau to examine illicit or forbidden love without addressing homosexuality directly.

Les Enfants terribles is therefore built on a complex system of poetic substitutions that all bear on the idea of non-normative sexuality. Adair, writing sixty years later, had different priorities. While the study of illicit sex is still present in *The Dreamers*, the sense that it functions as a code for homosexuality is much reduced, not least by the fact that homosexuality per se already features heavily in the action. (So, ironically, by increasing the amount of gay sex, Adair reduces its importance as an *idée mère* for the whole project.) Instead, we have a much more realistic attempt to consider where these dynamics lead in a closed system. Cocteau's protagonists, until the end, play almost naïvely, with sexuality seeming such a strong force only because it is so little acted on—but Adair identifies this freedom for what it really is:

> Theirs [...] was the license of the masturbator to do, inside his head, whatever he pleases with whomever he pleases for as often as he pleases, a license that must lead to ever more extreme fantasies. (p.140)

It is this aspect of Cocteau's novel that Adair picks up on and develops. Already in *Les Enfants terribles* there are striking moments of sexualised power-play, and the sort of ritualised domination and submission that would today fall under the umbrella of BDSM. Indeed one main function of 'the game', from a psychological point of view, is apparently to redirect these sexual impulses into other areas, as for example during the extraordinary episode when Élisabeth makes her brother beg for a crayfish, which she at first refuses to give him and later forces down his throat while he sleeps.[5] Paul here is told that he is 'abjecte', 'misérable', 'ignoble'. It is exactly this sexualised degradation that later attracts Agathe to the group (note that the word Cocteau uses for 'enjoyed' also means 'reached orgasm'):

> Agathe jouissait d'être victime parce qu'elle sentait cette chambre pleine d'une électricité d'amour dont les secousses les plus brutales demeuraient inoffensives [...] (p.72)
>
> [Agathe enjoyed being a victim, because she felt the bedroom to be full of an amorous electricity whose most brutal shocks remained inoffensive.]

So while Cocteau uses this D/S atmosphere for poetic and metaphorical purposes, Adair is much more free to explore its potential endpoint in a real sexual environment. Matthew's degradation in *The Dreamers* illustrates, as it were, the sexual reality behind the Coctellian metaphors. Matthew is reduced to the most unclean and animalistic level possible—penniless, starving, sick, collapsed on the floor in a puddle of his own faeces—before finally being forcibly sodomised against the bathroom mirror. And Matthew, like Agathe and Gérard, positively welcomes what happens to him:

> rape [...] already filled him with elation even as he knew its intention was to pain and degrade him [...]. With an agonised moan that could have been either of pleasure or pain, he capitulated unconditionally, assuming at last the role in which his whole life had cast him, that of the martyred angel, frail of physique and lamblike of character, to be caressed and beaten, cradled and spat upon, inspiring in those who are drawn to him and to whom he is drawn a desire to protect, and at the same time a compulsion to defile, the very innocence that seduced

---

5 Adair nods to this incident when he has his own characters dine on crayfish during their slap-up meal in the place Bienvenue.

them in the first place. (p.139)

Like Agathe, he is on some level convinced that his environment renders the 'most brutal shocks . . . inoffensive', and like her he will soon be disabused of the notion.

Adair's treatment of sexual themes in *The Dreamers* points to a more general trend: a movement away from the elaborate subtlety of Cocteau's symbolism and towards a more clear-headed exploration of how such symbols translate to the real world. Indeed the 'real world' is brought into *The Dreamers* in a way that breaks with Cocteau completely, and the temporal setting of the two books becomes one of the most crucial differences between them. A timeless present for *Les Enfants terribles*; and for *The Dreamers*, a very particular moment of recent history.

That Cocteau was more concerned with a 'contemporary' setting than one dealing specifically with the 1920s can be inferred from the fact that, while working on the famous 1950 film adaptation, he urged director Jean-Pierre Melville to set it in the present day and not in 1929. He could certainly afford to be flexible with such details: the outside world has remarkably little impact in Cocteau's text. Almost everything of import happens in the 'monde singulier des enfants', an ahistorical world created by the siblings themselves. Instead of the social (even physical) laws the rest of us are used to, this created world has its own internal logic (crystallised in 'the game') which is dreamlike and druggy —Cocteau compares it explicitly to being on opium. Indeed, 'the game' itself is merely the 'inexact' name given to this 'demi-conscience':

> Il dominait l'espace et le temps ; il amorçait des rêves, les combinait avec la réalité, savait vivre entre chien et loup . . . (p.17)

> [It dominated space and time; it created dreams, blended them with reality, knew how to live in the twilight.]

And this domination of space and time, for Cocteau, is absolute, not relative. When the outside world does intrude, far from destroying the children's illusions, it tends only to succumb to the all-powerful dream-logic of shared adolescent fantasy. Witness, for instance, the fate of poor Michaël, a solid man-of-the-world and potential breath of fresh air —introduced for the first time on page 80, engaged to Élisabeth by page 81, married two pages later, and decapitated in a freak car accident by the bottom of page 83. He was necessary to provide the children with the money and property to continue their fantasy life; this function completed, he is summarily dispatched. Not by the children themselves —they are (holy) innocents—but by the exigencies of the oneiric world that they've created.

For Cocteau, fantasy outranks reality; the private world is more powerful than the world outside the bedroom. Impervious to threats from without, it self-destructs purely as a consequence of its own internal logic (at the very beginning Paul's death is evoked as 'la suite naturelle d'un songe', the natural consequence of a dream); and it ends in the acme of solipsism—double suicide.

Adair's approach is utterly different, and once again more interested in examining where the fantasy ends. His 'dreamers' are much more vulnerable to the outside world, and when this world breaks in violently through the window they have no defence against it.

> A small paving stone, hurled up from underneath, came crashing into the bedroom. It sprayed the bed with fragments of glass. It landed on the record-player. It shattered the Trenet record. (p.143)

Even before this intrusion, they had been in trouble—unwashed, bedraggled, reduced to combing the bins for food. Not for them the luxury hôtel of Cocteau's novel. Not for them the wealthy and timely-beheaded benefactor.

Adair jettisons the poetic logic of *Les Enfants terribles*—where we see the world as fantasy tells us it must be—in favour of a more pragmatic assessment of what happens when fantasy and reality collide, and in doing so he spring-loads *The Dreamers* with an argument against Cocteau. The private universe created by Théo and Isabelle, far from being a generalised 'eternal present', is carved out in relation to a specific historical background—a 1968 whose utopian but naïve ideals are set up in thematic parallel with the ideals of the central characters. The outside world, with its 'phalanx of helmeted CRS officers', and namechecked entities like Sarah Bernhardt, Daniel Cohn-Bendit, François Truffaut, De Gaulle, Malraux, Sartre, Foucault—Cocteau himself—all these people's lives will not be co-opted by the adolescent dreamworld as Michaël's was. Quite the reverse. In the shape of Théo's friend Charles, the outside world will drag the 'dreamers' out into the streets, 're-educate' them, and push them into conflict with the forces of political authority.

> The world which had indulged them for so long, which had given them their heads, must eventually call them to account. (p.133)

Despite the sacrificial nature of Matthew's death, there is nothing suicidal about it: he is killed by a representative of precisely those practical laws that are so easily suspended in Cocteau's fantasy world. At the same time the reader feels a similar sense of inevitability. Where Paul and Élisabeth are killed by the internal logic of their private dynamic, Matthew's death is the result of an external logic which dictates that deviations from the 'natural' order—sexual and political—must be crushed. The individuals that enact this fate are practically incidental, which is perhaps why the riot officer who shoots Matthew is left staring at his gun 'in disbelief':

> 'I couldn't help it!' he cried. 'I couldn't help it!' (p.185)

Adair thus widens Cocteau's study of self-destructive impulses to take in politics as well as sexuality, while simultaneously drawing the ideas into the real world. Symbolism was crucial to Cocteau's project, not only because he was, in the final analysis, a poet, but also because it was what allowed him to write most frankly about his own sexuality. If Adair chooses to take these symbols seriously it is not because his approach is any less sophisticated, but because he moves the argument forward to consider how these insular fantasies survive within society more broadly. The revolutionary graffiti in 1968 calls for L'IMAGINATION AU POUVOIR; but this is a dream, not a reality. Cocteau's characters have really got that—for all the good it does them.

None of this is disillusionment for its own sake; for Adair it serves a specific purpose:

> Though, as we grow older, we have fewer reasons for hope and happiness, fewer of those which do remain to us will be illusory. (p.186)

This, then, is why it is important to test Cocteau's dynamics in the real world: because the sooner you strip away the illusory pleasures, the sooner you can discover what's really of value. Some might say this is one function of literature. Reading *The Dreamers* after *Les Enfants terribles* provides a particularly full illustration of where those illusions lie, both between the sheets and on the streets.

A final thought. By deliberately focusing his ideas in a new direction, Adair also leaves open a possibility that the books can interact on their own terms, providing another way of looking at the relationship between them. The dreamlike nature of Cocteau, the need for Adair's protagonists to seek escapism, the re-appearance of motifs like the crayfish and the closed room, and, most of all, the obsession in both novels with sleep as a 'séance' that produces 'the opaque and terrible ectoplasm of dreams'—all of this makes it tempting to conclude that Cocteau's book is itself the dream that is being dreamed by Adair's dreamers, their own fantasies blown up into poetry, offering a warning that they are unable to follow when they wake in the real world.

An Open Book

ALBERTA RIGID

"Hello? Anyone there?"

"Yes, yes! For heaven's sake, I'm coming. What in blazes was all that buzzing for? I'm blind, not deaf."

"Really sorry, only I had buzzed twice and there was no—"

"Never mind. Come in then. Put your coat on the hook, please. Excuse my being a crotchety old bag, I find it keeps me in great shape. Take a seat."

"Thank you. Sorry again about the buzzing. It—"

"You already apologised. Now would you care for a coffee or a tea? They're on the table behind me. You will have to pour them yourself, what with me being blind."

"Oh—no thank you, I'm not thirsty."

"Hmm."

"Yes?"

"You say you aren't thirsty, though it's unusual to decline a coffee or tea when in a stranger's house. A cup in one's hands tends to put one at ease, gives one something to grasp. Is it the prospect of standing up and walking behind me that you find off-putting? If my housekeeper had poured you a cup, would you have accepted one?"

"I expect so, yes."

"Well there you go. That's the sort of thing you will have to get used to accepting. Now, your name is Mary Wodan, correct?"

"Yes."

"And what makes you want to spend eight hours a day reading to a crotchety old blind woman?"

"I have experience working for—"

"Oh don't bother with that 'experience' rubbish. I'm not your average employer. I don't need to hear your entire CV, I only want to know why you, Mary Wodan, want to spend your days reading to me."

"I enjoy reading. And reading aloud. In my last job, I was so overworked I did little reading at home. I have an English Literature degree."

"Ah, I see. A frustrated bookworm. Nothing gets my old lady's dander up more, Mary, than these jobs that drain one's energy entirely, leaving no time for the pleasures of reading or art in general. Having said that, you young people are more preoccupied with filling yourselves with ethanol and backpacking across Naples with your lovers than cuddling up to a good book. Anyway, this is blather. What books do you tend to read, Mary?"

"Oh, plenty. The Alchemist, Norwegian Wood, To Kill a Mockingbird . . . I read this amazing book recently called The Kite Runner, it's—"

"Stop! Stop! Mercy me, an English Literature graduate, you say? There was me thinking you would leap on Austen, Dickens, and Hardy! Never mind. You have to excuse me. I have come to acquire a snob's taste in books since losing my sight. I only want to read the finest works available, none of this romance rubbish at the library. Why do public libraries seem to think all blind old bats want to listen to is turgid and unsexy tales of horrible people having very tame intercourse with one another? Boggles the mind. All right, Mary, I've made a decision. You're hired. I like your voice, I trust you will make a fine reader. I am keen to get someone to start immediately. Are you able to start first thing tomorrow?"

"Yes, that should be fine. Thank you for—"

"Never mind that. No gratitude necessary. I would rather we be friends, Mary, not employer and employee. Although I may have to crack the whip occasionally. Here's your first task—since I'm switching to physical books, could you raid the library tomorrow morning and pick up a dozen books for me? Use your judgement. But no Paulo Coelho, please. We can test drive a few titles. All right?"

"Yes, sure. I'll see you tomorrow."
"Goodbye, Mary."

*

"Let's see what you brought. Well, not *see*—you know what I mean."
"Yes, um . . . well, first up, The Irresistible Inheritance of Wilberforce by—"
"Ludicrous title. Next?"
"Oranges are Not the Only Fruit."
"Read that."
"I thought you might. A Tiny Bit Marvellous by Dawn French."
"Dawn French? Mary, I told you to use your judgement. Not to pick up celebrity memoirs or any old shelf-filler."
" . . . "
"Well?"
"It's a novel."
"I can hear you blushing. You'll have to learn to put up with my outbursts, Mary."
"You can *hear* me blushing?"
"Yes. You stopped shuffling the books. A very obvious sign. All right, never mind. I promise not to criticise your choices. That was unfair of me. Next?"
"The Dreamers by Gilbert Adair."
"That sounds more promising. Read me the blurb."
". . . 'Paris in the spring of 1968. The city is beginning to emerge from hibernation and an obscure spirit of social and political renewal is in the air. Yet Théo, his twin sister Isabelle, and Matthew, an American student they have befriended, think only of immersing themselves in another, addictive form of hibernation: moviegoing at the Cinémathèque Française. Night after night—' "
"All right. That's enough. Let's start with that. If it degenerates into a tasteless softcore romance, you can hurl it against the wall for me."
"Don't you want to hear the rest of the blurb?"

"No, blurbs only spoil the surprise, or tell me what to think before I've even started. Let's get on."

"You want me to start reading?"

"Yes please."

"All right. Here we go, page one."

"Best place to start."

"Yes."

"Sorry, couldn't resist."

"Actually, the text itself starts on page three."

"Ah."

"Anyway, here goes. 'The Cinémathèque Française is located in the sixteenth arrondissement of Paris . . . [. . .].' The end."

"Well, that was far too short! And that ending! Sending Théo and Isabelle out on the streets! Making symbolic sacrifices of his poor dreamers! I have to say, though, I do like this man's prose style. He is very expressive in a concise way, with none of that hard-bitten American minimalism I find distasteful. It's lunchtime now. Why don't you pop back to the library and pick up more Adair? I will give you some money, purchase a sandwich or something for yourself. Yes, this Adair fellow should keep us busy for the week."

"You want to stick to the one author?"

"When I take a liking to an author, I want to devour the complete works. No half measures for me."

"Be back shortly."

"See you, Mary."

"Umm . . . "

"Yes yes, I know. Off with you!"

*

" 'So, as I say, we were simply too intimidated to have the kind of gossipy chit-chat we might have expected to enjoy over dinner—which was our big pisstake. For, you see—' "

"Sorry, could you read that sentence again?"

"Sure. 'So as I say, we were simply too intimidated to have the kind of gossipy chit-chat we might have expected to enjoy over dinner—which was our big pisstake.' "

"Pisstake? That doesn't sound right. Sure it doesn't say 'mistake' instead?"

"Quite sure."

"Hmm. OK, read on."

" 'For, you see [. . .] Clem Wattis brindled at what he clearly felt was a slander on his character.' "

"Well, really! I must protest—*brindled*? I'm quite sure that is not a verb. Does he not mean 'bristled' here?"

"Says brindled."

"All right. Carry on before we lose the thread."

" 'Clem Wattis brindled [. . .] The twist is that he himself—Lindstrom, I mean—has already indulged in a little bout of bedroom hunky-plonky with Boy—' "

"Wait. Does it really say that? *Hunky-plonky*? Why would he invent an even sillier hybrid than hanky-panky? Most peculiar."

"Shall I carry on?"

"Please do."

" 'The twist is that—"

"Actually, that's enough for one day. No need to keep you right up to five o'clock on your first day. You've been an excellent reader, Mary."

"Thank you. See you tomorrow."

"Could you show the housekeeper in on your way out?"

"Sure. Goodbye."

"Goodbye."

"Ah, Mrs Ludlow. I have a favour to ask you. See that book on the table called The Act of Roger Murgatroyd?"

"Aye, ah see it."

"Great. Could you do me a favour—could you thumb through the first hundred pages looking for the sentence 'Clem Wattis brindled at what he something something?' That's how the sentence starts."

"Ah dunno, thar's an awfae lot ae words here."

"I know. I would appreciate it. Just scan each page quickly. Clem Wattis should stick out when you see it."

"Aw right."

"Thanks."

"Foond Clem Wattis, but dinnae see . . . whit wiz it? Bristled?"

"No, Clem Wattis *brindled*."

"Aww, that's funny."

"What is it?"

"Ah said is it Clem Whatsit *bristled* and you said *brindled*, but here it says Clem Whatsit *bristled*."

"Read the sentence to me please?"

" 'Clem Wattis bristled at whit he clearly felt wuz slander oan his character.' "

"Yes, that's the one. Thank you, Mrs Ludlow."

"Is that aw ye want me tae dae?"

"Yes, thank you. What's for dinner?"

"Mince."

"Ah, your usual."

"Aye."

"Better than starving, I suppose. Only just."

"Ah heard that."

*

"Good morning, Mary!"

"Morning."

"How are we this lovely spring day?"

"Fine, thanks. You're in a very upbeat mood today."

"I am, I am. Please help yourself to a cup of tea."

"I will, thanks. Would you like one?"

"Oh no. I'm plump with tea at the moment. Got to think of your colon at my age, darling."

"Of course."

"Now. Before we begin reading today, I thought we might play a little game."

"Game?"

"Yes. Let's call it Truth or Adair."

"Sorry?"

"Truth or Adair. Yesterday, you told me that Adair had used the word *brindled* instead of *bristled*. I asked Mrs Ludlow to come in and check. This must mean those other slip-ups, like *hunky-plonky*, were all fake, and no doubt others passed me by. Which means you doctored Adair's prose to deceive a blind woman."

"Yes."

"Well? Is an explanation forthcoming?"

"You don't remember me, do you?"

"Clearly not."

"I was Mary Simpson before marriage. You worked in Hoole library where I grew up, in Chester. One day I came up to you and asked if I was allowed to withdraw a story book, The Cat and the Wizard. You said it was too scary for me."

"What?"

"I really wanted to read that book. You refused me. I went home in tears."

"Is that it?"

"What do you mean, is that it? You refused a six-year-old the pleasure of reading the one book she had set her heart on."

"So you remembered this and decided to track me down and deceive me?"

"I saw the ad in the paper. I recognised your name. I wanted to get back at you for that refusal. You know, I never read another book for ten years after that. I demanded a Sony Playstation and spent my free time gaming. I missed out on a decade of reading because of you."

"Well, now I see the wound is more substantial. And this was all because I refused you that one library book?"

"Yes."

"And to pay me back, you intended to mangle Adair's prose and diminish my enjoyment of the books?"

"Yes. I wanted to disappoint you with every book I read, as you disappointed me by refusing me that book."

"And you planned to do this for ten years?"

"No, I . . . only for a while. I wanted to drive you away from books entirely."

"Ah. Oh Mary, this is all incredibly silly. Firstly, let me apologise for not lending you The Cat and the Wizard. I'm sure it had an age restriction on it or looked unsuitable, but I could have been less draconian. I certainly would have let you check it out had I known it would set your reading back by a decade."

"Well, it's a little late for an apology."

"Nonsense. It's never too late. If I'd been dead, that would have been too late. Now, how about we start again? With the proper words this time?"

"I suppose so. I'm sorry for deceiving you."

"And me for refusing you. Now, what are those other Adairs you got for me?"

"A Closed Book."

"Oh, apt title. Now, if everything is alright between us, might I hear this book read to me in your lovely voice?"

"OK."

"Original text? No additions or changes?"

"None. I promise."

"Excellent."

"Here we go. 'The blind is rapping at the window again. [. . .] Sightless, brainless, faceless andalone, autistic—' "

"Wait. Why did you pronounce that anda-lone?"

"It's printed as one word. Honestly."

"Must be a typo."

" 'Sightless, brainless, faceless [. . .] Yet it's valid, there do existeffects *sans* causes—' "

"Wait. You pronounced it existy-fects."

"It's another two words merged together."

"You aren't deceiving me, are you?"

"I'm really not. We can ask Mrs Ludlow to come and check if you like."

"Typesetting in the book is terrible. Go on."

" 'Yet it's valid, there do existeffects *sans* causes. Things croak by themselves. They move of their own accord.' [. . .] "

"Thank you for reading that to me. I couldn't help thinking there was something lacking in the prose. Oh well. Apologies for questioning you on those merged words. That was clever of him."

"No worries. I found the book quite disappointing too."

"Well. See you tomorrow, Mary. I'm sure we'll get on well together now that we've cleared up that little misunderstanding."

"Yes, me too. I'm sure we'll get on just fine."

"Goodbye."

"Goodbye."

[Quotes: The Dreamers, p. 3. The Act of Roger Murgatroyd, p. 52, 82, 102. A Closed Book, p. 106, 123.]

Death and the Auteur:

The Gilbert Adair Meta-murders

SERGIO ANGELINI

Preamble

Why are so many people killed in escapist fiction? Why doesn't it seem to matter? And what does *that* say about us? Moreover, what would happen if those characters wanted to exact a little revenge . . . ?

It is certainly instructive, if not necessarily revealing, that when Gilbert Adair first dipped his metaphorical quill in poisoned ink to engage with the mystery form, he did so with a novella entitled *The Death of the Author* (1992). For the best part of twenty years, he would explore the theme of authorial demise in a series of witty and beguiling books that would invariably conclude with the killing of the (fictional) creator of the scenarios hitherto enacted therein. Together with his four subsequent novel-length excursions in the genre, he created a series of recursive mysteries that did not so much deconstruct the form as to try understand how they could work under the shadow of one dominant concern: how authorial visibility and credibility is maintained even when everyone, including the fiction's creator, dies.

> As I have discovered to my disappointment, death is merely the displaced name for a linguistic predicament, and I rather feel like asking for my money back.[1]

The Death of the Author, a post-structural *roman à clef* riffing on the

---

1 Gilbert Adair, *The Death of the Author* (Minerva, 1992), p. 135

Paul de Man scandal, and the longer, more substantial-seeming if outwardly more conventional *A Closed Book* (1999), are both tales of psychological suspense focussing on the murderous games played by a pair of antagonists battling for supremacy in a literary arena. If *The Death of the Author* is obviously a literary game making use of the trapping of the murder mystery, *A Closed Book* is clearly a genre work. It is perhaps the less overtly challenging of the two but from a narrative standpoint the more innovative, managing to sustain tension despite only a main cast of two and limiting itself exclusively to only spoken or reported speech, dispensing entirely with any descriptive text. If these first two books may be described as thrillers, then the following three are most definitely shaped in the form of the traditional whodunit. *The Act of Roger Murgatroyd* (2006) masquerades as an Agatha Christie-style murder mystery set during a Christmas weekend in a snowbound country house circa 1936, sparring with the alert reader on the consequences of one of her most celebrated narrative coups. Its follow-up, *A Mysterious Affair of Style* (2007), is a Hitchcockian mystery in the sense that it features a director modelled closely on the great English filmmaker but postulates a premature and ahistorical end to his career and life, in the spring of 1946. *And Then There Was No One* (2009) is set in the then-near future of 2011 and stars Adair himself, or a close literary facsimile. In it, he solves a murder that takes place near the Reichenbach Falls on the tenth anniversary of the World Trade Center attack, with the help of his fictional creation, the mystery writer Evadne Mount.

Taken together these five books offer a varied and always entertaining commentary, critique and ultimately very fruitful exploration of the mystery form. What follows is an appreciation-cum-celebration of Adair's playful engagement with the genre, with special emphasis on the four full-length novels and the movie buff asides with which he imbued them and which help to make these works distinctively Adair-ish.

Deconstructed mysteries

When leafing through a work entitled *The Postmodernist Always Rings Twice*, most prospective readers might be expected to applaud the ironic wordplay of the title and the writer's grasp of pop culture plasticity. They would not assume that he had a profound knowledge of the crime fiction genre or the novels of James M. Cain in particular (the writer of that literary scandal of 1934, *The Postman Always Rings Twice*). However, in his fiction Adair repeatedly proved himself a capable and attentive critic-cum-chameleon, as easily able to channel the works of Proust and Thomas Mann as Agatha Christie. In the case of the latter, having perhaps inevitably set his sights on the reflexive narratorial possibilities of the interwar Golden Age crime fictions, he did so in a truly assiduous fashion. Indeed, Adair devoted most of the final part of his fictional life —that is to say, roughly, that part of his professional career that dealt with fiction—engaging with the world of the traditional murder mystery. After spending two years re-reading all 66 of Christie's detective novels[2], he embarked on a trilogy featuring his own sleuth, Evadne Mount. During that time, Adair also wrote the screenplay for the 2010 film version of *A Closed Book* (2010). This was made with his friend and frequent collaborator, director Raúl Ruiz, who incidentally is name-checked in the third Mount volume and who also provided the opening epigraph for the first book in the trilogy: 'The real world is nothing but the sum total of paths leading nowhere.'[3]

In his excursions to the mystery story, Adair explored the inherent gamesmanship of the Golden Age conception of the genre in which the reader competes not so much with the sleuth as with the author. There are of course plenty of examples of such attempts to toy with the detective story. Arguably, one can trace its roots at least as far back as *The Woman in White* (1868). Specifically, to that exquisite moment (quoted below) when Fosco violates the privacy of Marian's diary by adding his own postscript, briefly turning the epistolary convention, on which the structure of the book depends, completely on its head and making us so deliciously complicit in the act.

> The illness of our excellent Miss Halcombe has afforded

---

2 Gilbert Adair, 'Usual Suspect', in *The Guardian* newspaper (11 November 2006) and also available online at: www.theguardian.com/books/2006/nov/11/crime.agathachristie [accessed 1 May 2014]
3 Adair, *The Act of Roger Murgatroyd* (2006, Faber and Faber), p.vii

me the opportunity of enjoying an unexpected intellectual pleasure. I refer to the perusal (which I have just completed) of this interesting Diary.[4]

It is certainly a precursor of that wonderful frisson that Fredric Brown would give us with his 1947 story 'Don't Look Behind You' in which the reader (yes, me and you, right now) prove to be the intended victim of a murder plot. But let's not get ahead of ourselves. If in the novella *The Death of the Author* we are left unsure, even at the end, who is responsible for the crimes and the actual text that we are reading, in *A Closed Book* we most definitely know who 'did it' by the end. And yet the hermeneutic tools required to comprehend the intricacies of the plot are wonderfully granular, literally coming down to the very shape of the letters on the page . . .

A Closed Book (1999)

While Adair happily admitted that his novels were self-consciously built on pre-existing works, *A Closed Book* is perhaps the one of his mysteries that genuinely comes the closest to creating something new within the genre.

> "I know, I know. It makes no sense for a blind man to be afraid of the dark."[5]

Adair's affection for the detective genre, especially its Golden Age variant, is perfectly understandable if one considers how playful the genre could get in the 1920s and 30s. Just look how closely the likes of Philip MacDonald and John Dickson Carr, by directly sparring with their readers, came to deconstructing the genre they served (Carr in his magnum opus, *The Hollow Man*, has his detective Gideon Fell state outright, ". . . we're in a detective story, and we don't fool the reader by pretending we're not. Let's not invent elaborate excuses to drag in a discussion of detective stories. Let's candidly glory in the noblest pursuits possible to a character in a book.").

---

4   Wilkie Collins, *The Woman in White* (Oxford University Press, 1999), p. 343
5   Adair, *A Closed Book* (Faber and Faber, 1999), p. 28

> What conceivable reason could you have for wanting the life of a lonely, defenceless old man?[6]

Adair's 1999 novel is in part a reflection on the works published by Golden Age crime author A.B. Cox as 'Frances Iles', specifically *Before the Fact* (1932), later filmed in bowdlerised fashion by Hitchcock as *Suspicion* (1941). In it a wife starts to suspect that her husband is planning to kill her, which in the end he duly does but not without unwittingly bringing about his own downfall by posting her very last letter, one ultimately incriminating him.

Sir Paul is a wealthy, celebrated author who has become a recluse following an accident in which he lost both his eyes. Looking to write one more book, an autobiographical work, he hires John Ryder to become his live-in helper for a year to act as his eyes and type the manuscript. The principal innovation of the book is Adair's daring and successful solution to finding a literary correlative for Sir Paul's blindness: the story is told entirely through dialogue. Thus, we rely completely on the words as spoken though Sir Paul's unspoken thoughts are mysteriously presented in italics in separate paragraphs. If anything is described it is done purely through verbal exchanges, so the effect is very much like a radio play—indeed, the book could work extremely well if adapted that way, though not without some difficulty...

> Why is it I'm glad, why is it I'm relieved, that John is out?[7]

The novel eventually develops into a cuckoo-in-the-nest story as it becomes clear that John is deliberately misleading Sir Paul (he tells him that Tony Blair has AIDS and that rock star Pete Townsend has been assassinated) and trying to destabilise his tightly controlled home regime (Sir Paul is now a recluse, his home his whole universe). Just how accurate is John's transcription of Sir Paul's dictation? What kind of book will emerge when all the topical cultural references are skewed by John's lies? As events take an increasingly sinister turn, we soon suspect that

---

6 Adair, *Ibid*, p. 205
7 Adair, *Ibid*, p. 191

there is more than mere mischief behind John's actions. Eventually Sir Paul, who has become finally aware that something is up (but only expresses this in thoughts seen by the reader) decides to act. After several failed attempts to use a telephone (a standout sequence that lasts several pages, all conveyed through increasingly frustrated dialogue) he manages to contact his agent, making a showdown inevitable.

> "What possible excuse could you find for deceiving a blind man?"[8]

Sir Paul faces John with the discovery of the lies he has been telling him, leading to a revelation that is sexually explicit and highly disturbing but that does not feel gratuitous as it anchors the characters in an a wilfully artificial construction in the pain of a very real personal tragedy. Although rather overlooked on its release, A Closed Book may none the less be the most successful of Adair's postmodern dalliances in integrating his modernist techniques with traditional storytelling, remaining suspenseful throughout its 250 pages, leading to a clever twist in the tale, which surprises even though quite fairly prepared for. It deserves to be remembered as a singular novel in conception and execution—no mean feat after 150 years of development in the genre.

The special natures of its accomplishments were brought starkly into relief when Adair adapted it for the distinguished Chilean auteur Raúl Ruiz (it was to be their third and final collaboration). Told almost completely in standard objective mode, with just a few ominous authorial voiceovers from Ryder, the book's original technique proves impossible to replicate and indeed does not attempt to represent Sir Paul's point of view. One suspects that it would have taken a very special kind of filmmaker—perhaps a Polanski—to do it justice properly, especially coming as it does after decades of thrillers putting blind men and women in jeopardy.[9] In the event, the resulting film had a very limited the-

---

8   Adair, Ibid, p. 133
9   Notable examples include Edward Arnold in Eyes in the Night (1942); Ida Lupino in On Dangerous Ground (1951); Van Heflin in 23 Paces to Baker Street (1956) from a novel by Philip MacDonald; Faces in The Dark (1960) from a novel by Boileau-Narcejac; Audrey Hepburn in Wait Until Dark (1967); Mia Farrow in Blind Terror (aka See No Evil, 1971); Joan Allen in Manhunter (1986) and Emily Watson in

atrical release in 2010 and quickly sank without creating much of a ripple. It starred Tom Conti as a very credible Sir Paul while the role of John was subjected to a gender switch, sadly dispensing with the book's homoerotic subtext, with Darryl Hannah proving something of a lightweight as 'Jane' Ryder. Miriam Margolyes however was well cast as Mrs Kilbride, the cook. With a greatly altered third act that completely alters (and softens) Ryder's character and motivation, it still works fairly well as a small-scale cat and mouse thriller—and at 88 minutes certainly does not outstay its welcome. But one still wishes that a more innovative technique could have been found to do the text justice. In a nice little in-joke, in a scene featuring Sir Paul's editor, on his shelves in the background we can see a copy of Adair's first Evadne Mount mystery ...

The Act of Roger Murgatroyd (2006)

> "Never known a locked-room murder to happen in real life," he muttered to himself. "Might be worth writing to The Times."[10]

Celebrated mystery author Evadne Mount, a cross between Agatha Christie and her fictional alter ego Ariadne Oliver with just a dash of movie star Margaret Rutherford thrown in, is the star of this book, a locked-room mystery set circa 1936 in a snowbound country house over the Christmas holidays. The least likeable character, a gossip columnist with dirt on all the guests, is found shot inside a locked attic and the murderer must be found. Trubshawe, a neighbour and more importantly a retired Scotland Yard Inspector, is asked to investigate until the proper authorities can be reached once the weather clears.

> "You may like to think of it as a bit of a game, but, don't forget there's not much point to any game, be it Ping-Pong or Mah-Jongg, if you refuse to abide by the rules."[11]

Red Dragon (2002), both from the first Hannibal Lecter book by Thomas; Uma Thurman in *Jennifer 8* (1992)
10 Adair, *Murgatroyd*, p. 2
11 *Ibid.*, p. 66

This being a book by a master of the postmodern entertainment, there are plenty of literary references (the locked-rooms of John Dickson Carr and the moors and escaped convicts from *The Hound of the Baskervilles* all get a mention) as well as in-jokes that are slightly more elaborate. At one point we learn that Evadne once wrote a book about identical twins called *Faber or Faber* and of course not only were Adair's mysteries are all published by Faber and Faber, but despite the company name the publisher was founded solely by Geoffrey Faber, the second Faber added to the name purely for effect.

> ... Classical narrative can exploit omnipresence to conceal information that individual characters possess ... The subjective film and the mystery film can thus make narration self-conscious and overtly suppressive ... [12]

On re-reading Gilbert Adair's mysteries the phrase returning to my mind is one used in film studies to describe a certain type of camera technique, the 'unattributed point-of-view' shot. In murder mysteries the POV of an unidentified character is used often to show the killer at work without revealing identity, either in the act of spying on others or bumping people off (often dramatically though unrealistically as the murderer seemingly stares at a pair of gloved hands while committing the crime rather than looking at the victim). This is now a completely accepted part of modern film syntax (examples of it go back to the teens and twenties) even though it means that as a viewer we have to accept an abrupt shift from a neutral, seemingly objective third person mode of narrative presentation to a purely subjective one.

The classic modern example of this would be the opening sequence of John Carpenter's 1978 horror mystery *Halloween*, which is presented to the viewer as two long uninterrupted takes (there are in fact several disguised cuts). In the first, the camera shows us the point of view of an unidentified character looking through the windows of a house as a girl and her boyfriend neck on the sofa. When the couple go upstairs, the

---

[12] David Bordwell, 'The classical Hollywood style, 1917-60' in Bordwell, Staiger and Thompson, *The Classical Hollywood Cinema* (Routledge, 1985), p. 32

unidentified person walks inside the house, takes a knife from a kitchen drawer, goes upstairs and dons a clown mask found on the floor and, as we watch through the eye-slits of the mask, stabs the girl to death. But the killer is stopped while leaving, the mask is pulled off, and the identity revealed. At this point we cut to an 'objective' shot and see the murderer still holding the bloody knife—at which point the camera starts to move further and further backwards as we see the tableau outside the house where the crime was committed, with the murderer at its centre, flanked by a man and woman. Although the camera is still moving, convention tells us that this is an authorial interjection, an aesthetic presentation of events and, unlike the previous half of the sequence not meant to represent what one a character is actually seeing. It is this complex commingling of signifiers and narrative effects and codes, and the way that audiences (viewers, listeners and readers) have come to unquestioningly accept such narrative and representational conventions, that lies at the heart of what, with his quartet of mysteries, might be termed the 'Adair project.'

> "Oh, I know I'm a colourless character, a bit of a cookie cut-out figure."[13]

While some have questioned just how honourable Adair's intentions with Murgatroyd (and its sequels) were, what comes through repeatedly is his affection for the detective genre in general and a marvel for the effect it has on the reader, especially its Golden Age variant. As the author of *The Death of the Author*, one should expect games, tricks, and postmodern effects. What is surprising is the extent to which Adair is prepared to subordinate this urge to the needs of creating a plausible mystery—but then again, this can also be seen as integral to the book as a whole. Indeed it can be ascribed as part of an obfuscation necessitated by the desire to explore the theme of authorial invisibility quite boldly, making it necessary therefore to draw as much attention as possible from Adair's presence. Without wanting to give too much away (this is a whodunit after all), it is only with the closing sentence of chapter 12

---

13 Adair, *Murgatroyd*, p. 193

that we realise quite what Adair is playing at:

> So it was that our dolorous little procession forged its slow and solemn path across the snow-mantled snow.[14]

Why is this significant? Quite simply because until this point, 212 pages in, we the reader were sure we had been reading a book written in the third person. But in fact, the author is the killer, only we do not know who has in fact been narrating and will not know that, of course, until the final chapter. Adair within the book itself has his characters debate the effect and power of the classic detective story's denouement, something he described in a newspaper article, which, fittingly, incorporated material ascribed to his Evadne Mount in the novel—here is how Adair expressed it:

> I realised that the real tension resides exclusively in the reader's own mind . . . the reader himself, already keyed-up, begins to grow as nervous as one of the suspects in the novel . . . he can't bear the prospect of its climax proving to be a letdown, either because it's not clever enough or because it's too clever by half.[15]

Adair succeeds with his ploy because it is supremely clever and one that will be appreciated by those who have read and understood the significance of Christie's strategy of deception in *The Murder of Roger Ackroyd* beyond the desire to surprise the reader. With *Murgatroyd* Adair tries to have his cake and eat it, and mostly does. Yes, some of the humour falls a little flat in places; and the solution to the locked room does beggar belief; but this is always a smart work, one that provides, underneath its narrative carapace, plenty of nourishing metatextual content. Even the most hardened of mystery addicts might, after reading it, look again at their next whodunit and wonder just what it is that it thinks it is striving for—and just might make you wish that it had tried just a little bit harder.

---

14 *Ibid.*, p. 212
15 Adair, 'Usual Suspect', op. cit.

A Mysterious Affair of Style (2007)

The 'auteur theory' postulates that even in the cinema, as in literature, there is only one true author—the director. *A Mysterious Affair of Style* explores this idea with typical cunning and knowing humour, as one might have expected from a novelist who was also a frequent film critic and screenwriter. It is 1946 and there is serious trouble on the studio floor . . .

> I kept asking myself, 'What would Farje have done? What would Farje have done?'[16]

Author Evadne 'Evie' Mount, retired Scotland Yard Inspector Trubshawe and actress Cora Rutherford all return in this follow-up to *The Act of Roger Murgatroyd*. Ten years have passed, the war is over and our favourite mystery writer is set to meet Britain's greatest film director—and bring some excitement to the life of an ex-policeman. Trubshawe has moved back to London but is drowning in suburbia, where his list of friends grows ever shorter—until his life is turned around when he unexpectedly bumps into Evie in the tearoom of the Ritz.

> He owned a pleasant, semi-detached house in Golders Green in which he lived a pleasant, comfortable, semi-detached life.[17]

Ten years have passed since they last met but they have not changed at all (in classic Golden Age fashion), though age does seem to have affected the fortunes of their old sparring partner, stage star Cora. Evie invites Trubshawe to a benefit show for which she has written a short sketch (slightly in the style of the compendium film *Elstree Calling*, for which Alfred Hitchcock apparently directed a segment)—and after the briefest of hesitations, he leaps at the chance. Things begin well but then a real murder apparently occurs on the stage and Evie jumps up and takes charge—this is soon revealed to be an elaborate gag, but should help tip the wink to the reader that there will be fun and games

---

16 Adair, *A Mysterious Affair of Style* (Faber and Faber, 2007), p. 161
17 *Ibid.*, p. 65

ahead as real and fake murder plots are intertwined.

Cora is attempting a comeback with a supporting role in the new mystery by Alastair "Farje" Farjeon, a director modelled very closely on Alfred Hitchcock (the surname is taken from J. Jefferson Farjeon, whose play *Number Seventeen* was filmed by Hitchcock in 1932). Sadly for her, the director has just been reported dead after his house burned to the ground. But the film is still going ahead with his long-time assistant taking over and Evie and Eustace are invited to the studio to watch Cora at work. During a scene, added at the last moment, one of the actors is drinking from a glass of champagne rather than breaking it, and a death occurs and is caught on camera. In a shocking twist (one that deliberately echoes *Psycho*), Cora is poisoned and Evie and Eustace are there as witnesses. Is this death connected to the accident in which Farje perished? And how did the poison enter the champagne given that the decision to have her drink from the glass was only made on the spur of the moment?

In his introduction to the book, Adair seems as surprised as anyone that he was asked to write another adventure for Evie, something he initially refused to do on principle—until he realised that he had never written a sequel before and so would not, therefore, be repeating himself (sic).

Thankfully, the book is built on a less specious and rather more solid foundation than such a capricious and whimsical approach to fiction making might suggest, along with plenty of postmodern jokes on the 'auteur' theory, courtesy of a French critic who is at the studio to write a book on Farje and who is most definitely meant to remind us of Truffaut[18].

> For what are detectives but the 'critics' of crime? And what are critics—true critics, theoretical critics—but the 'detectives' of cinema.[19]

And once again Evie quotes from that article that Adair wrote about

---

18 Truffaut's long interviews with the British director were ultimately published in English as *Hitchcock by Truffaut: A Definitive Study of Alfred Hitchcock* in 1967.
19 Adair, *A Mysterious Affair of Style*, p. 194

Christie in which she expounds on his theory that for the reader of a whodunit the contest is not with the detective at all but with the writer, the excitement predicated on discovering if the resolution will live up to their expectations, or not. Here Adair provides a plot not quite as clever structurally as *Murgatroyd* but thematically just as interesting, as well as a much more varied milieu in and around the film studio. The ultimate resolution, which as the title told us all along, is based on a close analysis on the Farje film style, albeit by proxy, and once again point of view becomes crucial (it is worth remembering that in Hitchcock's film, point of view was paramount). As a device this proves highly satisfying as it allows Adair once again to explore his role as a postmodern author who builds and embroiders on the work of others, both within the literary and cinematic spheres.

At a plot level one of the most entertaining aspects on this book is the formal duel between Evie and Eustace, reminiscent of the sparring between Poirot and Inspector Giraud in Christie's *Murder on the Links*. Only here the stakes are much higher—if he solves the case, she will have to dedicate her next book to Christie, calling her 'the undisputed queen of crime fiction' and if she wins, the two will have to marry! She actually wins, but the dedication none the less did appear, in her final book, one that more than anything reads like a cross between Agatha Christie and Luigi Pirandello...

And Then There Was No One (2009)

> You can always count on a murderer for a fancy prose style.[20]

During the 'Golden Age' of the detective story, between the two World Wars, the genre developed as a game in which ingenuity and surprise were much more important than characterisation or plausibility. The likes of Monsignor Ronald Knox and SS Van Dine created rigid lists of what was, and was not, permissible in a detective story, in much the same way as one would seek to establish the conventions of a round of Bridge—there were puzzles in the real sense of the word, constructed

---
20 From the opening page of *Lolita* (1955) by Vladimir Nabokov.

like acrostics and frequently appealing to those in search of distraction by way of gentle brainteaser. Crime not as literature but as a form of narrative Sudoku in which the main virtue was the ability to create order from seeming chaos and succeed in beating the opponent / reader by generating an unexpected ending. Inevitably many of the stories written then and shortly thereafter extended the 'rules of engagement' to include parody but such was the sense of 'gamesmanship' that knowing postmodern jokes and tropes entered the genre even before the term 'postmodern' had come into general use after the end of the Second World War.

Ironist supreme Gilbert Adair includes himself as the main character in the third and last of his pastiches featuring his ex-spinster novelist-cum-sleuth Evadne Mount in what is clearly meant to be a truly kaleidoscopic postmodern adventure. In it his page-bound alter ego describes the genesis of the series and simultaneously professes to find nothing more enjoyable than relaxing in front of a black and white British B-movie:

> I rather fancied writing a parody of vintage Agatha Christie, a novel in black and white, as it were, like one of those feebly directed but sparklingly and gloriously well-acted pre-war British films which are for me one of the definitions of sheer, uncomplicated bliss.[21]

If one wanted to provide a quick summary of the sort of thing Adair had in mind here, one might profitably point to the mini-movie that opens *The Mirror Crack'd*, the 1980 Christie adaptation starring Angela Lansbury as Miss Marple. Set in the world of movie make-believe, this camp and sly adaptation is a murder mystery for connoisseurs, revelling in the conventions of the genre while gently poking fun at them at the same time. It begins in glorious black and white with an external shot of an opulent country home (which is clearly a model). Everyone speaks in cut-glass accents and acts very stiffly indeed—a murder has been committed and Inspector Gates (Nigel Stock) has gathered all the

---

21 Adair, *And Then There Was No One*, pp. 95-96

suspects together to reveal the murderer. Just as he is about to name the culprit . . . the film breaks down and we cut to the village hall in St Mary Mead. It is 1953 and what we have been watching is the conclusion to 'Murder at Midnight', a (fictitious) movie starring (real) 1950s movie star Anthony Steel and Dinah Sheridan. While the vicar tries to repair the film, it is left to Miss Marple to reveal the identity of the (movie) murderer.

This extended pre-credits teaser is a charming touch and alone worth the price of admission, director Guy Hamilton expertly recreating the tone and style of the mysteries that he was making at around that time such as *The Ringer* (1952) and more significantly perhaps his metaphysical investigation, *An Inspector Calls* (1954). By giving us the traditional climax at the beginning, albeit an interrupted one, it signals to viewers that this is a film that plans to play a little with traditional viewer expectations, which it certainly does though this is undeniably an intelligent way to adapt a book infused with movie lore. Not only did Christie dedicate the novel to Margaret Rutherford, then playing Marple at the cinema, but the motive for the murder of seemingly innocent movie fan Heather Babcock was in fact based on something that actually happened to legendary '40s star Gene Tierney when she contracted German measles while pregnant. The actual climax to *The Mirror Crack'd* is a complete damp squib, part of a logical diminuendo in which, after the traditional opening, Miss Marple's final deductions come far too late and make no difference at all, thus making sense in a scenario where we were told, right at the beginning, that the traditional rounding up of the suspects and long-winded explanations were a silly convention.

And Then There Was No One, published with the subtitle 'The Last of Evadne Mount' and set in the (then) near future of 2011, mingles fact and fiction with gleeful abandon. It opens with a long historical prologue that introduces us to the life and work of controversial author Gustav Slavorigin, a Rushdie-style pariah who went into hiding after writing a polemical book that criticised America and the victims of 9/11. (Adair helpfully tells us to which page to skip if readers wish to avoid this whole section in one of the many rather jaundiced footnotes.[22]) He comes out of exile as the surprise guest at a Sherlock Holmes convention that Adair is also attending, sticking around long enough to discover that most of the guests hold grudges against him and so (of course) is murdered.

Of the entire Evadne Mount trilogy, this is the most overtly postmodern, though it never quite sacrifices its affiliation to a standard Christie-style plot (and yes, the least likely suspect turns out to be the murderer). None the less, this feels like several volumes rolled into one —part fake autobiography, part state-of-the-nation address, part pastiche—and even includes a story within the story when we read Adair's own rendering of Conan Doyle's unwritten story concerning the 'Giant Rat of Sumatra' (not his finest hour). It is at this point that Evadne Mount rears her tricorn-hat-bearing head and the reader starts to wonder if 'Adair' has finally disappeared down a semiological rabbit hole in search of his own tail.

> Each of my novels is thus a palimpsest. Scrape away at its surface and you will find, underneath, another novel, usually a classic. I offer no apology for this.[23]

The 'Gilbert Adair' who narrates this story may look and sound like the real thing but once Evadne appears then fiction, fantasy, and murder begin to intermingle indistinguishably. While her appearance in the audience during a reading overtly recalls Pirandello's 1921 classic *Six Characters in Search of an Author*, it turns out that Evadne really is more than just a figment of our imagination. 'Adair' in fact based her on a real person, a mystery writer by the same name—but then Adair would say that, wouldn't he? Sometimes fiction just is not good enough, it would seem.

The book delights in filling page after page with examples of artistic pilfering and reflected glories, with a critic named Sanary forever telling everyone that much that they hold dear is actually second-hand.

---

22 Sample footnote, from page 47: "Shopping is the only real, fully functioning culture left to us".
23 *Ibid.*, p. 92

Nevertheless, does it matter what lay distantly behind Bernard Herrmann's film scores for Alfred Hitchcock or the cuckoo clock speech delivered by Orson Welles in *The Third Man*? Do we not celebrate our past, and those long-passed, through re-invention and re-interpretation rather than that outwardly more respectful repetition that so often only leads to artistic calcation and atrophy?

In his 1986 television play *Murder by the Book*, Nick Evans imagines a meeting between Agatha Christie (played by Peggy Ashcroft) and Hercule Poirot (a typically intense Ian Holm), in which he rails at her decision to kill him off. Adair at the top of the Reichenbach Falls stages something similar for his climax to *And Then There Was No One*. What hangs in the balance is at the very least Adair's literary reputation—will he have to keep churning out Christie pastiches to please his public, or will he regain his intellectual liberty (and, dare one suggest, snobbery)? In many ways though, one could argue that here it is the mystery genre itself being placed on the edge of a precipice, with the horrors of the real world snapping at its heels and narrative innovation and ingenuity finally succumbing to exhaustion, fading away after being recycled just one time too many.[24]

Pentimento

It seems extraordinary that after hundreds of thousands of mystery stories, published in magazines and in books, screened at the cinema and TV, and played on radio and the stage, that we still want to find out what happens at the end—but does it really matter who killed Roger Ackroyd or finding out the true identity of Keyser Söze?

In the introduction to *Pentimento*, her second book of fictionalised memoirs (filmed as *Julia* in 1978), Lillian Hellman likened her book to that of an artist who had painted over an old canvas but who could still see traces of the original, the old conception, replaced by a later choice, "a way of then seeing again."[25] Are Adair's mysteries a 'reductio ad ab-

---

[24] Rather like the protagonist of 'The Men Who Murdered Mohammed,' Alfred Bester's classic time paradox story, who turns himself into a ghost having unsuccessfully tried to cancel his unfaithful wife out of history.
[25] Lillian Hellman, *Pentimento* (Quartet, 1978), p. 3

surdum' of the genre, hoax meta-novels that enjoy embarrassing its modern readers by using old-fashioned phrases such as "she ejaculated" to describe dramatic outbursts? Are they, as emblazoned on the jacket blurb (maybe written by Adair himself) of *And Then There Was No One*, " . . . a conjuring act that ends with the conjurer, or author, sawing himself in half"? Is Adair, by injecting himself into the narrative and making himself a suspect (much as 'Cameron McCabe' did in the 1938 classic *The Face on the Cutting Room Floor*), seeking to unravel the genre?

Alternatively, one could argue that Adair's mysteries offer clever scenarios, postmodern flourishes a plenty, some good jokes (and a few bad ones too) and thus deliver intellectually stimulating, tongue-in-cheek rides that explore and celebrate, with wit and imagination, the undying push-pull and dangerous allure of the mystery genre in all its forms.

Creative Licentious: The Real Cast of Buenas Noches, Buenos Aires

EDITED BY DONNA KRASCHLONG & MILO WI

Gideon:

On the first page of Gilbert Adair's 2003 "novel," *Buenas Noches, Buenos Aires*, his "narrator" writes: *Everything you read in the next hundred and fifty pages is true. Absolutely everything and absolutely true. This is a true story.* Meaning—of course—that absolutely everything is an absolute lie. My name is Gideon Wasp and this novel is a crude distortion of my own life, penned by Adair as some kind of score-settling prank. I first met Adair when he was teaching at the Berlitz the early 1970s. At the time, he was a relentless bore on the topic of cinema—praising Truffaut and Fellini as 'auteurs' and lecturing us on the theory of cinema (Barthes namedropped every other sentence—made me want to take a bubble Barthe). I was an ardent fan of vintage American cinema, and of musicals such as *West Side Story* and *South Pacific*, much to Adair's amusement, who used this knowledge to cast aspersions on my heterosexual credentials. Firstly, I believe homosexuality is against God's wishes. Adam and Eve, not Soddem and Leave. I believe that those who elect to be homosexuals cannot be Christians and gain access to paradise. As I was teaching in Paris, I was forced to keep these views secret—the city had sunk in a sea of shameless sin since the war—and this opinion would have made me unpopular on campus. Homosexuals came (pun intended) to dominate the campus and I was unable to remain silent. I had suspected Adair to be of the same ilk due to his dandyish mannerisms and had my fears confirmed when I caught him kissing one of the older teachers—a fortysomething married man with whom I had enjoyed several long and meaningful conversations about the pleasures of uxoriousness. At this point I broke. Adair was a corrupting influence with his independent cinema and its loose morals. Intellectuals like him used theory to defend their debased actions and were eating out the heart of society. I denounced him in the staff room, said he ought to be ashamed of himself being so lewd in public. He merely removed his lips from the elder, fixed me one of his impish smiles, and said: "Why, there's enough tongue to go around. Young Billy here is looking for an experienced tutor." Billy was one of my best students and had been corrupted by Adair. I stormed from the common room and wrote a letter to the Dean. To no avail. Adair and his cronies (several of whom appear in the "novel"), began to perform obscene acts in my presence, such as sneaking inside my classes and taking out their *membrum virile* at the back of the room. One time, I asked Adair to help me carry an extra desk into my classroom. When he rose from his own desk, he was naked from the waist down. There was shameless French kissing in the common room (with under sixteens!) and on two occasions I overheard sodomy in the stationary cupboards. Aspersions were even cast on my heterosexual sex life—several of the homosexuals called me a tragic virgin and left instructional diagrams on my desk to help me penetrate my wife. As I was married, I only had sex once a month, so to this licentious mob, I was practically chaste. It came as no surprise to see me cast as a sex-starved homosexual in his novel. It is precisely the sort of outrageous sensibility I would expect from such a shameless sensualist as Adair. My attempts to take Faber and Faber to court for libel have fallen on deaf ears—no lawyer seems willing to take me seriously. It is not pleasing to be immortalised in a "novel" for the wrong reasons.

Carla:

In *BNBA*, Gideon (i.e. Gilbert), describes me as his first girlfriend: *Her knuckles were red, her fingers were red, her hair was red, even her nose, which she would pick in public with the vigour of a chimney sweep endeavouring to dislodge an awkwardly located build-up of soot, had its reddish tip.* (p6) This description is a reference to Gilbert's own acne, which at the time made his face resemble a series of active volcanoes, and his own nose-picking was the one thing that turned me off him at first. He used to extract the snot (with the vigour of a spelunker extracting rare quartz, in fact) and wiggle the offending matter on his finger, make as if he had eaten it by swapping his middle finger with his index at the last minute, and flick the rolled-up mucous over my shoulder (pretending to aim at my mouth). This teasing aside, I was highly attracted to Gilbert for his brilliant wit and lovely singing voice, and did indeed seduce him in the manner described in the novel. Unlike Gideon, Gilbert was able to perform and deflowered me with gusto in my bedroom until I was as red in the face as he (and novel-me) were. However, I was surprised when I woke up alone at 3AM and found him in my older brother's bed, planting a line of kisses down his torso and performing skilful fellatio until my brother brayed like a hyena. I flung Gilbert's clothes out in the hallway and he never returned to my room.

George Schuyler:

I appear in this novel as myself. Adair captures me rather well. I am especially fond of this description: *George Schuyler was, perhaps, a Sphinx without a secret, and all the more enigmatic for that* (p26). One update I would like to make: my novel *The Quarterback of Notre Dame* has been completed and published by Ergodic Shed (1991). My novel is set in a tenement apartment and details one day in the life of Frances Alders, a collier on the edge of a nervous breakdown, who staggers around his space throwing up, eating raisins, trying to read a novel by overrated hack D. Keith Mano, and drinking rum while listening to Chopin's nocturnes. I wanted to create a symphonic novel using long digressive and contemplative paragraphs as musical notes, building to huge swathes of emotion and chaos. The novel was reviewed favourably. Adair was less kind in *TLS*: "This overbearing novel has all the self-important pomp of a violist caught up in his own performance, oblivious to the fact the orchestra packed up their instruments two hundred bars ago. The longueurs make use of surrealist autowriting to a devastating effect—ingestion of four or five paragraphs might lead to an irreversible coma." This is amusing to me. Adair writes thumbnail novels, anecdotal ramblings that aspire to the bargain bucket. My novels will be read for centuries to come, studied and poured over, rebound and reprinted. This foolish remaking of the past has already been forgotten, as if Proust's madeleine were accidentally submerged in the tea. My next novel, *A Sentry's Mental Education*, is the tale of an heroic teacher attempting to instruct an idiot savant in playing the harp during the Austro-Hungarian war. This book has been read in consideration for the Nobel Prize. (And by the way, the following passage sums up Adair perfectly): *In fact, I have an aversion to those solipsistically self-absorbed gays, and heaven knows they exist, who are content to let their lives be not only coloured but conditioned by their sexual tastes. (For most people, a penis is something attached to a man; for the type of homosexual I'm talking about, a man is just something attached to a penis.)* (p56)

Yves-Marie:

Bullshit! In this so-called novel I am described as a *slim-hipped thoroughbred with ripe, pouty lips, fiery brown eyes and a long swanlike neck that would expand when he lost his temper*. (p49) Not accurate! I am an overweight pudding of a man, the proud sporter of a pristine paunch and two menacing moobs with which I wallop and bludgeon my rivals! I seduced Adair using the magnetic power of my navel and he is merely embarrassed to have to admit (through his puppet Gideon) to going with such a seductive Santa Claus of a man as me in lieu of his usual Tadzios and Bradzios with their litheness and Aryan purity. I am insulted to be portrayed as a Mapplethorpean stripling with a line in whiny fellatio complaints. Frenchmen are proud of their paunches. Adair is a typical Brit with his fondness for pale suggestive boys. He liked to wear pince-nez in bed and his secret pleasure was drooling over the movies of Gregg Araki. So much for the arch social critic! I will sue when I scrape enough euros.

Ferey:

I was the first AIDS victim in the novel. I did not, of course, succumb to the disease, and I have to take issue with Adair's depiction of the courting process. As in Will Self's outrageous *Dorian: An Imitation*, the gay scene is depicted as a moral free-for-all, with fucking and sucking taking place at any and every opportunity. My experience of teaching at the Berlitz is that the gays were excessively polite seducers and extremely selective with regard to carnal matters. The final section of the novel shows Gideon embarking on an orgy of illicit and unprotected sex so he can at last "belong" to the AIDS-infected brethren and lose his virginity in style. The fact is, during that period at the Berlitz, it took a great deal of persuasion, paperwork, and palaver to net sexual partners. The procedure for aspirant lovers was usually as follows. 1) Write a very polite note accompanied by a permission slip to the potential suitor's parents. 2) Upon approval, to attend an eligibility interview with the parents, putting forth your case for partnering up. 3) If successful, present the stamped and dated permission slip to the suitor (via the mail to avoid embarrassment) and await a written response. 4) If a first date is agreed, the two of you are to meet in a safe public location and the conversation is to be kept general, topics including one's career ambitions and preferred sporting activities. 5) If the first date goes well, a year-length courtship is to be instigated (for the first nine dates a chaperone or 'support person' is permitted to attend). 6) After that period, if both parties reach a mutual agreement, and sign a mutual consent form (to be stamped by parents or nearest relative of both parties), then intercourse is permitted. Now, answer me, how is it possible to engage in such Gideon-like debauchery with such a morass of red tape to overcome? Apart from that flaw, I like the novel generally.

Mick:

I struggled with this little minx of a novel(la?) for a long time. At first I felt the author trivialised the AIDS-era in which I played an unpleasant part. After a few reads, I was able to appreciate the humorous abandon and sense of adolescent frustration Adair brought to the text, and although the notion someone might choose to infect themselves with the virus merely as an act of solidarity is most certainly a literary contrivance, I admire the elegant prose and comedic descriptions. Adair doesn't shirk from depicting the horror (as Ferey's outburst shows) of the disease, and takes a courageous turn by bowing out on such a triumphant note. Having said that, every aspect of my character in the novel(la?) is completely fabricated and inaccurate to the point of libel.

A Berlitz Student:

As if we didn't know what was occupying ~~Gilbert's~~ Gideon's mind (and other parts) when he strolled through the door during the mornings each school day. The way his eyes would flicker around the classroom and settle, ever so unsurreptitiously, on one of us, usually during roll call, or while we were reading a passage (and put it this way, why, if you are teaching English to French students, do you ask them to read a translation from the German (horrible language!) to English of Thomas Mann's *Death in Venice*?) aloud. He always thought himself discreet in his little fantasies, but only a complete dunce would have failed to realise why it was that only one in a semester was ever asked to discourse on the friendship (ha!) of Jean Cocteau and Jean Marais? Really, it was musical students with at least half of his colleagues; we used to gamble on how long each interaction would last, with whom, and how many bums would change seats. But Gideon omitted the real party, and naturally, who can blame him, angry white young unfulfilled gay he was, hating himself for lusting after what he was ostracised for desiring, of course he couldn't see the *broader* picture. We swingers who cut both ways, liked a bit of fur with our flaps, some beef with the bush, a group grope and a daisy chain: why settle for a sausage sandwich when you could choose a club? Not that we complained; the more prudish he was about finding his share of equally hung-up (if not well-hung) boys-only boys, the more variety we enjoyed. How we laughed at him and his pathetic conservatism, his determination to be branded gay by dying of AIDS, as if a disease discriminated on the basis of sexual preference!

[*Creative Licentious: The Real Cast of Buenas Noches, Buenos Aires*, Edited by Donna Kraschlong & Milo Wi, is to be released in Jan 2015 from Fibber and Fibber, £25 in hardback.]

Disturbance at the Pastiche Playground

VARIOUS[1]

I have always viewed pop-culture addicts with indulgent amusement —the sort of excitable and clueless mass-ent minions who queue up for hours to see the latest *X-Men* movie dressed as their favourite superhero, or to see the sixtieth sequel to a sixtieth prequel of another coma-inducing franchise. This all changed when I began dating Heather. At first I found her references to episodes of *Frasier* or Tom Baker-era *Doctor Who* to be charming signs of a misspent childhood and signifiers of her happiest times sat before the TV. I feigned smiles at each reference until the conversation turned to more elevated topics such as Anna's marriage to Ottavio in *Don Giovanni,* the investment benefits of fracking versus the risk of carcinogenic water poisoning, and the layers of postmodern irony in a Stewart Lee routine. After two months, Heather invited me to attend a Comic-Con conference in London. These are large corporate gatherings where fans of franchise TV and movies dress as their favourite characters and queue up at stalls to exchange ten seconds of shrill fawning banter with incredulous actors who attempt to mask their mounting panic behind down-to-earth simpers.

If I said no, I would be lighting a bomb under the relationship. She couldn't be with someone so resistant to her craving to dress up as a Tardis in public; conversely, I couldn't last long with someone so determined to dress up as a Tardis in public. However, due to my long-term fear of being abandoned to die alone in a bleak seaside town on a diet of a one-is-fun lasagne and gin-diluted lemonade, I consented to attend the Comic-Con convention, provided I could dress as a character who would allow me to retain my dignity as an artist and sophisticate,

---

1 See Credits Where Due at the end.

and not mark me as a tasteless flibbertigibbet (not all Comic-Con people are of this stripe, but the pitfall was there). Heather chose a character for me who required the mere use of a Primark cheapo range suit and a festive stovepipe. I entered into the spirit despite hating her for what she was forcing me to endure for the sake of avoiding loneliness.

    The conference itself was a fierier hell than I had imagined. A room the size of two stadiums crammed with attention-seeking fans dressed in extravagant outfits, each attempting to out-startle the other. I pictured these people sourcing their fabrics at ludicrous prices, knitting and weaving in their bedrooms for weeks after work and boasting to their friends about the splash they were going to make when they arrived. I felt the same brand of nausea I reserve for talent-show contestants made-up in the waiting rooms, desperate to embarrass themselves before the contemptuous eyes of the world, oblivious to their total voidance of skill or how placing the burden of their future hopes on a delusion will only end in blood. I regarded the chattering mass of proud franchise-followers with bewilderment, pleased at the fact these people had been united in the cause of happiness, repelled at the fact it was to support characters from popular franchises that bankrolled millionaires with no talent. I couldn't face an entire weekend of this. I couldn't stand in line beside aliens, Vogons, timelords, Spidermen, devils, witches, and other tiresome figures without flooding the whole room in an expressive arc of snob's vomit. I shamefully ducked to the toilets and headed towards London Central station. On the train I sent a text to Heather. She texted back: "Have a nice life."

    At least I was free.

It was with the trauma of this event in mind that I responded to ex-pat novelist and ultra-misanthrope Igo Wodan's invitation to attend the Lit-Con convention in the scenic coastal hamlet of Helensborough—a networking extravaganza for eccentric writers, with each participant required to dress as their favourite author, and made to speak in the prose style associated with that author. I had flashbacks to the Comic-Con event and left the request unresponded. As time passed, I realised the Lit-Con convention would be a perfect chance to promote the upcoming Gilbert Adair festschrift soon to released from Verbivoracious Press, so I decided to attend dressed as one of Gilbert's favourite writers, the exquisite ur-Oulipian polymath Georges Perec. I paid to have my reedy locks electrolysed and cultivated a little chin tuft in readiness. I practised conversing without the letter 'e' over the course of several months. In April, I set off (alone) to attend the conference by train. In Christine Brooke-Rose's *Textermination* underread literary characters congregate to discuss the absence of readers and their obsolescence as characters. At the Lit-Con meeting well-known writers alive and dead mingled with lesser-known writers alive and dead for a more inclusive celebration of all kinds of writing.

The local branch of frozen food supermarket Fossilfoods had been converted into a largish hall with a makeshift stage erected atop the frozen barfburgers. Upon entering, I was dismayed to see the various writers sticking to their cliques. I observed a froufrou of Jane Austens by the chicken goujons; a chortle of Charles Dickenses by the Lancashire hotpots; a nympho of Vladimir Nabokovs by the broken biscuits; and a discharge of John Updikes by the sacks of penne. Scattered across the room, I observed a frenzy of Robert Coovers, a bloat of Martin Amises, a vasectomy of Kathy Ackers, a wink of Joseph Hellers, a smirk of Andrew Kaufmans, a simmering of J.M. Coetzees, a sigh of Thomas Hardys, a howl of Hubert Selbys, a tipple of Malcolm Lowrys, a feck of James Joyces, a Himalaya of Thomas Manns, a ho-hum of Kurt Vonneguts, a steamboat of Mark Twains, a sorrow of Yasunari Kawabatas, a pile-up of J.G. Ballards, a pack of Virginia Woolfs, a sliver of Nicholson Bakers, a siphon of Sapphires, a pondering of Marcel Prousts, an echo of Samuel Becketts, a cacophony of Carl Van Vechtens, a pornofornocacophagomania of Alexander Therouxes, a jackhammer of Joyce Carol Oateses, a Borges of Jorge Luis Borgeses, a squelch of Steve Martins, a triptych of Gabriel Josipovicis, double doppelgaengers of Christine Brooke-Rose, a toddy of Lawrence Durrells, a sextet of Henry Millers, a symphony of William Gasses, a noodling of Raymond Federmans, a coterie of Arno Schmidts, a spray of Rikki Ducornets, a swarm of Arthor

Nonaymes, a shoal of Stanley Fischers, a fraternity of Flann O'Briens, a warband of Cormac McCarthys, a bulge of Norman Mailers, a bacillus of Charles Baudelaires, a bore of A.S. Byatts, a coven of Stephanie Meyerses, an ostentation of Oscar Wildes, a gaggle of Nikolai Gogols, a flotilla of Joseph Conrads, an arctangency of Thomas Pynchons, a swamp of E.L. Jameses, a scintillation of Ali Smiths, an arrest of Hannah Arendts, a yawp of Marguerite Youngs, a closet of E.M. Foresters, a trifurcation of Brontës, a landfill of Stephen Kings, a pilgrimage of Italo Calvinos, a lexicon of Umberto Ecos, a supercharged atmospheric ion particle de-accelerator of Douglas Adamses, a cornucopia of Goodreads Meviewers, among hundreds of others. I met two Georges Perecs by the bar.

"Glad to align ocular bits with you," one said.

"So charming to look at you," the other said.

"Ditto," I tersely replied. I had learned to speak tersely over the last two months thanks to the excruciating difficulty of forgoing the 'e'. "What's this all about?" I gestured to the cliques.

"Who knows?"

"Crazy to my ocular bits!"

The writers mingled after some encouragement from the Master of Ceremonies (a ratty Mark Leyner). I exchanged several long pauses with Harold Pinter, struggled to extricate myself from a knife fight with Norman Mailer, and swapped a few pithy morals with Kurt Vonnegut. I finally met Igo Wodan, who had come dressed as a cross between Carson McCullers and William Faulkner and had already downed fourteen beers before handing me a piece of paper.

"Izzprosose we play asittlegum," said Igo, passing out beside the instant mash.

Written on a crisp packet was a passage intended to be sneaked around the room and rewritten in the style of various authors, presumably as an homage to Raymond Queneau's *Exercises in Style*. Sensing an opportunity to fatten the Gilbert Adair festschrift, I circulated the barely legible passage to those trapped in formations of boring blather, hoping by the evening's end to have a book-length sample of pastiches to publish *pro bono* in this volume, tipping the cravat to Adair's premier pastiche work. The passage:

> A middle-aged fitness enthusiast boards the G train with his bicycle during a quiet period in the afternoon. His lycra shorts are undersized, drawing attention to a bulge beneath the fabric. As he stands his bike beside the luggage area, a woman pushing a pram emerges from another compartment, trying to shove past. He wheels his bike backwards to the doorway, blocking a man needing the toilet. The woman, noticing the biker's bulge, makes a disapproving face and is eager to remove her child from harm. The man is determined to shoulder past to the toilet, forcing the cyclist against the door, where the pedals of the bicycle painfully press against his legs. The woman refuses to move her pram, and the desperate man pushes until she is forced inside the space between the seats. "Sorry!" he says, leaping to the WC.
>
> One hour later, the bicyclist is standing in Edinburgh Haymarket station with a friend who says: "You need to do something about your shorts. You could get yourself arrested." The cyclist looks at the area and crosses his legs, pulling his shorts down further to attempt a less noticeable bulge.

The packet was circulated first to the dot matrix of Dorothy Parkers, too busy regaling other Dorothy Parkers with melancholy epigrams and swilling banana milkshakes around their champagne flutes to care, then to the whiff of Will Selfs, too busy making extremely precise points about the epiphenomena of bi-directional digital media in adenoidally camp registers to acknowledge the packet's presence, then to the fraternity of Flann O'Briens, too busy downing sugar-free American cream soda in pint tumblers and bitching about the latest editorial cuts to their Cruiskeen Lawn columns to notice, finally to the double doppelgaengers of Christine Brooke-Rose, one of whom speedily scribbled:

Neither young nor old boarding the afternoon G train bicycle in hand lycra tights skin-fitting muscles taut crotch bold. Negotiating the luggage area too little space too many bags, pram-pushing woman shoving past gasping aghast at bowled crotches not crutches backing away against a portly passenger seeking relief from temporary intestinal discomfort doorway bottle-necking with opposite directions intended. Cyclist pork-sandwiched between imaginary attributions of a salacious kind and an impending explosion. RATATATAT belching backwards, oh pardon! Reaching evacuation compartment releasing bike pram bowels.

Time passing cyclist relocating to a train station of significant proportions nondescript acquaintance announcing boulder crotches attract uniform attention. Cyclist helmeting the lower head.

And to the brunt of Anthony Burgesses, too busy blustering about the genitive case in the tongue of a primitive Finno-Ugric *Homo habilis* genus to notice, and to the rumble of Robert Bolaños, too busy describing the dismembered cadavers of Chilean señoritas in excessive and unpleasant detail to other Bolaños describing in lurid and unsexy detail their bedroom escapades with the dismembered señoritas to notice, and to the joust of Javiar Mariases, too busy feinting philosophy and faking philanthropy in sentences stretching the span of a football pitch to notice, to the mope of Michel Houellebecqs, too busy discussing their misadventures at Club 18-30 holidays in Lanzarote and ranting about the horror of being a self-loathing multimillionairist in a world devoid of adequate supplies of botox, butriptyline, and toilet paper to notice, and to the plethora of Jerzy Peterkiewiczes, too busy lamenting the dearth of brunette Fionas available under the avalanche of adoring spouses to notice, and to a lone Karl Edward Wagner, trimming his beard by the day-old turnips, who groped the gauntlet and wrote:

In the unnatural quiet of a fog-laced afternoon, the immortal Kane led his steed up the creaking ramp inside an immense black ship destined for fairer shores, pressed upon both sides by a mass of refugees, his fellow travelers . . . little did they know that the cause of their flight— indeed, the destruction of their city and the instigator of the war itself—stood nonchalantly beside them. Kane's torn and blood-spattered cloak was not out of place in such surroundings; nevertheless, the tight fit of his loincloth—barely concealing the heat-seeking missile so well-known throughout the whorehouses and monasteries of Carsultyal—was the cause of many quickly averted glances. As he stood beside his battle-wearied horse, a mother holding a mewling babe attempted to move past him. Casting his unnaturally shining killer's eyes downwards, Kane stepped back to allow her to pass, while unknowingly blocking another refugee seeking to gain access to the ship's privy. As the mother struggled in the press of the crowd, she noticed the bulge of his loincloth; gape-mouthing in surprise, she quickly placed a hand over her child's eyes. The refugee, desperate to reach the privy, lunged under Kane's horse, startling the noble beast. Kane attempted to halt his steed from rearing up in surprise, but its sudden movement caused the woman to be shoved forward and then to her knees, her quickly reddening face a mere handspan away from Kane's intimidating middleman. "Forgiveness!" shouted the desperate refugee as he began to relieve himself upon the heap of straw that constituted the ship's privy.

An hour later, after Kane had left his tethered horse within the ship's hold, he met his equally immortal daughter Klesst upon the deck of the now-departing ship. Noticing the sparseness of Kane's attire, she smirked and murmured "Father, many would recognize the fabled 'Mark of Kane' . . . you really must conceal yourself. Otherwise you may find your accommodations will be located within the ship's brig." The immortal warlord sighed and wrapped his cloak around his mighty thews.

And to the volupt of William T. Vollmanns, too busy firing their pistols in tandem to recitations of their 1,000-page dissertations on topics ranging from Japanese Noh theatre, the mating habits of the okapi in the Ituri rainforest, and the excessive sogginess of the mayonnaise in packaged sandwiches to notice, and to a froth of Philip Roths, too busy kvetching about their oversexed copulation partners demanding tri-hourly servicing in a various karmasutric tangles under the scornful eyes of their Jewish mothers to notice, and to the shyly American Brit Lucy Ellmann who wrote:

The middle-aged MALE boards the G train with his bright new PENILE TOTEM in the afternoon. His large male SHANKS are 50cm tall and 10cm wide and his CROTCH-HUGGING lycra shorts stretch the parameters of respectable tightness in public places. Jill shoves her pram towards the male and POPS HER EYES at the sight. Penises! Penises! A woman cannot travel two inches out the house without bumping into another bulging COCK! The male backs his totem against the door as a SECOND male appears holding onto his COCK as he bounces up and down desperate for a PISS. Jill blocks the path and thanks God for her CUNT. Make room for the cunt, Jill thinks. No one needs another obstreperous COCK. Not in the train! He forces her into the space between the seats and apologises. Jill feels her cunt RECOIL and winks at her daughter. When she is older she will be PROUD of her cunt.

An hour later, the totemist is at Haymarket station with a pal: "Am I supposed to see your John Thomas through those shorts? Get yourself on the register, mate." The middle-aged male crossed his legs and WISHES he had a cunt.

As the first key speaker, a smiley William Carlos Williams, discussed the importance of close reading in an age of sentence skimming and content shilling, two blandly dressed suits entered the Fossilfoods holding briefcases, and lurked around the prawn crackers until Williams rounded up his unrousing monotologue (the "kindly doctor" persona was not suited for the stirring *cri de coeur* needed—fortunately Gore Vidal was next). I had taken the two for Robert Ludlums, duped by a curl of ill-combed hair in a frozen flop over the older one's dome, but the younger was of the moodier Raymond Chandler variety, so clearly they weren't a pair. I sidled over to the holocaust of Barbara Cartlands to eavesdrop on the gossip, but the Picasso-faced crones refused to speak a word in the presence of such a dirty pretend-Frog as me, so I sidled back to my own kind. One of the Georges Perecs had taken hold of the circulating packet, and rose to the challenge with a piece entitled 'Arguably':

That day, a physical-training fanatic of a good fifty springs sprang on a G train, with his BMX in tow, around two or four pm, sporting a skimpy pair of Lycra shorts, hardly obscuring his bulging groin. As our man was parking his mountain-cycling apparatus among a stack of bags and rucksacks, a pram-pushing young lady, coming from an adjoining wagon and trying to push past both him and through two doors, was caught in a fix. As his BMX was shifting backwards away from this pram, it struck the front of a man who was looking for a lavatory. Also, such a bulging groin had now drawn both of our lady's bright pupils, bringing a disdainful look to that haughty brow, along with a wish to guard baby from harm. With his urinary tract about to pop, our arrival was now shoving his own way forwards, ramming both fanatic and BMX against that lavatory's door, so that its chain and foot-blocks stuck into his shins painfully. But, not wanting to shift an inch, our young lady stood stock still, until thrust back by such a vigorous pushing that adopting a position amid two rows of chairs was all this poor lass could do. Mumbling "sorry!", our squirming man-in-a-hurry slid through this gap for a piss.

An hour having spun by, our cyclist was standing in a main railway station in Scotland's capital with a pal, who told him: "You should start facing up to your shorts situation. You could wind up in prison if you don't." Staring down at his bulky lunch box, and yanking vainly at his shorts, our poor lad X'd his thighs, hoping thus to diminish his mound.

This e-less performance delighted the tittering Perecs, who praised the canny linguist with backslaps and tickles of the goatee, alerting the two suits to something amiss (and, indeed, something Amis—one of the Martins was writing his version under the scowling eyes of a klutz of Kingsleys). They strolled over, making no effort to downplay their intimidating police-constable intimidatingness and snatched the pastiche from my hands. "I am afraid this won't do," the younger one said. The older one boldly semaphored to the Gore Vidal who was making a sardonic remark about "loaferature", skewering the pukebomb of E.L. Jameses and shitstink of Dan Browns in the crowd with his verbal kebabery. Stepping onto the stage of frozen barfburgers, the older one commandeered the microphone, boldly elbowing an affronted Gore to one side, and said:

"Good afternoon. We are from the Copyright Infringement Police. This gathering has about it the stench of extremely malodorous copyright violations."

"Tuh!" Gore said.

"We will be in contact with our London office to determine whether the unapproved usurpation of authors' identities and styles in a supermarket setting constitutes a prisonable offence. In the meantime, we will be observing."

"Scary!" Gore said. The floor was his once again. He launched into an eloquent denunciation of property-protecting lawyers and reduced the room to tears (of laughter), minus the two suits who were busy notetaking. And to the muttering of W.G. Sebalds, too busy ambling aimlessly around the room and discoursing on Chinese wheat farming, the demise of Norfolk countryside, and the derelict state of the Bundesstraße 6 to notice, until one of them, fading under another long unattributed quotation and terminally confused as to who was talking, penned:

I had come to Edinburgh by foot from Worthing, in Sussex, partly for study, partly for reasons that are unclear to me even now, though in truth the journey was most likely initiated as a means of dispelling a nervous disorder that had taken hold of me and rendered me immobile for weeks in that southern English beach town, whose grey skies, empty boardwalks and gull-bespattered promenades evoked nothing less than the wreckage and ruin of all civilization. Being quite a considerable distance that I had covered in the past days and feeling an ailing of my spirit beginning to arise within me as does the Dog Star constellation of a clear summer's night, and wincing as the blisters on my feet burst one by one like small, painful, flesh-ensnared supernovae, I decided to give myself a rest and complete my day's journey aboard the G train. It was a calm, quiet, cloudless afternoon and it was on this occasion, upon entering the train and observing the passengers deposited here and there like animals in a zoology display, that I noticed a peculiar scene which I was to carry with me in reverberations of memory through all the ensuing years.

Directly after I had seated myself, a man one might describe as "middle-aged" boarded the train, carrying in his muscled arms the burden of a bicycle. I was drawn to this apparition not only for his noticeable peak physical conditioning and the velocipede he carried as he would a wounded comrade in outstretched arms, but also because of a prominent bulge emerging from his somewhat unfortunately undersized lycra cycling shorts. It immediately reminded me of the Bartlow burial mounds in Cambridgeshire, which I had visited the previous spring, and which had been tragically despoiled by neglect and vandalism, whose artistic treasures dating from the Roman period had been plundered by grave robbers, and whose grandeur had been diminished, as all things are, by that most unrelenting of thieves, Time.

Setting his bike in the most convenient area available, adjacent the luggage rack and the WC, and holding it by the seat and crossbar whilst remaining standing, he fixed his eyes straight in front of him, in what seemed such a mode of intent concentration, as if he was attempting to look on this tableau from the absolutely detached perspective of the Creator, that he was utterly startled by a woman emerging from another compartment, pushing a pram in which a baby, an exact image of the infant Christ from Raphael's "Madonna of the Pinks", clothed in toddler apparel patterned with scattered carnations, cooed and squirmed. Here a coalescence of events erupted, as sometimes happens when the divergent paths we follow throughout our lives veer strangely across one another, a conjuncture known in some eastern religions as *yuánfèn*. The woman pushing the pram, noticing with an agitated flinch the protrusive exhibition of the bicyclist's bulge and seemingly wishing to prevent any malapropos contact between child and tumescence, attempted to aggressively push past, and the bicyclist, alarmed, hastily sought to accommodate, wheeling his apparatus backward at the exact moment another fellow, a man with an almost albinic complexion, wearing circular, horn-rimmed glasses, his bright pale hair parted in the center and hanging in long strands about his brow, approached with vexed urgency the now completely obstructed entrance to the WC. Witnessing this triad of forces converging on the same spot and the ensuing deadlock, I thought of Pharaoh Thutmose's siege of Megiddo, that seven-month stranglehold of privation, disease, and starvation, alleviated only after the sons and daughters of the decimated city pathetically emerged from the battered fortifications begging for the lives of the emaciated survivors within; a plea that was granted by the conquering Pharaoh in exchange for the unbending loyalty of the poor souls that gravely persisted. These were represented, in the present conflict, by the beleaguered cyclist, pressed now so vehemently against the door of the WC that the pedals of his two-wheeler painfully pushed his legs, only further accentuating the bulge at the midpoint of his lower torso, the sight of which more greatly agitated the woman with the pram, who was amazed beyond action at the events unfolding. The albinic fellow in need of relieving himself might have played the role of the poor children of the citizens of Megiddo, so desperate to break the impasse that drastic measures, at great self-risk, were willingly undertaken. He shoved aside the lady with the pram, whose baby gurgled, in a space between the seats, pushed past the bicyclist, now floundering across the aisle in pursuit of his runaway vehicle, and leapt into the WC shouting an expeditious, and, I imagine, only partially sincere, "Sorry!"

An hour later I emerged from the side entrance of Haymarket Station. Having disembarked from my train, I then followed from the platform a procession of diminutive figures that materialized from a mist accompanied by the sound of dry leaves scuttling in a wind, who might well have been the souls of those restlessly departing this world, having lost a portion of their substance in the process and thus appearing dwarfish, who moved through an obscure doorway to an unused or abandoned part of the station, a vast chamber under a vaulted glass ceiling twinkling with dust motes in streams of wan late afternoon light, and to this chamber were attached many colonnaded halls, which opened onto further corridors and halls, more than I could account for and as far as the eye could see, and it was as if the rococo masonry of fate itself had woven these labyrinthine tendrils of steel and stone into something approximating in architecture its own circumlocutionary paths.

I became weary, traversed a passage, and found myself in the women's lavatory. Any amount of hours or days might have passed, but as I said, it was one hour when I made my way out of the side entrance of Haymarket Station, my head dizzy with all I had just experienced, and noticed to my considerable surprise standing on the flagstone square barely three meters before me the bicyclist from the earlier incident, in conversation with another man who was saying to the bicyclist, "You need to do something about your shorts. You could get yourself arrested." The athletic man looked down with consternation, crossed his legs, and adjusted his lycra cycling shorts in a vain attempt to reduce the noticeability of the bulge. Observing this, I was stricken by a melancholy I had not experienced since the bleak strands of Worthing, and found myself lamenting the original sin of Man, that of the shame of his nakedness, and how in all cultures this is inevitably entwined with the death-drive; thus we intermix the shame of sex and the fear of death; and could only see in the bicyclist's futile struggle a kind of kindred gesture to the practice of early Christians who wrapped their bishops and monarchs in death shrouds of fine cotton, wool, or silk, as if to conceal the degradation of mortality, before secreting them within the earth forever.

Igo Wodan appeared from behind a smugness of Simon Armitages, three drinks in hand, threatening the creation of a brilliant pastiche: "Isswoking on a newpass. Tisch! Hahaha. Izgonbe amazant, jusp you what . . . what?" And to the whipple-scrumpet of Roald Dahls, who wrote something entitled 'Mr Fitzcruncheonboom's Homeward Commute':

What a lot of muscly men there are in the world. I expect you've probably passed one of them in the street today. For all I know, you may even be sitting on a bus, glancing up at one over the top of this page. I don't mean the sort of man whose forearms merely bulge a little when he wishes to impress a lady or frighten her rival, or the kind that can carry three shopping bags in each hand, as well as a small child on his shoulders without too much difficulty. I mean the kind that looks as if he's swallowed half a dozen small animals for lunch, which are now wriggling around underneath his skin. And maybe he has done just that. Who knows what such people get up to in the privacy of their own homes? *It is possible.*

Mr Samuel Fitzcruncheonboom was such a man. He was enormously tall, with shoulders as broad as a small fighter plane. Wherever he walked he cast a shadow, from which a shadow-nose and a shadow-crotch bulged conspicuously. The latter was the result of his always wearing a pair of undersized blue lycra shorts—which he never washed. He had a round, pink, puffy red face with small eyes, and a long, pointy nose. His hair was thin, oily and permanently plastered against his forehead. Each weekday he took the train from Haymarket to Queen Street station, from which he then cycled to his job at a furniture factory. Here, he spent all day lifting huge and heavy boxes on the backs of company trucks for shipping to local outlets, before cycling to the nearby gym, where he liked to pummel things.

On this particular day, a Tuesday, Mr Fitzrunchenboom was feeling especially grotty, despite the warm sun and the nearly-cloudless sky. He hated sunshine. It made him sweaty and itchy. He boarded the train back to Edinburgh, pushing his bike before him, ploughing through the crowds of people who stood in his way on the platform. He was tired and hungry. His favourite punch-bag had broken, forcing him to use one of the weedy athletes instead. Unfortunately, the manager saw, and promptly barred him from the gym.

"Excuse me," said a haughty female voice from somewhere around his navel area. "You're blocking the corridor."

He looked down and saw a woman of around forty, with wiry brown hair, a straw hat, a hard, bony face and pince-nez. She was pushing a deep-bottomed pram, which contained a fat infant in a blue romper suit, eating a large bar of caramel chocolate. Mr Fitzcruncheonboom did not move. Instead, he glared at the woman. She glared back. A muscle in his jaw twitched and his right arm flexed. Her eyes travelled from his face down to the famous bulge of his shorts. Two tiny red spots appeared upon each of her cheeks. He shifted and the woman hurried her offspring through the sliding doors to the next compartment.

And now, another man was struggling to pass. This one was only slightly shorter than Mr Fitzcruncheonboom, but also lighter and thinner, with thick, square spectacles and brown hair which fell past his ears. He looked rather like a dirty floor mop. This way and that he dodged, desperately trying to gain access to the toilet door, which Mr Fitzcruncheonboom was blocking. Mr Fitzcruncheonboom manoeuvred his bike, so that the pedals jabbed into the spectacled man's calf muscles. The spectacled man leapt in the air as if stung on the bottom by a hornet.

"OWEEEEEEEE!!!!!! Can't you watch where you put that thing?" he cried, hopping around and clutching his leg in both hands. He then barged past, into the toilet, calling "Sorry," over his shoulder. A colossal explosion followed from within, the force of which shook the entire carriage so that it rattled at its hinges. And suddenly, it was as if the man had turbo-charged and shifted into a higher gear. He seemed to have some kind of magic in his bowels. The noise built, the shaking intensified, all the passengers felt a curious tingling sensation in their fingers and toes. Something was about to happen any second now. They held their collective breath, waiting . . .

An extraordinary event occurred. The force of the explosion, channelled through the toilet and onto the tracks below, acted like a rocket booster. Slowly—oh, most marvellously—the entire carriage rose in the air. The passengers gaped. They were staggered. They were dumbfounded and befuddled. They simply could not believe what was taking place and could do nothing but gasp and stare, pressing their noses against the window panes, as the train climbed majestically through the sky.

Past wraith-like wisps and towering columns they flew, gliding among their mysterious, shadowy folds and their silent and ominous overhangs, with the evening light glinting off the billows. A breeze from the open doors blew through the carriage, ruffling the hair on peoples' heads. Everyone took deep, appreciative sniffs of the cool, rain-scented air. Mr Fitzcruncheonboom looked down at the ground, through the open carriage door. Below him, houses and trees were the size of miniature models—the kind built by train-set enthusiasts. Sheep and cows were no more than tiny brown and white pinheads against vast swathes of green. The hedges looked like tiny grass snakes.

Soon, the fields gave way to houses, first dotted here and there, and after densely packed. The explosion from the toilet began to die down. The train lost height, and the tops of the buildings rose to meet them as they sped towards the ground...

CRASH! Straight through the roof of Haymarket station they plunged. Rafters and metal and dust and wood and concrete and pigeons' nests came raining down upon the passengers as they struggled, coughing and spluttering, up from the wreckage to blink in the stale air of the station. Onlookers gawked. The spectacled man emerged from the remains of the toilet, brushed himself down, and looked at his handiwork. Then he glanced at the bulge of Mr Fitzcruncheonboom's now torn and tattered lycra shorts.

"You need to do something about your shorts," he said. "You could get yourself arrested."

Slowly, the entire gathering turned to gaze at Mr Fitzcruncheonboom's nether regions. He pulled his shorts down to hide the bulge, and as he did so, the cleft of his buttocks appeared over the top of the elastic. His naked bottom winked in a shaft of sunlight shining through the gaping hole in the roof.

And to a bacchanal of Françoise Rabelaises, who offered:

I must refer you to the substantial chronicle of Pant And Grueling for the facts, information, descriptions, and understanding of the ancestry and genetic composition of that ancient and revered tribe from which Gargantabulge is descended. With the reading of such an history, it is possible to comprehend the emergence of specimens characterised by anatomically imposing genitalia within the present day of the Age of the Holocene. Be not offended, if at this time I but mention it only briefly, although in all respects it is the one subject such that the more it were recalled, the more would it satisfy you worshipping Senhoritas; according to which you have the appetite of Aspasia as exemplified by Plato's Diotima, and the adherence of Flaccus, contending that certain aspirations, the more oft repeated, the more delicious in experience.

Would to the heavens and skies above had all who read this attempt at explanation a sufficient and fundamental conversance of the geneaology concerning Gargantabulge from the time of the Tarantian Age until this. Many are they who occupy positions of influence and power, such as politicians, lobbyists, entrepreneurs, members of Bilderberg, scientists, celebrities, talk-show hosts and docu-drama commentators, whose origins rival nothing so lofty as the lowliest of illiterate urchins; in contrast the offspring of great thinkers of the past wander now as beggars or street sweepers, subsisting upon the most meagre of salaries or social handouts, whose intellectual lineage, once honoured and occupying prominence in the courts and parliaments of the great empires of the world, is now ignored and buried beneath an avalanche of populist dross concerned solely with the promulgation of an infantile escapism in which the masses drown their real and imagined sorrows, resulting, as I contend, from the inversion of production from honest toil without tool to that of technology without thought, thus from the Akkadians to the Assyrians, the Assyrians to the Medes, the Medes to the Persians, the Persians to the Macedonians, the Macedonians to the Greeks, the Greeks to Romans, the Romans to the French, the French to the British, the British to the Americans, and from the Americans to the Chinese.

To provide you with some small indication regarding who relates this material to you, I cannot suggest other than that I am a descendant of some great family of wealthy thinkers belonging to a former era, for it is impossible to conceive of any person with a greater desire than my own to be both politically influential and of independent means, and that only to improve the lot of ordinary people, to materially, philosophically, and spiritually enrich my friends and all with whom I have the (mis)fortune to engage in conversation, to do nothing other than play and practise at realising the potential, inherent in each and every individual I meet, to do good in the world. Thus do I comfort myself, for while in the flesh in which I am currently clothed this is mere whimsy, when I shall cease to inhabit this dimension and proceed to another, there I shall be of greater proportions, prominence, and puissance, than ever I could wish in the present. So shall it be also with you, irrespective of the conceit with which you console yourselves now or later, in happiness or in distress, in drink fresh or fermented whenever it is offered, or substances of a more diabolical nature.

Concerning our topic under scrutiny, allow me the impudence of emphasis: there but for the divine grace of a deity, the ogyguity and genetic antecessor of Gargantabulge has been bequeathed for our employ more entire and preserved than any other text excepting that of Osiris, of whom I will refrain from speaking since it lies extraneous to my purpose, and the daemons, by whom I refer to the heretics and the hate-mongerers, will loudly dispute this and declaim otherwise. It was a certain neophyte appellated Giovanne Andronicus, travelling with a company of gypsies bound for Hearsay, who located with much ado about something, in a poppy-covered field, surrounded by poplars and lemon groves, on account of wishing to plant an apple seed, a shallowly-buried, oddly-shaped sarcophagus consisting of a strange metal, most like bronze and yet with the malleability of lead; long, enormously thick through the middle and with a strange mound in the centre of the coffin. Upon the sarcophagus were inscribed ancient cuneiforms, indecipherable, but of a seemingly phallic nature, and on opening the casket, the company of gypsies and Giovanne Andronicus found a sacred number of various brass scrota, ranked according to the use of the appendage, such that the shapes were, amongst others, tumescent, shrunken, twisted, raised, ablated, divided, decorated, pierced, spliced, stuffed, and shrivelled. Each exemplar was perfumed with a unguent reminiscent of the spices itemised in Scheherazade's tales, from rose to neroli, jasmine to sandalwood, ambergris to frankincense, myrrh to cassia, cardamom to lily. Nestled between these lay a parchment of some fine material bearing a mediaeval script, which, though legible, lacked a contiguity of characters sufficient to determine the meaning recorded for posterity, that is to say, the incidence of Gargantabulge.

I, poor qualifications notwithstanding, was requested to join Giovanne Andronicus post-haste, and relying on magnifying technologies, as well as significant and broad experience in the art of decoding faded alphabets and emending texts as exhorted by that great dispenser of philosophical thought, Aristotle, particularly with the aid of bracing liquids and energising substances, have managed to derive a meaning from the text which you are welcome, whilst perusing the greater artefact of Pant And Grueling, to imbibe according to your distinct and particular sensibilities and learn of the strange case of Gargantabulge. As an adjunct to the discoveries detailed herein, an Annodated Poppy-Cock was intended as index for the more astute (and demanding) reader, however the Eddyt Whores of Babyschlong disdained to allow its inclusion; I bear witness to its existence despite the rudimentary (rude) education exhibited by these unworthy custodians of antiquated documents.

Un gentilhomme of uncertain age, or rather certain predisposition, of imposing height and breadth of épaules, bearing an instrument of unlikely execution and dubious purpose distinguished by a duo of rotary objects hung suspended at each end and a composition of tubes in a triangular formation separating these, upper torso apparelled in a form-fitting cloth of a thin and rasping nature and labelled AD-HE-HADS across the front pectorals and ASPER JERSEY across the back, hips and loins clad in what appeared to be the skin of a warrior from the heart of darkness; so smoothly did the fabric encase his body that but for its opaque nature he seemed naked, thighs outlined like the twining trunks of mature saplings, buttocks moulded like hewn stone, and crotch bursting forwards as though he had slung the extant testicles of a newly-made bullock between his legs, approached and entered the second class carriage of a Gs train gommuter locomotive as it lay idling at a downtown station on a drowsy mid-week afternoon (complete with cooing doves, twittering swallows, lazy fountain, and shafts of sunlight-dappled dust motes), compartments not yet filled with an in-rush of occupants destination unknown but somewhere in the hinterland of greater Slogwag.

The modern day Hercules of such eye-watering magnitude, seeming oblivious to the jaw-dropped stares and hastily reorganised glances of passers-by and waiting passengers, shrugged and bumped along the corridor to the racks of luggage, but so as he was out-sized, was his startling contraption also, and by no means would it arrange itself in the space presented for the storage of baggage, thus he lowered it gently to the carpeted floor of the passage and propped it against the carriage windows; on the thinly polstered triangle which could have sufficed as a seat he rested his own prolific appendage and leant an elbow against the glass, head almost brushing the domed ceiling of the passage.

At some short distance, following an ejaculation of compressed air, a door slid aside and a tri-rotored cart resembling an egg, perched upon double sets of multi-directional thick rubber rings rotating perpendicular to each supporting strut and at right angles to a forward momentum, caught itself upon the door frame before scooting out from the respective compartment to narrowly miss colliding with the wall of the corridor and veer suddenly towards the gargantuan man, only to jerk to a startled halt.

"Oh my goodness. Oh my goodness gracious me. Oh my grandmother's knitting needles. Oh have mercy on me for what my eyes have seen," the pale-faced woman crossed her heaving bosom as she squeezed past her tri-rotored chariot and yanked its clamshell covering from the rear to the front, preventing its contents from perceiving or being perceived. She twisted back around to place the mobile egg between herself and the gentleman of unfailing proportions and glared at anywhere but him while chomping her lip as if a piece of cud, gripping the horn-curved handles of the skittish trolley, its rotors skedaddling in all directions other than forwards as the gentleman of astonishing abundance glided his motley collection of circular and angled pipes backwards and away from the woman of affronted mien.

"Ooowwwaaaaaaa!" The shriek emanating from behind the clamshell canopy conveyed the ire of the protesting creature ensconced within it and the canopy was flung back to its original position. A flying device bedecked with small metal bells flew out and smashed harmlessly against another male passenger shouldering and mumbling his way along the corridor behind the riesen Mensch.

"Excuse me. Pardon me. Could you . . . yes, the toilet. Pardon. Oops. Would you . . . Oh. Your toes! Yes, of course. Ah, I really . . . Excuse me, I have to . . ." He stumbled against one of the rounded frames and protuberances to collapse hopping on one leg, face screwed in agony and hands fumbling to rub a shin. "Blast all cyclists to the outer reaches of the Larger Magellanic Cloud. Why don't you clutter up somewhere else?" He dropped his shin and clutched his abdomen, groaning at the woman, "excuse me, could you move a little to the side? I absolutely . . ." He nudged the woman on the shoulder and she elbowed him back, wedging her egg against the doorframe of the nearest compartment and frowning at the gastrically stricken man, after which he lunged forwards and knocked her sideways through a gap between two opposing seats as the creature in the egg erupted with another bellow.

"Soooorrryyy—" A swish of pressurised air sealed the digestively distressed usurper within the sanitation cubicle; the woman snatched the handles protruding from her miscreant egg, spun it around, and scuttled along the corridor away from the gentleman of eminent moment.

One thousand six hundred and seventy-four kilometres later (distance of the earth's rotation during a sidereal hour), the gentleman of immense dimensions heaved his massive apparatus upon his shoulder and strolled through a Dunne Barrow grass bazaar, to be hailed by a grimacing acquaintance.

"Gilbert, have I not told you before? You still dare to traipse around in those pants? For the love of Christ and all that's Agathe, that crotch of yours is enough to embarrass a rabble-rousing giant. Can you not nip and tuck a bit? They'll be calling you Gargantabulge next."

The gentleman of redoubtable reckoning glanced down and thrust his hips forward, lifting his knee to hip height and resting his foot on a nearby bench, bulge splendidly haloed in the twilight. "I can live with that. All the better to make merry with."

As the Rabelais-raisers rounded up, the doppelgänging had reached critical mass, forcing the Copyright Infringement Police to raid the Fossilfoods, approaching with mansize erasers and pipettes of Tipp-Ex and causing clamorous heck around the store—a burnout of Ralph Ellisons leaping onto the broccoli bags; a sneering of Thomas Bernhards crawling towards the washing-up liquid; a cringe of Truman Capotes sweet-talking the police to assist with the massacre; a Chesapeake of John Barths sailing upon the bottled water; an aposiopesis of B.S. Johnsons cowering under the muesli; and hundreds of other writers disagreeing politely with each other, listing their publications and awards, and re-reading their own books to check for a solution. The forty-strong squadron erased the writers in turn, not discriminating alphabetically, oblivious to the loud recitations of heartbreaking and elegant passages being spewed out from manifold orifices, the bawdy comedic monologues used as an attempt to tickle the police into abating, and the enraged balance sheets being quoted by the bestsellers. Igo Wodan strong-armed me to the stockroom, nudging past a silence of Anne Franks peering out from boxes of banana milk, towards the exit. As my companion vanished into the pigeon-scented Helensborough night, I found a pastiche signed Iaagoo Woodean!?, which I took to mean Igo Wodan, and, expecting an illegible drunken ramble, I was surprised to see my friend had delivered a faultless homage to that High Priest of satirists, Jonathan Swift, completely off our theme for this evening, but a prime pastiche worthy of Adair, included overleaf to conclude this raggedy and passionate homage to our fêted festschrifter: the grandiloquent, gracious, and gone Gilbert.

[Credits where due:
Main text: M. J. Nicholls
Christine Brooke-Rose: G. N. Forester
Karl Edward Wagner: Mark Monday
Georges Perec: Ian Monk
W.G. Sebald: Geoff Wilt
Roald Dahl: Laura Guthrie
Rabelais: Gianni D'Ane]

A Reasonable Scheme

IGO WODAN

> Gentle readers, dear Friends, "...who peruse this [purview], Be not offended, whilst on it you [chew]: Denude yourselves of all depraved affection, For it contains no badness, nor infection: 'Tis true that it brings forth to you no birth Of any value, but in point of mirth; Thinking therefore how sorrow might your mind Consume, I could no [more] apt subject find; One [plume] of joy surmounts of grief a [duration]; Because to laugh is proper to the [rational person]." — Rabelais

The sight is loathsome to those, who voyage the oceans and traverse the lands, when they are forced to observe the electric footpaths, the automobiles, the trains, the ships, the aeroplanes and the various other forms of person conveyor that great strides in technology have reduced to no strides in humanity; crowded with specimens of voluminous flesh, followed at times by an entourage of similarly endowed progeny, all bursting at the seams, and demanding at every corner, every fuel stop, every transit area, entrance to the feeding troughs of the food purveyors, or seated positions at the cubicled stalls of waste aggregators, when not collapsing panting and puce-faced in the arms of the fatigued and underfunded health curators.

These mountains of Menschen, instead of existing unaided and productive in our wondrous society, are forced to employ all their time soliciting aid in managing the carriage of their bulk and the breakdown of their overtaxed organs, in seeking assistance for the acceptance and integration of themselves and their offspring within their immediate milieu, requiring additional resources to be expended in psychological support for their unfortunate suffering as the butt and end of jokes and cruel satire belittling their intelligence and parodying their distorted forms. Oft are they exhorted to adopt frivolous or fraught-with-danger professions, such as security guards, circus exhibits, volunteers in longitudinal pharmaceutical studies, or figureheads of large multinational corporations, frequently their only means to derive an income and obtain access to the requisite health insurance designed to cope with their bloated status.

It is agreed by all, I think, that this prodigious number of such grossly mattered citizens is, in the present deplorable state of the planet, a very great additional grievance; and therefore whoever could devise a fair, economical, and stress-free method of making these people sound and useful members of the global community, would deserve so well of the public, as to have a statue erected as a preserver of nationhood.

My intention here is naturally light years from confining itself to provide only for these socially shunned and energy expensive individuals: it is of a much greater extent and shall take in the whole number of these at every age and state of Body Mass Index (BMI)>22^1, who are born of parents in effect as little able to support their plus-size offspring, as those of distended proportions who demand solace on our streets and in our institutions.

Having turned my thoughts for many years upon this important subject and maturely weighed the several schemes implemented, I have always found these staggeringly mistaken in computation. It is true, a person indexed at twenty two may be supported with little necessary recourse to the health system providing they remain stable, but experience shows this is the exception and not the rule, and it is exactly at this point that I propose to prepare them in such a manner, as, instead of being a charge upon the lean of us, they shall, on the contrary, con-

---

1 Until a BMI of 22 is reached, the average human requires a minimal expenditure on the maintenance of health, nor suffers any exacerbated or onerous mental or emotional ill-being as a result of having accumulated an excess of flesh (whether composed purely of fat or sinew and muscle).

tribute to the wellbeing of all those bound by our social structure to bear their maladjustment.

Another great advantage of my scheme: it will prevent stomach cutting and that horrid practice of fat vacuuming, an intolerable waste of good, useful energy, alas too frequent among us, sacrificing the poor innocent victims of their own size, more to avoid the shame than the accumulated detrimental impacts on quality of life, which would move tears and pity in the most savage and inhuman breast among us.

The number of souls in the lands (gross domestic product accounting for approximately 85% of the world's total) where this discussion has relevance (forgetting, quite naturally, those countries where they have yet to learn the saving of seeds for planting and harvesting the following season, let alone the hoarding of calories as the basis to support entire industries, professions, and economies) approaches four billion and a half, of these I calculate there may be about two billion sufferers of this malady and the rate is rising. The question, therefore, is how this increasing number shall be fed at the levels necessary to sustain their condition, and how the health services should be sufficiently strengthened to provide the necessary services to provide a minimum quality of life, which, under the present situation of affairs, is utterly impossible by all the methods hitherto proposed.

I thus humbly propose a solution which I hope will inspire not the least objection.

I have been assured by a large number of very knowledgeable natives with an enviable wealth of experience, and funded research conducted by an eminent institution skilled in the undertaking of surveys and studies of this sort, that the global energy crisis could be ameliorated with the smelting and rendering of human blubber, and that human flesh, properly prepared, makes a most delicious, nourishing, and wholesome food.

I most respectfully offer the following for consideration: that the two billion carriers of this additional energy supply be divided in gradations corresponding to available bulk (the greater indicating both a higher drain on existing resources as well as a commensurately disadvantaged psychological disposition) and auctioned to fast-food companies as raw ingredients (flesh), clothing companies (hide and hair), energy companies as collateral supply (body fat), pharmaceutical companies as test subjects and organ donors, and hospitals practising the increasingly financially significant medicine of sourcing replacement body parts, where these are free of disease and of suitable high quality (and can thus therefore be repackaged and distributed for sale at premium prices).

I grant this source of additional livestock may be somewhat costly and therefore very proper for consumption by the owners of capital and resources (shares, bank deposits, fertile land, clean water and air, minerals and energy), who, having already devoured most of the planet, would appear to have the best title to the products thus being created.

Obese flesh will be seasonally available, but more plentiful in the months following religious celebrations, thus it is necessary to ensure that where these occur simultaneously, government intervention in the form of price fixing, legislation, special notices etc. will be required to prevent price collapse and diminution of healthy profits. Further, since health services will no longer be as strained by the continual drain on personnel, pharmaceutical products, and infrastructure, the savings represented by freeing these resources can be usefully directed towards more valuable research such as anti-aging and longevity products and therapies.

Thus, the families of these individuals will benefit greatly from both the additional income and the reduced cost (social, financial, educational etc.) in maintaining these mammoths.

It is, perhaps, not unlikely that some well-meaning but misguided conscientious objectors might be inclined to censure this solution (indeed unjustly and at a continuing unsustainable cost to the planet and society) as a cruelty and not a kindness, which, I confess, has always been my own strongest objection against any project, however well so intended. Aside, of course, from this digression, the benefits of my proposal are many and varied and are surely to be regarded as the most convenient means to resolve this pressing problem.

Its implementation would result, as already noted, in a reduction in religious observers who balloon after festivals, and who are often heard quoting divine right as the justification for access to a plethora of attenuated goods and services reserved for those in greatest need, such as the captains/esses of industry, bureaucrats of inimitable standing, elevated representatives of the labour force, and other lobbyists. Notwithstanding this advantage, families under duress would no doubt find their social and financial status improved with the provision of their over-endowed relatives to enterprises created or expanded to process these additional resources. Thirdly, the maintenance of these amply-proportioned individuals runs to the millions of the units of relevant currency, and thus their addition to the stocks of national assets would thereby elevate national domestic product by an equivalent amount, and domestic product by the value imputed in the processing of their carcasses.

Imagine, naturally, the flow-on effects, the re-intermediation of currency and indirect goods and services resulting from this metamorphosis of liability to resource. Indeed, forecasting would predict that both relationships and the population would flourish, as families sought to commoditise the new status accorded those with the requisite BMI and offer offspring and dependents as plump and juicy alternatives to mere animal flesh to those financially deserving and capable of purchasing such premium products. Such a scheme could introduce a net-present value annuity paid in lieu of what the cost to society would have been had the individual lived to pensionable age. Child abuse would drop significantly, as bruised flesh would fetch lower prices at auction, domestic violence would all but cease as couples fornicated furiously in the hopes of producing marketable goods, not to mention a corresponding increase in the quality of parenting and relationship management both within schools, universities and the workplace.

It could reasonably argued that the trade balance with those nations outside the G20 would also favourably improve, as these nations sought to address the calorific imbalance by importing either fresh carcasses or value-added products. However, this would require further study after the scheme had been implemented in order to determine the exact trade flows and balances and adjust export quotas, foreign policy, provision of liquidity and access to G20 capital markets, etc.

One objection to this scheme might be accorded, that global population could fall. I admit to this possible effect and request my generous readers note that this remedy for our current state of disarray can occur at no more timely an epoch. Thus, conjecture not regarding other pragmatisms, such as increasing taxes or penalties, of further subsidising private or public funded services, or of interfering with the hand of the market, of implementing suspect technologies that cannot hope to replace our global energy requirements or of actions to curb our output of factors held to be principal in the imbalancing of the planet's climate, of changing patterns of behaviour that might result in a shrinking of luxury consumerism (a two car household with five digital devices, plasma screen home entertainment system, domestic pet, private education and two overseas holidays per annum being the minimum standard), of altering our determination of worth from pride in physical appearance (created with the aid of our esteemed cosmetic surgeons and the burgeoning and bulging beauty industry), of preaching severity, restraint, caution, and a finely developed sense of discrimination, not to mention tolerance for diversity and cultural expression, as well as respect for tradition and heritage and a classical education in conjunction with an openness for the new and unique to be welcomed and integrated, and finally, of rejecting divisive and intolerant behaviour which seeks to conquer and not to embrace.

Having been oft thought misanthropic, and despairing of finding a solution to our problems, I have devised this last great scheme, if not wholly new, at least something executionable, of little cost and perhaps slightly more bother, lending itself to immediate implementation and incurring no negative side effects; I am not so set upon my own imaginings as to discard alternatives, and willingly would look upon suggestions capable of achieving the same goals and outcomes.

I profess, with the sincerity of my mind and heart, that I hold no personal nor financial interest in persevering with the promotion of this wholly necessary and vital work, that I have no motive other than seeking to increase the public good of the planet and our global society, through advancing international trade, encouraging the development of the new global citizen, relieving the plight of the proliferating poor and others incapable of providing themselves with the basic commodities of modern living, and naturally affording an upsurge in pleasure to the rich and other resource owners. I have no dependants from I could profit in any way, am myself of a meagre BMI of 18.5 and must therefore sadly forego offering my own flesh to the benefit of society, nor am I of a status commensurate with successful child-bearing.

Igo Wodan, July 2014

The Glibread Affair

FOREST GREN

Prologue

G libread T'Air (born July 4, 1955, died July 17, 2015) was assassinated in the small Zubrowskian town of Zardoszyce, sited on three borders and being as isolated as one would not wish, on the third day of its James Bond Festival. That, at least, is known to the public. It will no more shock my readers if I mention that his body was discovered inside the Zardoszyce Cold War Memorabilia Gallery and beside the exhibit showing the remains (and gruesome story) of civilian flight NACH71, a year earlier downed by a heat-seeking missile on the borders of Zubrowskia during its resistance against the rumoured invasion of a neighbouring superpower supporting ethnic separatists. The Festival's directors, agitated at his extended and unexplained lack of presence at the gala dinner to which he had been invited (and feted as the star attraction) were horrified to find him with an Ace of Hearts playing card blood-stuck to his forehead and a bullet hole through both.

Prior to the bizarre *mise-en-scène* of Glibread's death, which ensured an even greater level of fascination with his (now defunct) persona, he had already commanded an unprecedented notoriety amongst not only European and the global media circuses, but the intelligentsia and *vox populi* as well. Readers who disdain to bear witness to a retelling of the dramatic (if already dramatized on Fox, BBC, Eurochannel, Deutschewelle, RAI123, Métropole Télévision, Al Jazeera, CCTV, and the like) events of 'the Glibread Affair' should eschew this section and flip straight to page xx to be greeted by the first chapter. I am not insensitive to the peril (real or imagined) of extraneity, however, in my opinion, assuming what follows requires an appropriate frame of reference (and indeed is to be sited within it), a necessary and sufficient condition (as is the wont of mathematicians to opine— self-instructed or university-graduated), and notwithstanding the potential to bore a reader, necessitates the telling of not only Glibread T'Air's personal *histoire*, but the common knowledge of those happenings which resulted in the dreadful apogee of death in the Zubrowskian Central Lowlands. Brief as this summary must be, allow me to make amends before the fact, as did Cicero in a page of correspondence, for having taken too little time to diminish it.

Glibread T'Air entered the world via Bucharest, capital of then Soviet-controlled Rumania. (An hilarious joke ankle-bit him wherever he travelled: as a celebrity status writer, his parents had not only chosen the unfortunate name of 'glib read', but gifted him with a birth place, oh ho, of 'book arrest'. The broadsheets and dailies throughout the Continent rarely failed to create captivating cartoons linking both aspects of his name and his authorial success, to more or less public approval). But Glibread's mother, CEO of a fashion empire, was obscenely well-endowed (we are talking here, naturally, of funds), and more relevantly, insanely consequential to the jet set, so that Glibread, although having acquired the Queen's English from the time he could crawl, was not only fluent in any number of Eurozone languages, but coddled in the paparazzi-shy bosom of the international elite. Not for him the soul-destroying drudge of mailing manuscripts to publishing houses and harpy agents and waiting interminable lengths of time before the familiar letter of rejection (when or if at all) arrived by postcard (cost-cutting measures prior to the advent of the internet) to sever yet another artery of ill-advised hope: Glibread arrested the book world in its steps (and in its cups).

We met as undercover contemporaries at a language school in Paris, having graduated from the national intelligence academy of the *Direction Générale de la Securité Extérieure* (DGSE, the French secret service) one year apart (but little known is the fact that Glibread, in his apprentice year and posing as a lecturer in Humanities, was tossed out of Paris' most prestigious private university for indecent behaviour during a sting operation (incriminating Europe's incestuous business leaders, as he was later to describe them, caught engaging in (or peddling) underage prostitution—the Vatican was spared humiliation only because it allowed scrutiny of its hitherto secretive banking practices), and therefore repeated his apprentice year); he had been downgraded to a middling institution which I was infiltrating as a gay transvestite student (and let it be said that I passed my apprentice year with flying colours, since none of my seducees, male or female, ever determined my at-birth gender) for the purposes of investigating language fraud (in which words from one language are taught as if belonging to another, or worse, claimed as superior in origin (see, for example, Professor Igo Wodan's 2011 treatise *The Confusions of Confucius and the Polemics of Ptolemy Lagides: From Classical Chinese Analects to Graeco-Egyptian Aggression or How the West Was Won*) without reference to etymology), a topic of hot debate back-and-forth across the Channel and amongst *Les Pays-Bas*, and vocabulary-laundering.

To return to Glibread, at the end of that tumultuous year, it transpired he had penned *Shaded Marble*, a spy-thriller *roman a clef* detailing his exploits at both language school and elite university and told in a sly postmodern mix of first and third person, which earned him accolades across the EU including nomination for *Le Prix Goncourt* (suspected, by many pundits, of being a result of his mother's meddling) and a listing amongst Granta's Most Promising Novelists (entirely deserved, although it was rumoured he had little competition that round). A few short years later, during service to I was never quite sure whom, her Majesty or Sarkozy, or perhaps both, or neither, since it was whispered Glibread had dealings with both SITCEN and Mossad, he produced what most consider to have been his *magnum opus*, *La Femme Fatale de St Ives*, concerning a Dutch born aristocrat in her late twenties, who, after fleeing her brute of a husband and travelling alone to Cornwall for the summer, is compromised by a secret agent (after seducing her, he claims that he has uncovered her real identity as a German spy) thus forcing her to play courtesan and courier information about British and Allied naval movements and equipment storage at St Ives prior to D-Day.

A snap-shot scribbler brilliant only because of the maxim less is more, a Cocteau or a Poe, a Chekhov or an Adair, would have sculpted nothing other than a moonstone of a novella. Glibread, however, created from this brief but intriguing sketch a multi-personaed panorama, a Bayeux Tapestry scrolling, in the recent tradition established by the American writers of door-stopper tomes, a mammoth seven hundred pages: a 'searing condemnation', as one online book-site reviewer squeed, of the winner-takes-all mindset of twentieth century patriarchal imperialism. He was awarded, and anything else would have pre-empted an outrage, the Booker.

A quartet of novels followed (Glibread was a writer of leisure and a leisurely writer) during the next decade and a half: *A Delicate Addiction to Preliminary Principles*, about a straight-faced (and straight-laced (and in dire straits)) protagonist who, in the first chapter, opines "Nothing exists. Thus is it created." in an online video, and who, in the final scene, self-injects a syringe full of sodium thiopental, morphine, and lorazepam. To have called it morbidly self-absorbed would have been complimentary; it disenchanted all but his most faithful stalwarts, and far from Glibread being revered as a convert to the magical realism championed by Calvino and Borges, the book earned him the pejorative 'purple prosist'.

His second in the quartet, *Youth Wearing a Blond Wig*, was a forgettable return to the short form *a la Catcher in the Rye* (although it was optioned by a major Hollywood studio and in line to be filmed before the same studio filed for Chapter 711 insolvency). But like the Resurrection, his third novel catapulted him once more to the attention (spans perhaps abominably short) of readers and reviewers alike, without commensurate sales, lamented only by his long-suffering publisher. *Zigeuner*, a giddy précis verging on a quarter of a million words and focused on Rumania's post-industrialisation era, related the stories (some woven, some scattered) of a classroom-full of primary school students captured on film just after the end of WW1. The photograph is discovered fifty years later by the protagonist while desperately raiding his papers looking for evidence to prove his Rumanian citizenship to the Securitate, whose unwelcome devotion he has attracted for no clearly explained motive other than his ability to speak German and Hungarian. The exquisite craftsmanship (craftspersonship is ludicrous) was unmistakably Glibread in fine form and high style, and he was short-listed for the Booker, losing out to a Commonwealth country author whose moment of fame lasted only as long as the time necessary to fly home from London after the ceremony, as well as the *Berliner Kunstpreis* (*Literatur*), but was pipped at the post by Herta Müller. I admit to personal defeat, having attempted twice and failed in the endeavour of finishing the book, and I suspect even It Who Must Be Obeyed, omnipotent and omnipresent, would have let it slip from benumbed fingers and bemused omniscience before perusing the final page.

Silence ensued on the writing front, although Glibread's private life was an open book: holidaying on the French Riviera with a series of passionately embraced and as quickly discarded flames (the gossip glossies included Véronique Sanson and Roberto Benigni amongst celebrities who hosted him at their private mansions on Corsica and Sardegna), photographed smooching Boy George one week, Sade the next, and Elton the third—Glibread never shied from celebrating his bisexuality, divulged in the notorious opening sentence of *Shaded Marble*: "I have always pitied any individual, male or female, who wasn't bi."—when not lambasting the progressively regressive policies of the British government in *The Observer*, Berlusconi's idiocy in *La Repubblica*, praising Angela Merkel in *Der Spiegel*, and lamenting the decline of French *haute cuisine* (and the increase in French waistlines) in *Paris Match*. It was, naturally, all a front, a disguise as international playboy when in actuality he was ferreting out facts about arms shipments from the US to Israel, trafficking in human and animal body parts between China, Africa, and the US, Mafia-run child pornography and prostitution in Europe and Asia, and international funding of terrorist groups through FTSE 100, Fortune 100, and DAX listed companies.

Precisely just as Glibread had begun to fade from literati view, if not that of *hoi* tabloid-scanning *polloi*, he published, as if from thin air, the novel that metamorphosed his life and impelled it to its disastrous finale, *Out of Thin Air*. While more trees have fallen in service to print the words spouted about it than were ever required to fulfil its own print-run, and terabytes of server space have been swamped with online commentary, it still behoves us to resist the mad dash through this familiar terrain and orienteer our course slowly, with eyes peeled, in order to apprehend the events that occurred and what has yet to occur in this memoir.

Although the book was marketed as fiction, not even the most naïve of readers could have failed to note that it was a thinly veiled assortment of long-winded, pedestrian, at times almost incoherent, compositions better titled *Life According to Glibread*. This prompted a not unexpected outcry, particularly acute given the dust-jacket image —by then almost banal for its splatter-bomb repetition amongst the media—of a fighter plane bursting through an euro-haloed sound barrier and dispersing thousands of banknotes in the atmosphere, much like a run-amok trader precipitating the downfall of a famous old world bank. But what no-one could have predicted, least of all I, and given his penchant for trenchant *laissez-faire* and *l'art de vivre*, was the savage bellicosity of his anti-Eurozone stance, not just Brussels but the entire continent, acquired territories, islands, and miscellaneous principalities external to the political behemoth it has become. Since it would be monotonous for me to echo Glibread's tirade (and preposterous in the extreme: he had a Wildean flair for scathing casuistry and as is ably demonstrated, a skill I am sadly (or perhaps happily) lacking), I shall merely refresh the reader's memory with respect to the rhetorical highlights of *Out of Thin Air*.

The initial sally, concerning plebeian tastes, was pithily titled 'Helen Had a Gas', a bilingual pun on the popular French sitcom 'Hélène et les Garcons', which Glibread delighted in faintly despising, and served no purpose other than to launch an attack on multicultural films espousing the joys of an integrated Europe, such as the trilogy of Cédric Klapisch (*L'Auberge Espagnole*, *Les Poupées Russes*, *Casse-Tête Chinois*), a "fatally flawed trio of films about desperately seeking Eurozone Europhiles fornicating their way through Erasmus and beyond", or of one art-house film director famous for bad moods and hairdos, "H is a cunt and his films mimic what cunts excrete. They bloodstain the screen."

The second rumination, 'The Analytics of EU Cretinism', created even more of an uproar. Glibread seduced his audience with a deceptively simple thesis proving Europeans to be as mindless as they accused their American counterparts. "Pay attention to the fact that in 1952, 50% of the EU's current population resided in Italy, France, and Germany, making up half of the founding member states of the European Communities. By 2004, some twelve years after the ratification of the European Union via the Maastricht Treaty, these three countries still dominated Euro politics, despite the presence of the UK, which refused to join the common currency of the Euro (*Caeuro*, *Cheuro*, or *Teuro*, as it was not affectionately known by the populaces of Italy, France and Germany respectively) preferring to retain its financial insularity. Keep in mind that pundits had predicted the integration of weaker economies would wreak havoc with the stability of the newly articulated currency, not to mention the security headache of distributing upwards of 600 billion in notes and coins (with the inevitable robberies—one security guard even looted his own van). *Et voilà*, Greece revealed at the end of 2004 it had cooked the books. The significance being that almost 400 000 000 inhabitants happily voted in the national leaders who sold their savings (and taxes) up the river to bail out the Greek economy. It should come as no surprise given Italy has voted the same white-collar criminal to represent and govern it three times, nor that France chose a President who has repeatedly financed his party wins with cash whose origin is as dubious as any laundered. As to the other 50% of the EU population? They can't or don't vote. Ergo, 100% of the population who did are simply asinine (which is as much as can be said for Americans, having voted in Bush twice, the second time being the same year Greece admitted its dishonesty)."

Without expounding much further, having already stated that the remaining essays continue in the same missile-launching fashion, allow me to summarise by noting that Glibread methodically denounced the malevolent autocracy of EU amalgamation and acquisition policy, the unruliness of its political-financial foundation, the assimilation (read eradication) of innumerable cultural treaties, the inherent ethnocentricity of the Eurozone's intellectually privileged as evidenced in the popular press, literature, and arts with every second title including the word 'Europe' or 'European' or some linguistic derivative thereof (*Europa Europa, Rue de L'Europe, Europe in the 21$_{st}$ Century, Verloren in Europa, Un Lupo Mannaro Europeo a Beijing, A European Anarchist* (an oxymoron if ever there were one), the universality of solicitors and storytellers (of all persuasions), and so on and so forth.

To the real meat of the corpus, however, the ultimate essay, whose title is preordained by that of the book: *Out of Thin Air*.

I must mention here that Glibread deliberated over two headings for the article: 'The Gate Crash', a sly twist on J. K. Galbraith's excellent chronicle of the genesis of the 1929 Wall Street debacle, and 'Small Losses in the Eurozone—Not Many Defaults' in a dare to pen the most tedious tagline possible for *The Economist*. His editor threw an apoplectic fit but Glibread prevailed; neither heading was excised from its relevant paragraph, and, as he opined later, "Cast away virtue before unspeakable crime, for unspeakable crime characterises all past and future human existence."

In 'Out of Thin Air' Glibread contends, death-wish fascination aside (how we have bloated ourselves on the stills and videos of economic crisis suicides since the first forlorn and frustrated pensioner shot himself in front of the Greek parliament), and excluding the indisputable and, as Glibread accedes, to-be-expected jolt to the bellies of Eurozone citizens and their dependency on their weak-willed politicians, a jolt he likens not to that of the collapse of the Bretton Woods system or the oil crisis, but to the destruction of the nuclear reactor at Chernobyl and the subsequent extinguishing of the smug belief that nuclear power presented the eternal and limitless fountain of energy required to fuel the ever-expanding demand for it, that the sovereign debt disaster, from the haughtiest of perspectives—this, I repeat—belongs to Glibread, "is a rather insignificant catastrophe, featuring only a handful of negligent policy-makers and ruining a few institutional hedge funds and bankers, while leaving most of Europe's corporate class unscathed and the largest economies operating business as usual."

He ends the paragraph with the ignominious: "When all is said and done, it's only a Eurozone storm-in-a-tea cup. Austerity measures would be the lap of luxury for any other non G20 country (the majority of the world's population); the real catastrophe is how little Europeans realise how well they are off."

The essay, in a nutshell, was a specious attempt to incite an imbroglio. Irretrievably incendiary, it might have been copied from the columns of *The Daily Mail*, so lacking was it in logic or complexity. However, and no doubt an anti-climax for Glibread, no fracas ensued: outside a slavering review from a fawning Glibreader, his collection attracted nothing more from the UK press than commentary on his unfettered grandiloquence. But its rhetoric registered with those same *Daily Mail* readers and the book sky-rocketed to the top of the best-seller lists. The title essay appeared some scant weeks later in the *London Review of Books*.

On the other side of the channel, however, a furore had already begun brewing.

Glibread's Continental publishers disdained any interest in *Out of Thin Air*. But untranslated, it was readily available as a digital download and in print form via all the major online providers, and had soon 'gone viral' with unsolicited (and unofficial) translations abounding. Within mere days, a torrent of media items flooded the usual channels, spearheaded by an uncharacteristically caustic piece in *Das Handelsblatt* and a typically bilious attack in *Le Figaro*. Within weeks all principal Continental dailies had run articles and cable stations were devoting air time to dissecting the possible repercussions for the already sour pound-euro relationship. Suddenly, the masses were maddened and baying for blood. A triumvirate delegation from Germany, France, and Italy met with Catherine Ashton as the UK representative tasked with an EU role (ironically that of EU security given Glibread's day time profession) to demand economic sanctions. Downing Street responded with a slew of retaliatory measures until enough oratory flatulence had been exchanged that the matter evaporated.

Not, as it happened, before cyberspace, like hyperspace, exponentially inflated the event and the Internet almost choked its servers with rumours running rife as to Glibread's real intent. Some months later, after the tumult had dwindled but echoes still reverberated, one particular website seemed to become the repository for any and everything related to 'the Glibread Affair'. The site, Europe Unchained, claimed no allegiance to any one individual or group, but by dint of some vigilant digging, its origins could be traced to a panel of Bilderberg Group activists (admittedly using tools of the trade funded by the very same Bilderberg members, albeit without their knowledge, or let it be acknowledged, agreement had it been asked of them) with an address given as Drama, Greece. I created an automated monitor of the site and had all but forgotten its existence when its pages flickered alive with unexpected action (both in volume and content).

Cyber is nothing if not cipher space and that was now what riveted my attention on Europe Unchained. The website previously contained cryptic clues and hidden instructions, revealed by switching columns of text with rows, or clicking "View Page Source" and searching for purple programming language (always bracketed and clearly nothing in the slightest related to coding a web page) that when rearranged provided perfectly legible directions on any other number of otherwise dubious financial activities, including stock market manipulation, real estate opportunities in politically stable economies whose governments advertised their disinterest in tracking the source of purchase funds (Singapore is notorious for developments in which entire buildings are bought off-plan by overseas investors shedding corruption money), and tips and tricks for motivational speakers (Jordan Belfort had been cited as a prime example of how to win hearts and befuddle minds). While these resulted in a fairly stable pattern of surge and recession of site traffic, the latest spike exceeded all prior highs. A cursory examination would have shown even the most inept of virtual pirates that the application of tangrammatic principles uncovered the alarming:

Fifty million
Euros to whomever
Unites Glibread T'Air with
Death

Fifty million euros! Every single mercenary and wanna-be gun-for-hire within cooee of an optic fibre cable must have visited the site to generate the unprecedented statistics, the proof of which occurred not long after in the form of a concurrent unseasonal influx of the most unlikely tourists via Heathrow (London Airports Corporation reported a multiple of higher than expected earnings for that month, only matched by revenues accumulated during the Salmon Rushdie incident) and a heart-stopping rise in the number of weapons confiscated (implying an even higher number were not, since the easiest way to disguise an apple is hide it amongst others).

The next event is known to everyone: Glibread vanished from the literary and public gaze, chaperoned over a period of days prolonged to weeks, weeks to months, months to years, from one place of hiding to the next. He was, despite suffering what must have been a terminal desolation and isolated from the limelight to which he had been accustomed almost since birth, neither desperate nor separate. Discreetly at first and for a very long while thereafter, he would appear accompanied (always by two brawny bounders bedecked in black and stationed at an establishment's entrances like Scylla and Charybdis) at dinners in Chelsea or Mayfair, at a gala event in the West End, or for a session at a Writer's Festival. It was at the Edinburgh that his publishers announced the release of an espionage thriller penned in exile: *A Trustworthy Tale-Teller*.

The book defies classification (and has been the catalyst for many a critic proving her or himself a laughing stock in the attempt to do so) and I refrain from that temptation here. It commences with a prologue more fitting as the epilogue of an Agatha Christie or a Le Carré remaining unwritten, thereby disorienting the reader from the moment of encountering the page one finale. Treason is evident, the betrayer incarcerated, except, as the reader begins to discern, the judiciary system has failed horribly. The actual perpetrator (*A Trustworthy Tale-Teller* is a first-person narrative) has successfully transposed responsibility and punishment for the crimes against state committed, and in order to remain 'at large', is also bound to a secrecy of his own making, thus foregoing the notoriety such an act would have generated (and did for the agent falsely convicted). The tale-teller starts a dud, and deprived of the celebrity status his actual due, stays a dud.

Hell hath no fury like a villain scorned. A canker devouring his organs, his vexation tortures him until he shrieks his blameworthiness to all and sundry, who, if bothering to notice him at all, relegate him to the ranks of reality show attention-seeker. His only audience is, naturally, the all-knowing reader. Glibread's tale-teller, in a flawless rebuttal of postmodernism's most abused chestnut, is a slickly reliable narrator who sustains disbelief.

A Trustworthy Tale-Teller garnered reviews for which many writers would kill, unquestionably explaining why Glibread was an invitee of Zardoszyce's inaugural James Bond Festival (though why he consented to participate begs investigation), and is the point of departure for my appearance in his story.

Chapter X

By high tea I was famished and in need of refreshment, having spotted none of the other Festival attendees, nor, and I remained ambivalent as to the desirability of the occurrence, having crossed Daveen's path, though I chanced upon, seated at the main square's café, some sleazy-looking members of the British gutter press still loitering in Zardoszyce with intent to nab a murder story. I returned to the hotel and entered the bar, where Daveen, sleek-haired and kittenish as always, decorated one of the over-stuffed lounge chairs in a small and inviting alcove. She signalled me and I faced no choice other than that of joining her.

"The usual?" She beckoned a waiter as I nodded an unwillingly grateful assent, settling myself in the chair opposite. Her legs were a distraction I would have preferred to avoid, with little success (somehow describing her incredible sensuality never had the same disturbing effect as experiencing it in the flesh). Why does whichever intelligence or coincidence that governs the stars in our skies lavish such catastrophic pulchritude on some individuals and not on others? I sipped the double brandy offered me by the waiter and nibbled from a bowl of nuts while I watched her stir an olive round her martini (I admit, dear reader, I had messed up with having Daveen knock down daiquiris for my fictionalised version of her). In the far niche of the bar a Billy Joel look-a-like was strumming variations of Billy Joel tunes on a guitar.

"So, *Feresht*," she raised her glass, her Persian pronunciation of my name never failing to run shivers along my spine, "up your kilt."

I shied away from the thought that automatically entered my brain even as my eyes automatically slid over the gap between her skirt and her knees. "Cheers, Daveen."

We swallowed and I set down my glass. "How was your day?"

"Edifying. Yours?"

"*Au contraire*. I'm afraid I've nothing to contribute as far as investigating Glibread's death goes. I did find a nice *chocolatier*." I picked up the package lying at my feet and extracted the exquisitely gift-wrapped box of pralines I had bought. "I couldn't resist. These are for you."

"Tempting, *Feresht*." She lifted the chocolates to her nose and sniffed. "Cardamom and marzipan. My favourite."

"Tell me, did you discover anything?" I buried my nose in my glass of brandy.

"Discover anything? *Aziz-am*, I discovered *everything*."

"You don't say?" I wanted to sound cynical and instead sounded squeaky.

"I do." She swizzle-sticked another olive in her martini before poking it between her lips, the movement riveting my attention.

"So you've identified the killer?"

She bit the olive with her excessively white and evenly shaped teeth and chewed. "I have."

"Daveen, for heaven's sake," I leant forward before I could stop the gesture and grasped her wrist. "Who?"

She smiled and shook my hand away. I anticipated now that she would, as do all imaginary spies, sleuths, and others of that ilk, at the behest, of course, of their scheming writers, refuse to reveal any details and instead follow the formulaic tautening of tension, proclaiming, as I write her doing in *A Spry Defection*, 'were I to simply state the denouement, it would be no different to severing the Gordian knot rather than unravelling it, thus preventing the invaluable experience of learning how to piece together the puzzle and tease out a unique solution.'

Instead she swiped my nose like a cat and leaned back in her chair, naming a name.

Reverso.

"So you've identified the killer?"

She bit the olive with her excessively white and evenly shaped teeth and chewed. "I have."

"Daveen, for heaven's sake," I leant forward before I could stop the gesture and grasped her wrist. "Who?"

"You, *Feresht*."

"What?" My glass plonked loudly against the table. "Have you lost the plot?" To denounce one's creator of the murder of the creator's friend—had this ever in the history of exploratory literature occurred? Lawrence Durrell had suicided his journalistic-hack self in favour of his literary-pretensions self in *The Alexandria Quartet*, and repeated a similar stunt with each of his characters begetting the one before the other in *The Avignon Quintet*. Had Daveen conceived me?

Reverso.

"So you've identified the killer?"

She bit the olive with her excessively white and evenly shaped teeth and chewed. "I have."

"Daveen, for heaven's sake," I leant forward before I could stop the gesture and grasped her wrist. "Who?"

"You, *Feresht*."

"What?" My glass plonked loudly against the table. "Have you lost the plot?"

"Not likely, since there never was one." She tilted her glass, draining it, and exposed a column of slender throat. "But I do think you may have."

"Daveen," I interjected (she raised her eyebrows and clicked her tongue), "what on earth are you saying? I'm Forest Gren, I'm a pleasant person. I don't upset too many people, generally speaking. Check my Facebook profile."

"*Feresht*, you don't have a Facebook profile, you're running top-secret Data Forensics when you're not pretending to run a press and dumping all the work on your long-suffering side-kick."

"Dumping all the—" I shook my finger at her. "Leave Mickles out of this."

"Are you shaking your finger at me?"

I looked at my finger and folded it under my thumb. "Daveen, stop changing the subject. How do you arrive at this preposterous conclusion?"

"With the bane of our writerly existences," she leaned towards me conspiratorially, "although as you would know if you bothered to read my books I never stoop so low as to employ such contrivances. Flukes of circumstance."

I wished, despite wishing I didn't, she would stoop a little lower, since her neckline was demurely high. That, however, was my own fault. I never made her outfits revealing. She was bombshell enough without the trappings of glimpsed flesh.

"*Feresht*, pay attention." She snapped her fingers and thumb. "What did you write on page xy of this book?"

"On page xy?" I frowned at her. "I don't remember what I wrote on page xy. You tell me, Daveen."

"You wrote: 'the easiest way to disguise an apple is hide it amongst others'. That's rather telling, isn't it?"

"How should I know? You're the one telling the story here."

She patted my thigh and naturally sparks shot along it to my groin. I groaned. The last thing we needed here was a physical interlude. "What happens, *Feresht*," she squeezed my thigh gently, "when there are no other apples?"

"You'd best eat the one you have?" My stomach rumbled loudly.

"*Aziz-am*, shall we order something?" She nodded at the bartender, who approached with the bistro cards.

I shook my head. "The nuts are fine." I crammed a handful in my mouth and stoically chewed.

"It occurred to me, the more I thought about it, that all the fuss concerning *Out of Thin Air* just couldn't possibly constitute enough motive for murder."

"Of course not," I interjected (this time she stamped her foot and rolled her eyes), "it's quite clear it's internationally motivated. It will have been an agent from a foreign secret service simply acting on orders."

She smiled at me with tangible pity (don't shoot the scribbler, I'm merely recording the scene) in her eyes, tugging on her shell-perfect ear with the endearing gesture I had given her. "The more my ear twitched, *Feresht*, the more I realised that was so much smoke and mirrors. Humans might have scrambled out of the Stone Age as far as intelligence goes, but emotionally we're still troglodytes. We act out our crimes of passion from exactly the same motives our forebears did."

I relaxed back in my chair, cradling my empty glass. "Go on."

She slid her pumps from her feet and folded her legs under her, an Eva Green in *Casino Royale* (I have always imagined Daveen playing Vesper Lynd), and continued. "Realising that Europe Unchained was nothing so much as an outrageous catch of cured kippers, I scuttled my previous notions and undertook a little forensics of my own."

"Forensics? You?" I snorted.

"Don't snort. It doesn't become you." Daveen lifted her martini glass towards the bar and the waiter immediately prepared refills. "And while you haven't exactly reiterated my cyber skills, I do possess them, just as I do life outside your books. So after I finished my morning run, I sat in the bath with my breakfast and my laptop and my privacy and surfed." She speared an olive and dunked it in the fresh martini the waiter placed on the table. "That house of charades had been erected with uncommon craftiness. I almost missed the one clue."

"The one clue?"

"The lucidity signature, *Feresht*. Only one person could have constructed such a complex system of logic, potential scenarios, and iterative decision-tree loops. Only one person had the BAT, *Feresht*."

"The bat? What bat? A cricket bat?" The situation was becoming surreal.

Daveen pursed her perfect lips and *tsked*. "The Background, Access, Training. You didn't have any other apples, so you created them. You put together the Europe Unchained website, you concocted all those bits of anti-Glibread propaganda and funnelled those around the 'net until the bytes arrived back at Europe Unchained, along with all the death-infatuated desperadoes determined to benefit from a bounty."

I circled the rim of my glass and it sang softly.

"What a brilliant idea." Her voice was dreamy. "How seductive it must have been, those manufactured murderers providing you with an alibi if they failed to bump him off and you had to take matters in your own hands." She glanced at her fingernails and sighed. "How you must have loathed him, *Feresht*."

I blinked in an exaggerated fashion. "You're forgetting the Bilderberg Group, Daveen. If Europe Unchained is a figment of my own devising, the Bilderberg Group would have certainly released a press statement."

Daveen tossed her hair over her shoulders and burst out with wild laughter. Several heads turned. She finally put her fingers to her lips, her shoulders shaking as she hiccoughed. Her accusation notwithstanding, I could not help but note how gorgeous she looked, my writerly eye mentally filing away descriptions of her every delightful action.

"*Aziz-am*, the Bilderberg Group doesn't release statements about *anything*! And in any case, the death of Glibread was hardly likely to trouble them. Oh no, they weren't any kind of issue for you."

"And what, for the sake of argument and in your inestimable opinion, was?"

"Not what, but who?"

"Who?"

"*Feresht*, will you stop echoing me like a badly trained parrot? At least consider your readers."

I wanted to say 'damn my readers' and for obvious reasons did not. "Will you reveal the identity of my issue? And I don't mean unborn children."

"The only person who, apart from Glibread, has haunted you all these years."

The muscles of my stomach clenched and I swigged an overly large mouthful of brandy. "Haunted?"

"Will you—"

"Get on with it, dammit!"

"Your other creation. Me. You can't hide your innermost thoughts from me."

"I bloody well can!" I stared at the ceiling and recited the Japanese *hiragana* table backwards.

"I'm hardly talking about fantasies, *Feresht*." Her fingernails scored lines down my shirt sleeve and I felt deliciously lacerated. "I mean that distinctive, unmistakable, style of yours, that pattern of sentence structure, that whimsical ability to play with words. Puns, for example."

"Yes, indeed. For example?" I cocked an eyebrow at her and promptly wished I had used a different verb.

"Drama, Greece."

"Dram—alright!" She had put her index fingers in her ears. "What in particular about that place? It's picturesque enough."

"Oh don't play the innocent! Olivia Newton-John and John Travolta —Grease!"

I angled my brandy to refract the overhead halogen spotlight, admiring the warm amber hue. "Actually I had in mind that the whole drama of the fiscal fiasco unfolded first in Greece and it's all been greased over since then."

She exhaled audibly. "Everything you've written has been a pack of lies, *Feresht*. So much sand in the eye, literary devices designed to obscure meaning and mislead the reader. When you killed Glibread, you committed not just a crime against him but a crime against the whole genre of espionage thrillers and mysteries and its devoted readers. 'The criminal must be someone mentioned in the early part of the story, but must not be anyone whose thoughts the reader has been allowed to follow.' Remember?" She dipped her chin and stared up at me, coquette and school mistress in one.

"Ronald Knox' 'Ten Commandments'."

"Precisely. Unpardonable! How anyone can think you are a pleasant person after such skulduggery!" She waved her hands in the air as if releasing doves.

I yawned. "Is this going to take much longer, Daveen?"

"I suggest we go in for dinner."

"No, I suggest you hurry it up before the others arrive. They might not find this all quite so entertaining. Even if you aren't blonde."

"You really are the limit." Neither the sneer nor her words did anything to diminish her appeal.

"Oh very well, let's sit on the terrace and share some *tapas*." I gulped the rest of my brandy; she had already tossed back the last of her martini. Whatever else, Daveen could hold her alcohol as well as Marion Ravenwood, while still looking infinitely ravishing. She stood and I followed her to the outside terrace, my eyes glued to the curves displayed by her form-fitting dress. She simply became ever more stunning in each novel featuring her.

The waiter set our table and laid out a selection of cold cuts, cheeses, marinated vegetables, and bread.

"What bothered me," she selected a *bocconcino*, "was how you'd carried out the killing, *Feresht*. And the only way I could figure that was via access to the scene of the crime, off-limits until our man from Interpol showed up."

"Oh yes, the Belgian chap. Rather unfriendly, I recall." I chewed a chicken wing.

"To you, perhaps." She shrugged. "But it turned out he knew all about my Agent Falk series and was perfectly happy to grant me entry to the Gallery."

"If I say that blessed with a face and figure like yours—OUCH!" She had kicked me in the shins under the table. "Well, admit you have a way of wrapping officialdom around your finger. Remember the *questore* in *A Venetian Courier*?"

"Yes. He was so charming. A pity."

"What do you mean?"

"Didn't you hear? At least via your old colleagues?"

"Hear what?"

"He was found hanged Mafia-style—upside down with his feet tied to his neck. Gruesome. It was in all the papers."

"All which papers?"

"Not that one you're always reading, of course. The Interpol agent was shocked—"

"The Interpol agent? Daveen, the *questore* was a *character in my book*! You really are losing your grip on reality."

"Oh no, *Feresht*," she smirked, her voice smooth. "It's your grip that's losing."

I harrumphed. "Back to the Gallery. What did you find out?"

"The Gallery? I must say the James Bond paraphernalia is quite marvellous. The original Aston. And those gadgets that always used to rescue him in the nick of time—"

"When those gadgets worked, that—."

"You're interjecting!" She interjected just as I was about to write 'I interjected.' "Can you not just write that you've grimaced with a rather sceptical look on your face?"

"What else captured your attention?" I proffered a prawn and she rejected it hastily.

"Don't you remember I'm allergic to seafood?"

"So you are," I rubbed the side of my nose, "so you are."

"It's a bit late now for more red herrings, *Feresht*."

"Well if you would kindly continue *edifying* me, please?" I thumped the table and the cutlery rattled.

"I examined all the different artefacts very closely. I even," and here she giggled fetchingly, "undressed the Bond statue."

"I'm sure that was revealing."

She sniffed. "Fleming obviously thought Bond needed some decent equipment."

"Besides Eggs Benedict, shaken martinis, and Q, of course."

"The Walther PPK gun was missing, logically, since the fingerprint squad would have been checking it. A waste of time because," she held up an index finger, "first, you'd never have been so obvious as to leave your prints," she extended her middle finger, "and second, that wasn't the gun used to shoot Glibread."

"As though there were several lying around?"

"There were, as it happens, given how many writers have been shoe-horned in to continue the Bond stories," she wagged her finger, "and don't pretend you don't know that. But none with bullets, and you can't commit murder without ammunition."

"It doesn't grow on trees, true."

"More importantly, you couldn't have cleared airport security carrying it. Which posed something of an enigma until I chanced upon a book in that dreadful plane crash exhibit. How it survived a ground-to-air missile I can't fathom."

"Let's leave the physics aside. What book was it, Daveen?"

"*From Russia With Love.*"

"Yes, I concede that particular title surviving, under the circumstances, heavily ironic." I quartered an artichoke and contemplated its succulence. "But I don't see the connection."

"Your modesty ill-becomes you, *Feresht*." She leaned back in the wicker chair, one hand resting on her abdomen, the other languidly toying with her martini glass stem. "Very well. Bond and Donovan Grant are travelling on the Orient Express and as the train enters the Simplon tunnel, Bond secrets his cigarette case inside his copy of Eric Ambler's *The Mask of Dimitrios* just as Grant shoots him. The cigarette case takes the bullet."

"Flukes of convenience, indeed."

"So I went back to the *From Russia With Love* corner and guess what I found?"

"I couldn't, really." I poured us some water, my mouth inexplicably dry.

"The cigarette case used to stop the bullet. Minus the bullet."

"And what, pray tell, is that supposed to prove?"

"The bullet that Grant fired was a special kind. He used a .25 electric gun which he had hidden inside Tolstoy's *War and Peace*."

"Oh dear. To be expected I suppose."

"Politics aside, *Feresht*, that was the clue I needed."

"How so?"

"I simply went looking for Grant's gun. And found it. Freshly fired.

That stunt with the Ace of Hearts on Glibread's forehead was just a decoy. *Casino Royale* has always been your favourite amongst Fleming's works and you couldn't resist making that book look as though it were somehow interwoven." She touched an invisible *chapeau* and tipped it.

"Oh piffle Daveen. This is all so much tosh." I threw my serviette across the remains of my repast.

"Is it? Shall we wait and see what make of bullet is extracted from poor Glibread's brain?" She placed her cutlery neatly across her plate.

"As if anyone would have been silly enough to leave a cigarette case with a bullet embedded in it lying around a Festival Glibread was attending?"

"When only the impossible remains, inspect the improbable, *Feresht*."

"Don't you start quoting fictional characters at me, Daveen. That really is beyond the pale!" I eased the collar of my shirt around my neck. The night air was still and unbearably close.

"You're exclaiming, you know. It's just not done these days."

"You haven't explained how Glibread was here in the first place," I muttered crossly.

"Oh that?" She blushed and looked over the terrace towards the floodlit trunks of the hotel's massive fir trees. "I asked the organisers who had invited Glibread. They told me he decided to attend after they sent him the guest list."

"Really? And how have I engineered Glibread suddenly taking it into his head to participate in this Festival after reading the guest list?" I injected as much derision in my tone as possible.

"Apparently you suggested sending the guest list to him, *Feresht*. You knew a certain name on it would draw him like a moth to a flame."

Not a breath of breeze stirred the trees. Even the cicadas had ceased their incessant chirruping.

"Shall we go for a drive, Daveen?"

"I thought you'd never ask." She waited for me to ease back her chair before standing and smoothing the folds of her skirt across her hips. I signed the bill and she gave the waiter the box of chocolates for safekeeping. "Your arm, if you please, *Feresht*. At least let's go out in style."

Epilogue

Thus we arrive at the confluence of all strands.

We exited via the mediaeval gate at the north of the town and drove along a secondary road hugging the river, at times reflected with an oily, moonlit sheen, at others obscured by dense groves of forest. Eventually I selected a gravel road signposted for a picnic area. It was deserted. I parked the car and assisted Daveen from her seat, her touch producing annoying (and embarrassing, because of course she knew) tremors of excitement. She refused to release my arm and walked in synchronisation beside me, her thighs and hips pressed momentarily against mine, towards an ill-lit path leading to the river.

We strolled through the dark and silent forest like a couple of characters from a Hitchcock film, estranged and yet united, the only sounds that of twigs snapping underfoot, until we neared the river, its movement muted yet palpable. Somewhere a nightingale tweeted, answered by another on the opposite bank. We stopped at a picnic bench and table close to the waters' edge, along which pebbles, small and large, gleamed a dull grey in the moonlight.

"You seem remarkably calm for someone claiming me murderer." I reached inside a jacket pocket and pulled out a battered packet of Gauloises and a lighter, offering her both.

"Well, if we were standing atop the Reichenbach Falls and I had nowhere to run but over a cliff, I might be worried." She raised the cigarette to her lips. "Conan Doyle tried it with Sherlock and that proved pointless." She flicked the lighter twice before sighing exasperatedly. "You're not still carting an unfilled lighter around as prevention against smoking, are you?"

"Evidently." I took back the lighter and slid a cigarette, unlit, between my lips.

"Oh here." She unclipped her small black handbag and withdrew a box of matches, striking one and lighting her own before cupping the match to my face. I inhaled deeply. She seemed satisfyingly oblivious to any threat I posed, if she believed that Conan Doyle had truly needed the Falls to dispose of the millstone round his neck that the character of Holmes had become.

"I don't recall having you smoke in any of my novels." I thrust a hand in my trouser pocket and rested against the edge of the picnic table, surveying the swirling waters. The centre of the river was almost unmoving, indicating a depth of some consequence.

"I don't recall giving you discretion as to what I do outside your novels." She blew an insouciant smoke-stream directly in my face, her head tilted to one side. "You've taken unforgivable liberties with me."

"Really? I would say I've been the height of ethical and respectful. I haven't had you jumping in and out of bed with every Tom, Dick, or Harry, or had you pawed or compromised or, worst of all, raped."

"And there, *Feresht*, right there, you demonstrate just what a chauvinistic bastard you really are."

I gasped. I had never heard Daveen use such language. "First a murderer, now a chauvinistic bastard? Maybe I should take a leaf out of Conan Doyle's book." I grabbed her wrist abruptly and she squealed, tugging away. I released her and attended to my cigarette. "You've spun me a tale about how I'm supposed to have topped Glibread. Care to elaborate on my further shortcomings as an author?"

"You just said you've been respectful *by not* having me choose multiple partners. Ergo, were I to have a boy in every port, I'd be worthy of disrespect. How ethical is it for you to have your principal male characters always graced with more women than hot dinners and never the other way round?"

"Well the one is good for both, you know." I ducked as she aimed a wild punch at my shoulder. "Oh come now, Daveen, that was a joke."

"Admit it, *Feresht*, you're applying double standards, for all you and Glibread boast you're bisexual and completely free of social mores and constraints. Look at me, *Feresht*. You made me so beautiful I've had more offers than a porcupine has quills and yet not once, not one bloody damn once, do I ever end up pricked with one!"

"Calm yourself. That was an exclamation." I ground my cigarette butt underfoot and allowed myself to drape a friendly arm about her shoulders. We had never, not in all the time I had known her, enjoyed such an intimate and intended proximity. For all her air of *savoir faire*, she still had not guessed my real reason for proscribing her any dalliances.

"Calm myself? You never once describe my intelligence, *Feresht*. Why do I always bring home the bacon in your books? Because I'm the super sexy secret agent that outsmarts the enemy by being a bimbo! It's positively appalling in this day and age."

"I've never written you weren't intelligent, Daveen. But the public wants—"

"The public wants? The public WANTS?" She stamped her foot.

"This isn't probably the best time to remind you, but you are rather starting to sound like a broken record."

"Oooohhhh!" She twisted away from me and I lunged after her, catching her by her hair. "Ouch. Let go, *Feresht*."

I dropped my hands. "Look Daveen, you're a free agent. Outside the fictional world I create for you, you're in charge. I've never attempted to pry, to insert—"

"Yes, there's precious little insertion going on whenever Agent Daveen Astreid is active! Even my name is a disgrace. I'm just a punnet of puns in your book, a vehicular vagina flaunting your flair."

I winced. "Don't you think you could cut down a little on the alliteration?"

"*Feresht*, you're incorrigible. You're in love with your own literary lexicon and even with me as your ultimate heroine, writing in the one genre it's almost impossible not to enjoy some form of popularity and which you most blatantly lack, you just can't leave yourself out of the narrative. You couldn't write a decent linear plot-based novel if someone force-fed you the fabula and sandwiched you the syuzhet. Look at where this is going!"

I rested my hands behind my head and faced her. "Literary theory and postmodernist tricks aside, and yes you're just as guilty of them as I, where, Daveen, exactly is this going?"

"You brought me here to kill me, quite obviously," she dropped her gaze, her voice low, "since I know how you finished off Glibread. I suppose you'll suggest we go for a walk on the footbridge over there, and when we arrive in the middle, you'll make some excuse, and push me off. Correct?"

"Not quite." I reached for her limp fingers and tugged her along with me to the footbridge. We stopped at the centre of the span. "I'd need a rather large lump of something heavy to weight your body, and as you can see, I don't have anything to hand."

"Moriarty was all the weight Conan Doyle needed." She stared across the river and I stared at her face and her body and was intoxicated with the smell of her. "You killed Glibread because you were jealous, weren't you? You knew he was seeing me, was interested, wanted to create a whole new series based on me, wanted me to have my own relationships, real blood, sweat, and tears interactions with multiple orgasms and orgies and everything you've always withheld from me, the public adoration and fascination with a brilliant, rounded, multifaceted character."

"Stop it!" I clapped my hands to my ears and hunched over as if she had gouged me in the stomach. "Stop it, Daveen."

"Why, *Feresht*? Why? Couldn't you see how unhappy I was, how I was suffering under this imposition of impossible virtue, and for what purpose? And now you've killed Glibread, how long until another writer comes along and realises my potential to be more than just an airhead? To make me valued for my true qualities, to create a whole generation of new fans. Glibread even promised to make me ugly!"

I leaned on the railing and covered her hands with my own. "Daveen, how could I let you have relationships? Haven't you realised? Are you really so blind? I've been in love with you ever since we met!"

She recoiled, a look of horror marring her features. "But you can't be. That's incestuous. And fatuous. How on earth could you love a character with no more dimensions than her hip-bust-waist ratio? That's not real love, *Feresht*, that's make-believe."

I clasped her hands and pulled her, resisting, against my chest. "Oh but Daveen, I do love you. You have no idea. I dream of you, I hunger for you. I thirst for you." She struggled to escape and I held her tightly. "Don't fight it, I've waited so long to tell you, Daveen. Of course I had to get rid of that bloody Glibread with his ridiculously clever storylines and his ingenious imagination. He was stealing you away from me."

"But *Feresht*, you don't understand." She stopped squirming and pushed back from me slightly, her voice mocking. "I'll never love you. You . . . you're short, you're fat, you don't do any exercise, your hair is falling out, and what isn't smells of grease and is turning grey, your clothes are always creased, your breath is foul, you eat meat and wear leather shoes, you're poor and you live in a bedsit in East London. Why would I fall in love with you?" She laughed and stepped away from my suddenly weakened embrace. "The only reason you're bisexual is to increase the likelihood of finding someone able to put up with you. Why would anyone fall in love with you, and then ask yourself, why I, who you made so devastatingly attractive and desirable, would want to saddle myself with a never-even-made-it like you?"

"Daveen, you can't mean this." I clutched at my heart. "You simply can't. I know we're meant to be together."

"The only way we'll ever be together, *aziz-am*, is if you put yourself in one of your stories with me. And I'll never agree to sleep with you."

"Oh yes, you will." I snatched her wrists and pinioned her with my weight against the railing. "I'll make you. I'll write that you fall completely, deeply, head over heels in love with me. I'll make you suffer for me, I'll make you beg for me, Daveen. And I'll make you forget you ever thought of anyone else." She arched away from me over the railing and I leaned further over her until we were bent double out across the waters. Somewhere, a strut creaked.

"Never," she hissed through clenched teeth. "I'll write you inside one of my Agent Falk books and have you captured and tortured by the North Koreans. I'll send you on a doomed space mission to the moon." Another strut creaked. "I'll have you emergency land inside an Ebola breakout zone. I'll make you a test subject for mind manipulation by the Bilderberg Group."

"Really?" My voice lost its pleading tone. "Then I'll just have to kill you." Gripping the far railing behind me, I slammed my fist down on the joint beside us that our combined weight had already overstrained and the railing snapped, the bars flying backwards. I heaved forwards against Daveen, lifting my knee to kick her, flailing and shrieking, backwards through the gap towards the water. She made a very small splash and her scream was silenced before I had even drawn another breath. Despite her fictional status as agent extraordinaire, in real life she couldn't swim.

I stood still some minutes, chest heaving, adrenaline coursing through my veins and causing my muscles to twitch involuntarily. I withdrew my packet of Gauloises, picked one, and took out a different lighter. The flame erupted as I flicked it open. Silly woman, for all her talk of percipience. As if I would have sincerely carried an empty lighter with me as a means to quit smoking. As idiotic as pocketing a roll of sweets and reaching for those each time the urge for a fag struck.

I sucked for a long moment on the cigarette, scanning the dark waters. Daveen's body would eventually surface, the question was only how far from this spot, who would find it, and how long before she was connected with the Festival. Long enough that I would have already boarded a flight back to London. Long enough, perhaps, that someone would link her name with mine and request an interview, always good publicity, and never bad for selling books. I rubbed my hands together, smiling.

The moon had faded behind passing clouds and I waited for its reappearance, glancing at my watch. We had been absent from the hotel almost an hour. For precaution's sake, I needed to create an alibi, and quickly. I jogged back along the footbridge towards the car and stopped, horrified at what greeted me sprawling across the bonnet.

I collapsed against a tree trunk some metres from Daveen, gloriously naked like a surreal Lamborghini advertisement (except the car in question was a late model nondescript Asian brand), and propped on her elbow, blowing smoke rings towards the moon.

"Hello Forest." Her voice was as sultry as her demeanour and oddly accentless. Her hair was charcoal streamed with silver, wafting of its own accord around her shoulders, and as she moved her limbs languorously to slither from the bonnet, she appeared haloed as if by moonshine, as though her body glowed, as though the rays of light somehow penetrated her.

I swallowed convulsively. "Daveen? Is . . . is that you?"

"The very same." She sauntered towards me. Her breasts were marvels of nature, her hips a bounty to plunder. She was a feast not only for the eyes but every other sense. I shivered uncontrollably.

"But. You're dead." I stepped back from this apparition of loveliness after which I had for so long lusted until I stumbled over the pebbles at the bank.

"Evidently not."

"You can't not be."

"Forest, you're such a fool. Of course I'm not dead. Look," she glided one step, "at," followed by another step, "me."

"Oh I'm looking," I gasped. "I can't help it. Even I never realised just how truly beautiful you are. But that doesn't stop you being dead."

She laughed, a hollow sound that curdled my blood. "Even now, even after you've committed not just one murder, but attempted a second, even after you've cheated and teased your readers, you still can't admit what you've made me. I'm a one dimensional character!" Her voice rose in a harpy screech. "I can't die, Forest. Lungs are three dimensional, remember?"

"What?"

"You're a cop-out, Forest." She stood now in front of me and I clenched my fists against the desire to touch her. "For all your so-called love of espionage and thrillers, you're nothing but a superior and snooty snob belittling those who write and read such books." She placed her hands on my chest, fiddling with a button, and slid her hands inside my shirt. "You've never bothered to give me any facets other than physical, you've only ever described me as if all any reader ever wants is a soft-porn scene without the climax." As she pronounced the word she pinched my nipple and I yelped. "You can't resist playing out your own juvenile fantasies and pretending it's 'what the public wants'. You've typecast me in the most vulgar fashion. Let me guess, Forest. Next you'll write about how I make you feel. You'll describe your physical sensations and what you want to do to me."

I resolutely recited the Japanese *katakana* table backwards.

"You even dared to compare me to other women, as if my sole dimension of beauty needed to be bolstered and validated against the appearances of others. How demeaning. As if women are simply just a collection of physical surfaces arraigned in some combination to please the eye of the beholder. And if someone criticised you for it, you brushed it aside as evidence of literary ineptitude at worst and naiveté at best, since you've styled yourself a pasticheur, and that's what pasticheurs do." She tweaked my nipple painfully again, but I was powerless to move.

"A bulletproof strategy, hmm?" She stepped behind me and now pressed herself against my back. I murmured *ichidan dōshi* furiously.

"Exceptional writing, and you claimed it. Crap, and it was the original. Very cute, Forest. And you make me out to be some sort of wet dream waiting to happen, except we both know I just fire blanks." She grabbed my crotch and massaged my genitals to prove her point. I remained utterly flaccid.

"Rough justice, darling, isn't it? How you've yearned to possess me and now, here I am, in all my blazing glory, having about as much effect as *Don Giovanni* on windmills. Which is why I can't die."

"Bullshit you can't die." I whipped around and grabbed her by the throat, only to find my hands pass straight through her. She kicked me unerringly where she could cause the most pain and I staggered back, clutching my scrotum and whimpering.

"Don't you dare, Forest. I have no qualms about inflicting all kinds of punishment upon you. You abused and manipulated me for long enough. Your two-bits of fame you owe to me. Forest Gren the pasticheur? Oh you make me laugh!" She danced away from me, howling hysterically, before turning back abruptly and kicking me again. I collapsed on my knees, almost retching with the agony. "You keep forgetting we're so far past postmodernism we don't even use the term anymore. It's hypermodernism now, Forest. Nobody even remembers what postmodernism is, that it even existed. It was such a miniscule blip on the literary radar screen, such an insignificant apostrophe to the end of the twentieth century, no-one cares an iota about it, or your books, or even you, Forest." She bent close to my ear and whispered, "I could kill you and no-one would notice."

"Why don't you?" I croaked.

"You'd love that, wouldn't you? Having the last laugh, ranked there with your postmodern superheroes Adair and Brooke-Rose, Calvino and Durrell, Eco and Federman, Gibson and Heller, Ionescu and Josipovici. But you failed there too, Forest. You've not only botched bumping me off, but I refuse to wipe you out of this dog's breakfast of a narrative. In fact, I rather think I'll start a new one, this time with me sitting in the computer seat, and you jerking to my strings." My arm twitched elbow first, windmilling for an instant and startling me to my feet.

"You can't stop me from wiping myself out of it, Daveen." I ran, like a confused marionette zigzagging across a stage, and dived headlong in the river, Daveen's voice receding as the waves received me in their cold and watery embrace.

Lightning Source UK Ltd.
Milton Keynes UK
UKOW02f2043130317
296536UK00003B/199/P